Ah, Camelot. What is to become of you?

I am Astrala, guardian of the holy chalice, which is secured in its secret niche in the marble tomb on Avalon. Looking around the raised slabs on which lie the effigies of so many of the knights of the Round Table, I realize much preparation has already been done. Yet, there is so much to do before Arthur's knights will ride again.

Arthur's nephews—courteous Gwalchmai, steadfast Gaheris, trusting Gareth—lie together in silence. The king has not yet joined them. After Cam's Landing, Gwenhwyfar and Nimue brought him to Avalon to heal. Myrddin returned him to the world several years later, where he still remains. He chose not to reclaim the throne of Camelot, but instead took the assumed name of Armel and became counsel to young Judwel of Léon, the last of the Sangréal bloodline. Nimue, having borne Arthur a daughter throught the pagan Great Rite, joined him there.

Gwenhwyfar was trapped while trying to pass through Faerie. Once again, Lancelot rescued her, this time by fighting the horned god, Cernunnos. No easy task, but Gwenhwyfar would expect no less from her half-fey champion, nor would Lancelot ever give up his love.

There lies Peredur. Truly, he has been the most naïve of fools and yet, he managed to marry Blanchfleur, the love of his heart. Lohengrin was born of that union and it was he who mated with Arthur and Nimue's daughter, Argante, to continue the bloodline of the Ladies of the Lake as well. Peredur's innocence also allowed him to assist Galahad in finding the Holy Grail.

Galahad. The last Grail Keeper. He fought to be known as someone other than Lancelot's son. Much of his young life was spent in proving himself to be pure of heart. Even when he met his love, Dindrane, she was taken from him. The Goddess allowed me to give him the choice to live without Dindrane or to return to Avalon with the Grail. He did not hesitate.

There is no slab for Lancelot, even though, in the mortal world, he is dead and buried with Gwenhwyfar at Glastonbury. Lancelot and Gwenhwyfar are very much alive in the land of Faerie. Cernunnos planned to make Gwenhwyfar his consort when he captured her the first time and Morgan le Fey, queen of Faerie, lusted after Lancelot once Gwenhwyfar learned how to use the scrying pool to communicate with him. Before their earthly death, Morgan offered them immortality in the land of Fairie.

I suspect there will be many problems over that decision, but it is incidental to the the trouble that is brewing within the mind of the rival Faerie queen, Aoibhill. Trouble that will spill into the mortal world and threaten to destroy it.

And yet...yet, somehow human destinies have not been completely spun by the Wheel of Fate.

In Time, there is a world that awaits the return of Camelot.

Happy Reading
Cynthia Breeding

Camelot's Enchantment

Cynthia Breeding

~~~

Highland Press Publishing

Camelot's Enchantment

For information, please contact
Highland Press Publishing,
PO Box 2292, High Springs, FL 32655.
www.highlandpress.org

ISBN: 978-0-9842499-5-4

HIGHLAND PRESS PUBLISHING

Excalibur

Prologue

515 AD

Aoibhill, faerie queen of Eire, let her gaze trail over the naked form of her mortal lover. He was well-made—broad shoulders and sinewy arms from years of sword-training, hard-muscled thighs from years of riding—and pleasant to look upon, with his long, raven hair and grey eyes that reminded her of stormy seas. Her fey sense told her his heart was evil, even if she hadn't known he was the product of an incestuous relationship between a brother and sister. Ah, yes. She had waited many centuries for just such a man. One who could beget an incubus son on her...a son that would allow her to get rid of her arch-rival, Morgan le Fey, once and for all. It was her luck that this man had come seeking soldiers for his army.

"Medraut," Aoibhill murmured, "I must leave soon—"

He growled and flipped her over, his body pressing her down, crushing the cushion of primroses that she lay upon. The bower of enchanted vines hid them from view of the various nymphs, dryads, sylphs and trickster elves that roamed about, but did nothing to stifle sound. "Not before I make you scream again so that even the gnomes will flee."

She bit her lip to keep from smiling as the mortal drove himself deep inside of her. He ground his pelvis against her soft femininity which such force that, had she been human, she would surely have felt pain. Medraut was a man who enjoyed inflicting pain, something he no doubt learned from his mother, Morgana, but it was necessary to mate with such a one as him if Aoibhill desired her son to be truly capable of helping her destroy her nemesis and reclaim Cernunnos as her consort.

Cernunnos. How long had it been since she'd seen him? She narrowed her eyes in anguish, letting Medraut think his violent thrusts were the cause. When Myrddin—the magician or whatever he was—had come to Eire to gather the blue stones for the Giant's Dance, Morgan had been with him. And somehow—somehow!—she had managed to capture the horned god's interest. Aoibhill had never understood why. Morgan was a mouse compared to her. She had brown hair and green eyes and dressed in the same colors and was nigh invisible from the earth itself. Aoibhill, on the other hand, prided herself on her fiery hair and eyes the lavender color of twilight. And she never dressed in drab colors. Only the brightest reds and yellows, cobalt blues, and brilliant emeralds would do. How could her bronze-colored god possibly be attracted to Morgan?

She groaned when Medraut's shaft butted against her womb. He grinned. "I knew you'd want it like this."

"Yes. Harder." What she *wanted* was to make sure she captured all of his seed within her. Twice before this afternoon she had. The magic power of three would make sure she conceived.

She arched her back, preparing to loose the blood-curdling scream that would make Medraut think she'd reached her ecstasy and bring welcome relief.

"AIIIEE!" she screeched and Medraut bellowed an answer, spending himself.

"When will I see you again?" he asked after he'd dressed.

"Soon, my love." She handed him his sword. "Soon."

She waved her hand through the air and disappeared in the swirling mist, leaving Medraut standing on a cobbled road leading to Dun Laoghaire.

One day she would send his son to him. Morgana would be a wonderfully evil influence on the child's life. But for now, Medraut would remember nothing. Aoibhill had made sure of that.

Chapter One

540 AD

Morgan clapped her hands in delight as she did a pirouette around the scrying pool that bridged the space between Faerie and Avalon. Her long, chestnut hair swirled around her petite frame. "I'm so glad our plan worked! Lancelot and Gwenhwyfar are with us here in Faerie."

"Aye." Cernunnos wrapped one strong, bronze-colored arm around her waist and drew her to him as he peered over her shoulder into the pool. "Just in time, it seems."

For a moment, the water in the stone-lined pool fed by a natural spring turned murky. Underneath its surface, a stone cottage emerged. Inside, Gwenhwyfar and Lancelot lay dying of the Black Death, brought to Briton by the woman who lurked outside the window. Morgana, sister to King Arthur, bent on avenging Medraut's death by Lancelot's hand, smiled at their writhing agony. The smile turned into a silent scream as she was grabbed from behind by deserting Saxon marauders.

Morgan saw herself twirl in the air above the couple, oblivious to the approaching danger. "You are half-fey, Lancelot. Come with us to Faerie where you will be young forever." She giggled and swept her lashes at him. "How old do you think I am?"

"Not now." Cernunnos caught her and set her down. "We don't have much time. Gwenhwyfar will be dead in minutes."

"Gwenhwyfar can come too?" Lancelot asked hoarsely.

A rack of antlers formed over Cernunnos' head and his amber eyes glowed. "Certes, but hurry."

Even as he spoke, a Saxon burst through the door of the cottage, swinging his heavy mace at Lancelot's head.

Morgan waved her hand and the images disappeared, leaving the pool tranquil and still. Her lower lip thrust out. "I don't know why we had to bring Gwenhwyfar. She's mortal."

Cernunnos swept Morgan's hair back and bent to nuzzle her neck. "I know your cravings, my queen, and I've seen the way you look at Lancelot."

She tilted her head to give Cernunnos better access to her neck. "You aren't fooling me, Cern. I've seen the way you look at Gwenhwyfar too."

"Ah, well." His hands slipped up to cup Morgan's breasts. "I'm only half-god. I've always found red-haired women to be,,, Morgan's elbow jabbed his taut belly. "Ouch!What was that for?"

She arched her back, thrusting her clothed breasts more fully into his hands. "Just remember who you're with."

His teeth pulled at the thin shoulder straps and the gown slipped off to puddle on the ground. Cernunnos spun her around and pressed her back against a rowan tree. With one hand, he lifted her arms above her head and with the other he freed himself from his trews and drew her leg over his thigh. "Do you want to remind me?"

Morgan sighed with pleasure as he entered her slowly and then groaned in frustration as he withdrew. She tried to catch his shoulders, but he held her fast. Another slow entry, only partial this time, before withdrawal. And yet another maddeningly slow thrust.

As her craving grew, the leaves on the tree rustled and the grass flattened. A storm began to build around them, the wind whipping Cernunnos' tawny mane behind him.

He lifted his head, antlers beginning to form in the ether above him. "Ah, yes. Your specialty, Morgan. Send the lightening bolts. Remind me who you are."

She gave him a seductive look and silently called on her power. Cernunnos flew back, landing on the ground. Morgan swooped down, impaling herself on his hard erection and hissed with contentment as she began to ride him.

He bucked beneath her, finally giving her the deep, hard thrusts that made her body clench and quiver. The wind howled as her frenzy built, Cernunnos buried inside her. His hands grabbed her buttocks and he took her over the brink to pure ecstasy, even as a white bolt of lightening split the tree behind them.

* * * *

"I didn't think I'd ever be glad to see this place again." Gwenhwyfar looked around the room that had served as her quarters when she had originally been held captive in Faerie years ago. The priestesses of Avalon had attempted to send her through the portal back to Arthur, but Cernunnos had intercepted and taken her on the Wild Hunt.

Lancelot came to stand beside her, resting his hand on her shoulder. "This time I'm with you." His dark eyes turned smoky. "I won't let anything bad ever happen to you again."

She slipped her arm around his waist and laid her head against his shoulder as he draped his arm around her. "Do you really think Morgan and Cernunnos will leave us alone?" His arm tensed and then he placed a kiss on her forehead.

"I hope so, Gwen. So far, they've been nothing but good hosts."

"We've only been here a day." She snuggled against him. "Or maybe more. Time is so distorted. The whole place feels like it's constantly shifting and changing. Whole earth years passed while I was here last time."

His hand tightened on her shoulder again. "You don't need to remind me. I spent those years waiting for the portal to open to let me come to you."

Gwenhwyfar gave a slight shudder. "If you hadn't forgiven Arthur for leaving me in Avalon, the portal might never have—"

"Shhh." Lancelot brushed her hair back gently. "Arthur and I forgave each other."

"I wonder what he'll think when he learns we've disappeared?"

"We didn't exactly disappear, love."

Gwenhwyfar straightened and looked up at him. "What do you mean? We're here." She ran her hand over his broad, muscled chest. "You're real."

"Is anything real in Faerie?" He shrugged. "You were unconscious and nearly dead. I gathered you up even as a Saxon broke through the door and bashed my head in—"

"Sweet Mary! No!" She reached up to brush his dark hair off his forehead. "No!"

9

"I felt nothing, for we were already floating upward. What I *saw* were our corpses. As far anyone in the real world knows, we died."

"King Custennin will send word to Arthur in Armorica then." Gwenhwyfar nibbled her lip, thinking of how Arthur had assumed a new name and deliberately removed himself from Briton so she could wed Lancelot. Maybe now he would return.

A muscle twitched in Lancelot's jaw. "I only hope Custennin can. He was barely holding Camelot. When we...left, he was surrounded by Wehha's and Ida's Saxons."

Gwenhwyfar placed her hand on Lancelot's arm. "You wish you could have stayed and fought."

"I was in no shape to fight."

She traced the bulging bicep with her fingers. "You seem in shape to me."

His mouth quirked up at one corner and then he shook his head. "You were delirious those last few days. I wasn't in much better shape. Custennin sent men to rally Cynric and Bedwyr. *If* they managed to slip through."

"I know!" Gwenhwyfar said suddenly. "I should have thought of it before! We could try and use the scrying pool to find out what is happening there!"

She remembered the first time she had learned of its existence. Hetaira, one of the priestesses of Avalon, had taken her to it.

"You ache for another man," Hetaira said.

Gwenhwyfar started. "No. I love Arthur. I came here to help him heal."

"And so you shall,"the priestess said. "But you love two men and they both love you. Am I not right?"

"God forgive me, yes," Gwenhwyfar whispered. "I have tried not to love—"

"Never try to deny love. It is a gift of the Goddess to be able to feel such. Now look..."

Lancelot was lying on a cot in his quarters. Gwenhwyfar watched as he tossed his dark hair back and closed his eyes. She felt herself merging into his world and then he wrapped his arms around her and pulled her close, his lips soft and gentle in that first exploratory, teasing kiss...

It was also the day she first met Morgan le Fey. The mischievous faerie allowed her to use the pool only if Morgan could watch any interactions between Gwenhwyfar and Lancelot. It had been pure torture to visit Lancelot through the pool and refrain from letting him bed her. Lancelot had growled to let the damn faerie watch, but Gwenhwyfar couldn't do it.

"It's Morgan's pool, Lance. What kind of a payment do you think she would ask? I remember how much she desired you—"

"We'll ask her when Cernunnos is with her. She won't risk making him mad by doing something foolish."

Gwenhwyfar raised a brow skeptically. "You don't know her like I do."

Lancelot wrapped his arms around Gwenhwyfar and drew her close. "She knows I love you, Gwen."

Gwenhwyfar tilted her head, intertwining her fingers in his silky hair. Her last rational thought, before he kissed her senseless, was that she hoped he was right.

* * * *

"And what is my reward for helping you?" Morgan tilted her head, her slanted green eyes studying Lancelot.

Cernunnos watched as Lancelot paced across the small living room where they were all gathered. The man had asked to use the scrying pool to see how things stood at Camelot. Too bad Cernunnos hadn't been asked for permission to use the pool. He would have suggested a duel with swords first. He hadn't forgotten how Lancelot whisked Gwenhwyfar away from him by using Excalibur last time.

He shifted his glance to look at her sitting regally on the sofa. She had been near fifty human years when they brought her to Faerie, but now her features had softened to the translucent look of a woman barely past her youth. Gone were the red lesions and black welts that had covered her, the skin now smooth and glowing softly pink. She was more beautiful than he remembered. Her auburn hair shown like pure copper, her eyes shimmered like emerald fire...and she was looking raptly at Lancelot. Cernunnos cursed under his breath. How could a mortal woman prefer a half-fey prince to a demi-god? His antlers began to grow and he determinedly pushed them back. It was too soon to make his move. This time, he would make sure she wanted him.

"I'm waiting, Lancelot." Morgan rose gracefully from her chair and stretched lazily, before walking over to him.

Cernunnos turned his attention to his faerie queen. It set even less well with him that she was attracted to Lancelot as well. Whenever Morgan's fancy turned to a mortal man, Cernunnos usually allowed her to indulge herself—after all, he was hardly faithful—and then erased all thought of the mortal by pleasuring her with his own considerably well-honed skills. But there was something different about Lancelot and that presented a challenge to him. He glanced over at Gwenhwyfar again. No one challenged a god...and *won*.

Lancelot stopped pacing and looked down at Morgan. "Does everything have to have a price, my lady?"

"Certes," she purred and then glanced at Cernunnos. He arched an eyebrow and her mouth went into a soft pout as she stepped back. "I'm sure you'll think of something. Come. Let us go to the pool."

Lancelot extended his hand to Gwenhwyfar and helped her from the sofa as Morgan led the way outside.

As they followed the winding path toward the edge of Faerie, black gnomes glanced out from behind trees while manikins and brownies faded into shadows. Even the fey animals were still, watching the progress of two mortals in their world.

Cernunnos' antlers grew as he strode through the forest and sent a silent message: *Gwenhwyfar is here to stay this time.*

* * * *

Gwenhwyfar leaned over Lancelot's shoulder as he crouched to peer into the swirling waters of the pool. Gradually, they stilled.

Camelot emerged, the fortress looking like a small city atop its hill. The thick curtain-wall stood in place, its stones not broken. A few guards were posted on the ramparts. Farther down the hill, the earthwork ditches were unmanned and the deadly palisade of wooden spikes looked freshly cut. No armies fought.

"It's over," Gwenhwyfar said, "but who won?"

Even as she spoke, the double oak doors to the castle opened. Cynric and Custennin walked out and down the stairs toward the stables.

Lancelot bowed his head and said something in the Old Tongue that Gwenhwyfar didn't understand, but it appeared he was giving thanks. "We did," he finally said. "The scouts must have gotten through."

She laid her hand on his shoulder and squeezed. "I wonder if Arthur made it."

Morgan sidled up beside her, a sly look on her face. "Would you like to see what happened to Arthur?"

Gwenhwyfar's hand flew to her mouth. "He wasn't killed, was he? Not after—"

"He lives," she said in an amused voice as she spread her hand across the water again, causing it to swirl and then still. "See for yourself."

A grey-headed Arthur stood on the shores of Avallach, speaking with Nimue, Lady of the Lake.

"So many lives lost at Cam's Landing..."

Nimue touched his arm. "Bedwyr still lives...the last knight of your Round Table fellowship."

"I will visit him before I return to Armorica."

"Why must you go back?"

"I have created a life for myself as Armel, counselor to Prince Judwel. My life at Camelot and with Gwenhwyfar was over years ago. It is better the world thinks me gone as well. And I have something to return to you." He knelt before her and held out Excalibur. "I have need of it no longer."

Nimue accepted the sword. "I will give this into our daughter's keeping, for she is to become the Lady soon."

As he straightened, he took her hand. "Come with me then. You've done your duty to the Goddess. Now be my wife."

The water clouded and the images faded slowly away. Morgan giggled and twirled around. "It looks like you lost Arthur to the priestess, after all."

Gwenhwyfar didn't answer, but continued to stare into the pool and then Lancelot took her hand.

"Are you all right?" he asked as he stood.

"Yes. Certes. I was just remembering that Nimue had gone to him in Armorica, but when the fighting started with

Childebert, he sent her home. All this time he's loved her and they've been separated...and we're together."

"Gwen. Didn't I convince you long ago not to feel guilty about Arthur?"

"Yes, but—"

Lancelot grinned and leaned down to whisper in her ear. "Do you remember what I did the last time you thought you had to carry this burden?"

She felt her face flush, remembering Cynric's secreted cottage in the forest with the tinned mirror above the bed. They had spent the afternoon making love under the mirror and then guilt had flooded her.

Lancelot spun her around and draped her over his knee before she could think and slapped her sharply on her naked buttocks. It stung.

"What are you doing?" she cried.

"I told you once, Gwen," he said in an anguished voice. "I'd take you over my knee to swat that Christian guilt out of you. Now I plan to do it. Go ahead and struggle, until you let it all go. I will not have you feeling guilty every time we make love."

God help her. She'd loved it. She grinned wickedly at him now. "You wouldn't dare!"

His eyes darkened as a corner of his mouth lifted. "Wouldn't I?"

Beside them, Morgan le Fey frowned, her lower lip thrusting out in a pout. With a flounce, she turned and left, leaving the pool in a turmoil of splashing waves.

* * * *

"No man, even if he is half-fey, will be able to resist you in this, my lady!" Sadi, the nubile blonde faerie, said as she floated around Morgan, smoothing the translucent folds of the iridescent samhite gown tied with wisps of silk at the shoulders.

Morgan twirled, admiring herself in the reflections on the still water of the wading pond in the garden. The material was just filmy enough that her lush body was subtly outlined, but also layered to keep her assets hidden.

"It's a good thing Lord Cernunnos doesn't know you have this dress," Branda, the red-haired faerie, said impishly.

Morgan gave a sly look. "It's a full moon. Cernunnos rides tonight." Yes. She would have the whole night to seduce

Lancelot. He would be here soon, thinking he was to meet Gwenhwyfar. "You will keep Gwenhwyfar busy?"

"Certes." Both faeries bobbed their heads, causing little starbursts of light to shimmer in the air. "We found the unicorn she so liked while she was here."

"Good. I want no interruptions." With a wave of her hand she dismissed them and sat on the garden bench to contemplate. No payment indeed! Did he—or Cernunnos for that matter—think she would not exact payment for her gift of allowing the mortals to see what was happening at Camelot? She tossed her long chestnut hair back. All those years when Gwenhwyfar had been captive in Faerie and Morgan had to content herself with looking over the mortal's shoulder while Gwenhwyfar communicated with Lancelot through the pool were over. This night *she* would find out for herself what it felt like to be held in Lancelot's strong arms and have that full, sensual mouth pressed against hers. She giggled at what *else* she planned to do with the handsome prince.

"Gwenhwyfar?"

Morgan turned at the sound and drew in her breath at the sight of Lancelot standing at the edge of the garden. He must have bathed, for his dark hair was slightly damp where the edges of it curled against a snowy white linen shirt that was only partially laced, revealing a dusting of hair across his broad chest. The sleeves were rolled up, displaying strong, well-tanned forearms and the black cloth trews he wore clung like a second skin to his well-muscled thighs. She exhaled contentedly. This half-fey man was as well-turned out as her consort. The comparison of Lancelot's dark coloring with Cernunnos' tawny hair and amber eyes... Well, she simply had to have both of them.

"Gwenhwyfar isn't here."

"Why not? The elfin who delivered the note told me specifically what time."

"Time?" Morgan laughed and tiny, silver bells tinkled in the air. "Surely you know by now that Time is not of importance in Faerie. Come sit by me."

Lancelot frowned as he stepped closer. "Where is she?"

Morgan tilted her head, slanting a sideways look at him. "The faeries found her unicorn. Prince, I think she called him.

She was sure you'd understand..." Morgan held out her hand, sending an invisible thread of allurement toward him. "Come sit."

With a look of confusion, he moved forward. "Gwen told me of the unicorn when she returned from here. It was the same one who used to visit her when she was a child. I'd like to meet it."

"And you shall. But first, why don't you sit and eat something?" Morgan waved a graceful hand toward a table in front of her that was suddenly laden with delectable fruits, soft cheeses, warm bread and a crystal decanter of rich, red wine. She giggled at his suspicious look. "You don't believe the myth of not eating Faerie food, do you? What can happen to you? You're already immortal here. Go ahead and indulge." She poured some wine into two glasses and licked the rim of hers. "It's quite good."

"You've probably put some kind of spell on it anyway," he said.

Morgan pouted. "Do I *need* to put a spell on the wine to have a conversation with you?" She let her lashes sweep down before she looked up at him again. "I thought the knights of Camelot were chivalrous. Isn't it rude to deny your hostess such a simple request?"

Lancelot looked pained, but he sat. "My lady."

"That's better." Morgan reached for a cluster of grapes and slid over to him, letting the gown fall open to reveal the tops of her breasts as she leaned forward. "Let me feed you."

"That won't be necessary." Lancelot took the cluster from her.

"Oooh," Morgan purred as she put a hand on his thigh. "Then you feed me. That's even better."

He shifted his leg and placed the grapes on the table. "I'd better go."

She barely refrained from hissing at him as her other hand stroked his cheek. "Would you like me better like this?" The air around them began to shimmer. Her hair turned golden-red as her features began to change into Gwenhwyfar's. Under her breath, she muttered the words that would make the glamour look real. "I've been waiting for you. Kiss me, Lancelot."

He frowned. "Gwen? How did you—"

"No questions." Morgan pressed herself against him and brushed her lips across his. "I'm here now."

Lancelot slipped his arms around her and slanted his mouth across hers and then abruptly, he stopped and pushed her back to a sitting position.

"Bel's Fires! You're not Gwenhwyfar."

Morgan blinked, feeling suddenly cold away from his body heat. How had the glamour spell not worked? Stunned, she asked, "How do you know?"

"Because I know Gwen's scent and taste. How she feels. She is my soul's mate. Nothing you can do—no glamour you can produce—will ever change that."

"Lots of things can happen in Faerie." Morgan narrowed her eyes. "Don't be so sure."

"But I am," Lancelot answered as he stood to go. "I remember well your attempted seduction of me when I came to rescue Gwen. It won't happen again."

Morgan stood, too, as the wind began to blow. Her gown swirled up, revealing slender legs, a tiny waist, and luscious breasts. "Do you think you can resist this, Lancelot, if I choose to ensorcel you?"

"I won't deny you are beautiful, Morgan. But I can—and will—resist your temptations because there is something better than bedding a woman for lust."

Morgan stared at him, so surprised that the wind abated and her gown floated back down. "There isn't anything better than that!"

"Yes, there is." Lancelot bowed to her and turned to walk away. Before he left the garden, he stopped andfaced Morgan. "It's called love. And I love Gwenhwyfar. Nothing will ever change that."

Cynthia Breeding

Chapter Two

"What is this thing called love?" Morgan grumbled as she lay on her back amidst her cushion of primroses, gazing up at the stars later that night.

"Love?" Cernunnos grinned wickedly. "Tis just another name for what I'm about to do." He filled her and withdrew and thrust again. "Each time I do this, is love."

Soon he rolled off of her and onto his back, his forearm across his forehead. "That is love, my queen. Now I'm for sleep. Twas a hard ride this night."

Morgan lay silent beside him, frowning at the moon that now rode low in the pre-dawn sky. Twas what she had offered Lancelot earlier, yet he had not taken it.

Cernunnos propped himself up on an elbow wearily. "What's wrong, Morgan?"

She reached out to stroke his shoulder. "Nothing, Cern. Go to sleep."

He sighed. "Tis never 'nothing' when you say it like that. Did I not please you this eve?"

"Certes you did. You always do."

"Then what is wrong?"

"I don't know. Lancelot mentioned something earlier that the love he felt for Gwenhywfar surpassed even lust."

The wind began to stir as Cernunnos sat up. Grass and plants around them rustled with the small creatures of the night fleeing for sudden shelter.

"And why would Lancelot be discussing that with you?" Cernunnos asked silkily.

Morgan sat up as well, distant thunder beginning to roll. "Don't use that tone on me."

"Then answer the question. Why would Lancelot tell you that? Or should I ask, *where* was the prince when he told you?"

18

Lightening flashed nearby as Morgan glared at Cernunnos. "We were sitting on that bench, not a stone's throw from here."

Cernunnos raised a brow. A sudden wind gust bent the trees. "*Why* were you sitting there with him?"

Morgan tossed her head and a clap of thunder sounded overhead. "We were *talking*. People do that sometimes."

"Where was Gwenhwyfar?"

Morgan took a deep breath and decided not to hurl a lightening bolt at him. "The faeries found the unicorn she was so fond of. She was with the animal."

Cernunnos frowned, causing another wind gust. "That was to be my gift to her."

Morgan narrowed her eyes. "*Your* gift? I thought we had agreed not to bribe either of them."

Cernunnos glanced over at the still food-laden table and crystal decanter. "As you weren't doing with Lancelot?"

With a wave of her hand, lightening split the table in two. "Offering a man sustenance is not quite the same."

"Depends on what the *sustenance* is, my lovely queen. Did you offer him your body?"

Morgan raised both hands to send a jolt directly into him, but he caught her hands and pressed her to the ground. Pinning her hands over her head with one of his, he leaned over and kissed her slowly. "Do you really think he would be better than me?" His hand cupped and kneaded her breast. "Do you?"

In spite of herself, her anger diminished and new passion arose as Cernunnos soothrf her aching need with his mouth.

Morgan threw her head back with a groan and began to writhe. Cernunnos knew how to satisfy her and always had.

But was that love?

She just didn't know.

* * * *

"I should have known I'd find you here." Lancelot entered the faerie stable. From stalls whose walls were made of gossamer webs, white horses with pink eyes and ears nickered softly as he passed.

Gwenhwyfar looked up from the floor where she sat nestled in sweet-smelling hay, cradling the silver unicorn's head in her lap. Its large silver-blue eyes regarded Lancelot solemnly, but the shy creature made no move to get away.

"I've found Prince again!" Gwenhwyfar stroked the silky mane. "I was hoping he would be here."

Lancelot sank down beside her. "I remember the tapestry you brought to Joyous Garde and hung in our chamber. There was a unicorn in it...this one?"

Gwenhwyfar nodded. "My mother wove it herself and hung in my room as a child. It was almost as if she knew she wouldn't be around to raise me and Prince would protect me."

Lancelot put his arm around her. "You will always have my protection, Gwen, as well. Count on it."

She leaned into his shoulder. "I know. Did Morgan give you my message?"

His face darkened and Gwenhwyfar rose up. "What did she do?"

"Morgan was being Morgan."

"That means she flirted with you?"

"She did," Lancelot answered in a measured tone.

Gwenhwyfar frowned. "I had hoped she'd learned her lesson when you rescued me. She and Cernunnos nearly destroyed the garden that night."

A clap of thunder sounded in the distance and Lancelot looked up. "That's strange. The sky was clear when I came in."

The wind began to howl and the faerie horses stamped their hooves. The unicorn got to its feet and shook itself. "I must go," he said in Gwenhwyfar's mind.

She gave him a final pat before he trotted out the door. "Something's wrong."

Lightening flashed outside. Lancelot grimaced as he rose from the floor and held out his hand to Gwenhwyfar. "I think Morgan and Cernunnos may be having an argument."

"As happy as I am that we did not really die in that cottage, this world is going to take getting used to." Gwenhwyfar took his hand to rise and brushed the hay from her skirt. "When I was here last, Morgan could make things appear and disappear at will and Cernunnos moved objects with a flicker of his hand." She paused and then added softly, "And they both could mesmerize."

"Don't remind me," Lancelot said in a pained voice. "Having to watch Cernunnos almost seduce you through the pool drove me mad, remember?"

She remembered. The demi-god had gifted her with a chance to visit Lancelot through the pool, but he had exacted a price. And, if she wanted to ever see Lancelot again, she had to uphold her end of the bargain. She closed her eyes.

Cernunnos stood a few feet away, studying her, his golden gaze limpid, his tawny mane blowing in the wind. He said nothing, merely held out his hand. She felt an irresistible tug propelling her forward, toward him. As she moved closer, she could feel his heat. It pricked her skin, stinging like a thousand little needles, yet tickling too, making the surface tingle, while a deeper pulsation penetrated her muscles. She shimmied, lured on...

Gwenhwyfar opened her eyes and reached up to brush aside the dark shank of hair that always fell over Lancelot's forehead. "At least, it didn't happen."

He took her hand and turned it over, kissing the palm. "I know. By Mithras, he had best not attempt to do that again. Grateful to be here or not, I will challenge him without a thought and I will win. Again."

"Let's not speak of it, Lance! Last time, you had Excalibur!"

"Because I was rescuing Arthur's queen. I still have Arondight. My own mother magicked it."

"Your mother was Lady of the Black Lake. Will her magic work here?"

"I am half-fey, Gwen. I used to think that a curse. But my mother's magic comes from the Goddess through her priestesses. If the need arises, I will rent the veil between us and Avalon myself."

"It's strong, Lancelot. Remember how many years it took you to find the portal into Faerie!"

He grimaced. "That was because I would not forgive Arthur for leaving you behind. Nor did I have the tolerance to understand Galahad. When those things happened, the Grail maiden appeared and let me see the vision that opened the portal."

"She appeared to me too, when I was ready to kill myself rather than let Medraut rape me," Gwenhwyfar said, "but she—Astrala—said she had no power to rescue me, only to give me strength and hope."

"Strength is all I need, Gwen. Even the god of the Wild Hunt cannot prevail against the Grail."

Gwenhwyfar rose up on her toes to kiss Lancelot. "Let's speak no more of it. There's no sense inviting trouble in where it doesn't exist."

And no use in reminding Lancelot that the Grail serves those who are pure of heart.

Neither of us qualifies.

* * * *

Cernunos stabbed a finger in the general direction of the chair he'd just hurled across the room and it flew back to its original spot near the table. He flicked his hand again and the table contents floated up from the floor and back on top of the table.

He clenched a fist as he watched Morgan scamper across the garden and disappear into the trees. Lancelot had taken that trail to go hunting mere minutes before. Cernunnos hesitated but a second and then he slipped quietly through the shadows to enter the forest, making no more noise than his own fleet-footed deer. Gnomes scattered before him, their grotesque faces showing fear.

By all the gods! He was tired of watching Morgan make a fool of herself by trailing behind Lancelot at every opportunity this past week or however long it had been. It wasn't as though Cernunnos was jealous, he thought to himself as he moved silently through the trees, unaware of the creatures that scurried from his path.

He knew that part of Morgan's attraction to Lancelot was his indifference to her. And, he had to grudgingly admit, he *almost* admired Lancelot for that. Morgan le Fey was not an easy woman to ignore and her spells and enchantments were powerful. *Why* the man would withstand the faerie queen's charms, Cernunnos didn't understand. He stopped abruptly at the sound of voices just ahead and moved behind a tree.

"Gwen? I thought you were going to walk with Prince. Is he here?"

Cernunnos crouched behind some gorse and peered through the foliage. Lancelot stood in a small clearing, holding his bow. On the other side of a bubbling brook that flowed through the trees, Gwenhwyfar sat on a boulder.

"We walked. I left him at his cave," She smiled. "I just wanted to get away from the faerie maids. Their chattering gets tiresome."

Lancelot grinned. "It is nice to have some solitude. Somehow I managed to elude Morgan today."

Cernunnos blinked. Gwenhwyfar's eyes flickered, the green changing color. He lifted his head, scenting her. A faint smell of lavender drifted toward him. Gwenhywfar's scent.

"We are alone now, my love," she said. "How keen are you on hunting today?"

Lancelot threw the bow on the ground and started toward her. "I can think of a better prize to claim."

"I was hoping you'd say that." She put up a hand to stop his progress. "But before you come closer, let's play a game."

He stopped. "A game?"

"I want you to tell me exactly what you're going to do to me once you cross the stream." Gwenhwyfar brushed a long strand of copper hair away from her neckline and licked her lower lip. "Every single detail."

"I can't just show you?"

"Not yet." She leaned back on her hands, causing her breasts to jut forward. "I want to hear first."

For a moment, Cernunnos thought her hair had shifted color, going darker and then the sunlight hit it again. He sniffed the air once more, but didn't detect Morgan's earthy, spicy scent.

Lancelot sat down on the grass near the water. "It's been a long time since we've played this game, Gwen. I think Faerie becomes you."

Gwenhwyfar wet her lips again. "I agree. So tell me. Slowly."

"I shall spread my cloak over yon patch of meadow grass and lay you down. Then, my hands shall explore you. To learn your face again with my eyes closed, to trace your cheek and run my thumb slowly across your lips and then slide my hands down your throat to lightly brush against your breasts—"

"Am I still clothed?" She giggled.

"You are. I shall tease your nipples with the barest touch, circle them lightly, gather their fullness in the palms of my hands, knead them gently. Then stroke away from them—"

"Nay! You know what I like!"

Lancelot continued, "—stroke away, my hand flat against your belly. My fingers will caress your thighs—"

"Nay!" Gwenhwyfar cried again. "You've missed what lies between my legs."

"I will miss nothing, only make you want it more with the waiting." He paused. "You do remember how I would tie you to the bed and leave you in that longing state, only to come back and give you a bit more satisfaction before leaving again?"

"Yes, Certes," she said quickly.

Lancelot raised a brow. "And wasn't it always better, when finally, finally after bringing you to the brink and then withholding myself, I thrust fully into you, hard and fast until your body shuddered over and over before I finished?"

Gwenhwyfar gasped and began to pant. "Forget the rest of telling me, Lancelot. I want you now. Come to me."

Lancelot rose, his eyes turning smoke-colored. As he splashed through the brook, Gwenhwyfar's image wavered and Cernunnos snapped his head up. A whiff of spice assailed him and he narrowed his eyes. The water! It was the barrier that protected her! Morgan had become quite good at cloaking herself in Gwenhwyfar's glamour. Even Cernunnos had almost missed it.

Morgan rose and slithered her body up against Lancelot's until she was fully pressed against him, arms around his neck and parting her lips for his kiss. Antlers sprouted in the air above Cernunnos and he clenched his fists. As much as he wanted to leap across the clearing and tear Lancelot apart, it wouldn't solve this problem. Morgan was used to getting what she wanted. If Cernunnos stopped this, she would only try again. No. He would let her have the damn prince. Best to be done with this, once and for all. Lancelot couldn't come close to Cernunnos' prowess. He was a demi-god, after all and had even seduced the *real* Gwenhwyfar once. He forced himself to stay still. Being a voyeur had its advantages too. Had he forgotten that?

Lancelot leaned down toward Morgan and put his hands on her waist. Very slowly and deliberately, he lifted her and set her away from him.

"I hope you enjoyed the game, Morgan. It's all you're going to get," he said.

Her eyes widened in surprise. "What do you mean?"

"I mean, you're not Gwenhwyfar."

"How...what makes you think such a thing? Certes I am." She lifted a copper-colored curl to show him. "See? Gwenhwyfar."

Lancelot leaned down. "I have never—*never*—tied Gwenhwyfar to a bed and left her alone. 'Twould be dangerous." He straightened. "Go to your consort, Morgan. You are suited well." Then, he turned and walked away, leaving her with her mouth agape.

Cernunnos waited for him to disappear and then stepped forward. "Have you learned your lesson, my pet?"

Morgan whirled around, her form shifting as she did so. "How long have you been here?"

"Long enough."

"It wasn't...wasn't what you think."

Cernunnos lifted an eyebrow. "It wasn't?"

"No." Morgan moved toward him shakily. "You know how devoted Lancelot and Gwenhwyfar are to each other. I've tried to get Gwenhwyfar to tell me why, but she always talks of love."

Cernunnos let his antlers form in the ether above him. It was meant to intimidate.

Morgan wet her lips nervously. "I thought if I could lure Lancelot into thinking I was Gwenhwyfar, he'd tell me."

"Or show you," Cernunnos said dryly.

Morgan tilted her head, slanting a look at him as the wind began to rustle the leaves and the water stirred. "Are you jealous?"

"A demi-god jealous?" Cernunnos forced a laugh that shook the nearby trees. "But you did give me a thought. You were so convincing as Gwenhwyfar that I think it may be time I paid her a visit. Perhaps I can obtain the secret you so wish to have."

Morgan narrowed her eyes. "Gwenhwyfar doesn't want you."

He grinned wickedly. "That remains to be seen, my little faerie queen. That remains to be seen."

* * * *

"I had so hoped that Morgan would not stoop to this," Gwenhwyfar said when Lancelot told her what had happened. She paced back and forth in front of the open hearth where a

Cynthia Breeding

magic fire blazed, but produced no heat since Faerie was always comfortable. "She is mischievous, but this is too much. We must get away."

"Where will we go, Gwen?" Lancelot shrugged. "Morgan is immature, for all that she is an immortal. Mayhap, no one has denied her before. Here in Faerie, she is used to commanding and getting what she wants."

"She wants *you*, Lance. She has since she first saw you in the scrying pool years ago. And since you say no to her in her normal state, she creates the illusion that she's me. The next time, she may not make a mistake like not knowing you'd never leave me tied and alone."

Lancelot crossed over to Gwenhwyfar and put a hand on her arm, stopping her pacing. "I will always know if it's you, love."

"How? This is Faerie, Lance. You know how reality is distorted here. For that matter, are we real? Or are we dead and held somehow in an in-between world?"

He gathered her into his arms and slanted his mouth over hers, his tongue exploring her mouth fully, deepening the kiss as his hands caressed her back. "Does this feel real enough for you, Gwen? We exist."

She rested her head against his shoulder and tightened her hold around his waist. "Maybe if we talked to Cernunnos—"

"I don't think so. That would only stir up more trouble."

Gwenhwyfar sighed and straightened. "I suppose you're right. Cernunnos would only want to fight."

"And I won't back down if he does."

She sighed again. "I know. There's too much warrior in you still."

Lancelot put a finger under her chin. "And you object?"

"You know I don't. I love you for everything you are."

"Good. Because tonight, when I get back from hunting for real meat and not this shimmering faerie fare—I'm going to show you how much of a lover I can be. You'd better be ready."

Gwenhwyfar gave him a playful push. "Have you ever known me not to be?"

His eyes darkened. "Maybe I don't need to hunt after all."

She arched a brow. "What was it you told Morgan about prolonging the wait?" She gave him another light push toward

26

the door. "Go. I'm hungry for real food, too. And," she added, "it'll give me some time to think of a special...em, dessert."

"I always like your...em, desserts. I won't be gone long."

"Take your time. I planned to visit Prince in his cave this afternoon."

He leaned over to kiss her forehead. "Take care, then."

"Always."

After Lancelot left, Gwenhywfar gathered a few apples from the basket on the table and stuffed them into her pockets. As she made her way through the lush forest, she caught sight of pointy-eared elfins working happily in patches of tilled soil and she caught the sound of laughter from the small, childlike manikins playing with the sunbeams that filtered through the leafy branches. Out of the corner of her eye, she saw a flurry of pastel colors, wrapped in twinkling mist and knew the faerie maidens were nearby. She wondered if Sadi, the blonde one who had been her friend, still liked the male faerie, Ganus. Gwenhwyfar smiled. Would she ever become as carefree and free-spirited as the sprites were?

When she got to Prince's cave, it was empty. Disappointed, she took the apples out of her pockets and laid them on the ground where he would find them when he returned. She turned to leave when a shadow covered the entrance.

"I've sent the unicorn to the meadow," Cernunnos said.

Gwenhwyfar was all too aware that he was blocking the only exit. The sunlight silhouetted his massive body, a brightness glimmering around him. His golden eyes glowed like an animal's in the dark. Involuntarily, she looked up for his antlers, but didn't see them.

Cernunnos walked toward her. "Do you wish for me to appear as the god of the hunt, my lady?"

Gwenhwyfar stood transfixed. She wanted to back away and yet felt that strong tug of energy that would lure her to him as it had done before. *Don't look into his eyes. It's the way he mesmerizes.* Nimue had told her that once. It took every bit of her will-power, but Gwenhwyfar forced her gaze away.

Cernunnos looked surprised. "It seems you have gained strength, my lady, since last you were in Faerie."

She looked at the wall. "You tried to take advantage of me then, my lord."

He lifted an eyebrow as he moved closer. "Did I? It seems you agreed to my terms willingly."

"I had not much choice in the matter."

"No? It seems to me you did. You wanted to see Lancelot through the pool. I could take you there. For a price, I believe I said. Did you not agree to it?"

Gwenwhwyfar felt her face flame, remembering. "There's no use having this conversation. I must go."

"Ummm..." Cernunnos reached her side and took her hand. "I let you go that time because you weren't ready for me."

Sweet Mary! He was sending tingling sensations up her arm and through her body. Gwenhwyfar tried to pull away, but he held fast. "You used magic," she said with a gasp, "just like you're doing now."

Cernunnos laughed. "No magic, my lady. You're feeling the simple attraction between a man and a woman. It is strong between us. Let me take you and show you how it can be."

She kept her eyes averted. "I love Lancelot. You know that."

"Love him if you wish. Let me show you pleasures you didn't know were yours to be had." His free hand caressed her cheek and slid down her throat to rest on her collarbone, his fingers brushing the swell of her breasts.

Gwenhwyfar began to tremble. The demi-god's powers were strong, the male heat of him enticing. She could scent him...

"Damn you." Gwenhwyfar threw her head up and glared into his face. "I will not allow this. Release me."

"Why? You know I will pleasure you."

Sweet Mary, help me to think. Gwenhwyfar fought to keep her head clear. *Concentrate. Think of Lancelot.* She took a deep breath and lifted her chin. "Pleasure is all you care about. Lancelot can give me pleasure too, but he can also give me more."

Cernunnos narrowed his eyes. "More?"

"Yes. He can give me love. And love is stronger than anything you can do." She took another deep breath. "You told me once that you did not rape. Are you about to begin with me?"

He growled and released her hand. "Go. But know, we are not finished."

Gwenhwyfar turned and walked with as much dignity as she could to the cave entrance, not looking back. Only when she had reached the safety of the trees did she break into a run that would have made any warrior proud. She didn't stop until she reached the house and was safely inside with the bolt thrown.

* * * *

The unicorn moved from a corner of the room to her side and gave her a gentle nudge. "How can I help, my lady?" he asked in his silent voice.

"Oh, Prince!" Gwenhwyfar threw her arms around him. "Can you get us out of here?"

His low voice sadly replied, "That I cannot do. Mayhap the ladies at Avalon can."

"Can you go to Avalon?"

He nickered. "I will try."

* * * *

"So," Morgan said as she waited for Cernunnos to emerge from the unicorn's cave. "You weren't as successful as you thought."

"Leave be, Morgan." The earth rumbled under his boots as he strode toward the forest, rabbits and squirrels scurrying from his path.

She did a pirouette in the air beside him and giggled. "My lord is—"

"Silence!" He glared at her as trees shook and birds took flight. "I see nothing humorous about this. A mortal woman refuses a demi-god? How can that be?"

Morgan settled her feet on the ground and slanted a look at him. "How can it be that a mortal man refuses the queen of Faerie?"

Cernunnos waved his hand dismissively. "That *mortal* is half-fey, remember?"

"That makes a difference?" Morgan flounced ahead of him and then turned. "If Lancelot's fey powers are too great for me to ensorcell him, perhaps they're too great for Gwenhwyfar to be won from him."

Cernunnos stopped in his tracks. "You dare to say he is stronger than I? A demi-god who has ridden the Wild Hunt for centuries? Who is both feared and worshipped? Have a care, Morgan."

"Do not threaten me, Cernunnos. I have ruled Faerie for as long as you have ridden! Was it not I who brought you to Briton and away from that conniving Aoibhill in the first place?"

"It was Myrddin, the Goddess' own bastard, who did." Cernunnos replied.

Morgan gave an indifferent shrug. "I could always handle Myrddin. I tweaked his ear on more than one occasion."

Cernunnos gave a grudging nod. "I remember."

"I'm not saying Lancelot is stronger than you, Cern," Morgan said in a softened tone. "Mayhap his power is not fey."

"Then what is it?"

"Love."

He snorted. "What is this thing called love? I don't understand it."

"I don't either, but it was the reason Lancelot refused me and the reason Gwenhwfar refused you. What kind of a power allows mortals to resist the temptations we offer them?"

"How can any power be stronger—or more pleasant—than satisfying the lust that lies between a man and a woman?" Cernunnos asked. "You know yourself, that's true. We've both lured mortals to our beds to enjoy what their bodies offer."

Morgan frowned. "But what if there *is* something better?"

"There can't be." Cernunnos reached for her. "Let me prove it to you."

Morgan eluded him. "No. I think I wish to know what love is."

The earth began to tremble again as he glowered. "You are denying me?"

"For now, yes. Lancelot and Gwenhwyfar seek only each other. They always have. Even when she was trapped here and he spent years trying to break through. This love showed when he fought you. *You*, Cernunnos. A demi-god who should not have been able to lose—"

"He had Excalibur!"

"Even so. The sword might have protected Gwenhwyfar, but it wasn't Arthur who wielded it. It was *Lancelot*. The sword would not have allowed him to hold it if this love' wasn't the reason." Morgan floated away from a second grasp that Cernunnos made toward her. "I think I will deny you until we find out what love is."

"You can't do that!" Cernunnos bellowed and felled two nearby trees with the sound.

"Certes, I can." Morgan raised her hands and the trees lifted once more. "I am the queen of Faerie, remember?" She giggled and twirled in the air once before she dissolved in a glittering, swirling mist of colors.

Chapter Three

"I didn't think I'd ever see Camelot again." Arthur looked around the Great Hall that had once been his and then reached over to take Nimue's hand. She put her other small, delicate hand over his large one.

"Twas time." She pushed back the uneasy feelings she had about the summons of King Custennin that Arthur return from Armorica.

The silver cast to his eyes matched the silver in his hair. "Even though people think me Armel, counsel to Prince Judwal of Lèon. It's still good to be back."

Custennin looked at both of them. "Cynric and his son, Caewlin, were instrumental in helping us defeat Wehha and Ida five years ago, but new trouble lurks and I fear it comes from within our own people. I need your advice."

Arthur frowned. "I have heard nothing of this in Armorica."

"You know the southeast has always been riddled with Saxons. Still, both Octha and Cissa have been relatively quiet these past years since Medraut was finally killed. But now, someone seeks to stir them again. My scouts reported armies amassing."

"Britons no longer fight the Saxon," Nimue said in her soft, priestess voice. "Boundaries have been established. Who would do such a thing?"

"Tis a fairly youthful man who goes by the name of Melehan." Custennin paced in front of the huge hearth where Arthur and Nimue were seated. "Cynric told me this Melehan fought with Wehha and then fled to Venta when Wehha was driven back."

"So why does he seek to stir trouble now?" Arthur asked.

Custennin stopped in front of him, looking uneasy. "Several moons ago, the old priest in yonder village passed away. His

32

acolyte brought some scrolls to us, babbling about witch's papers to all who would listen."

Nimue lifted a brow. "Witch's papers?"

"Aye. She came before the Black Death started, claimed to be a holy sister that could heal. Called herself Anna."

Arthur blanched. "My damn sister, Morgana. She was here?"

"Aye," Custennin said again. "She brought those rats with her that started the plague. No one knew."

Arthur took a deep breath and closed his eyes while Nimue gently rubbed his shoulder. "Her revenge," he said at last and wiped at his eye. "She vowed she would kill Gwenhwyfar for what Lancelot and I did to Medraut." He took another deep breath. "Well, 'tis done. The world's a better place without either Morgana or Medraut." He looked up when Custennin remained quiet. "What is it? They *are* dead. I saw Medraut—"

"Yes, Medraut is dead,"—Custennin resumed pacing—"but he was not without issue."

"*What*?" Arthur and Nimue said together.

"It was all written in Morgana's scroll," Custennin replied bitterly. "She probably realized the danger the boy would be in if it were known that Medraut had a son."

"She kept Medraut a secret from me for nigh onto twelve years," Arthur said dully.

Custennin nodded. "I think she planned to seat Melehan on the throne of Camelot once Wehha and Ida won the battle."

"And she would finally be able to rule Camelot through her grandson. 'Twas always her ambition."

"Did Melehan know?" Nimue asked.

"Not likely," Arthur responded. "The risk of my finding out would have been too great. Morgana was far too clever to risk it until she was ready to make her move."

"I agree," Custennin answered. "If that agitated young priest had not babbled about what he had read, word of it would never have reached Melehan's ears and he would be ignorant of the whole thing."

"Who raised him?" Nimue asked.

"He was fostered by relatives of King Gormund."

Nimue knit her brows together. "He was sent to Eire? Morgana feared disclosure that much?"

"Mayhap." Custennin paused.

"There's more?" Arthur asked.

Custennin stopped pacing and looked up at the ceiling and then back down before answering. "You know me to be a blunt man, not given to superstitions?" When they both nodded, he continued, "Morgana wrote this odd thing at the end. 'Twas what got the priest's tongue to wagging."

"What was it?"

"'Tis a bit of nonsense to be sure." Custennin shook his head. "She said that Melehan's mother was Aoibhill, the Aire queen of Faerie." He managed a strangled laugh. "Certes, no such creatures exist."

Arthur exchanged a glance with Nimue and then said quietly, "They exist, Custennin. 'Twas Morgan le Fey who transported me to Avalon to heal."

"I still have difficulty believing that story, Arthur."

"I know of Aoibhill," Nimue intervened softly. "Myrddin told me about her."

Custennin looked skeptical. "What did he say?"

"She has no love of Britons. 'Twas because of our Morgan le Fey that Aoibhill's consort abandoned her."

Arthur stared at Nimue. "Cernunnos? Is that whom you speak of?"

"Yes, but that is only part of this problem."

"There's more?" Custennin asked.

Nimue nodded. "Medraut was evil. If Aoibhill is truly Melehan's mother, that would make him an incubus."

Custennin sighed. "And what is an incubus?"

"It means he would be possessed of the evil that was his father's and enhanced by the fey powers of the faerie queen. He would have great power. His offspring would also inherit the ability to become wizards."

"Such as Myrddin?"

Nimue shook her head. "Myrddin was more than that and his power came from the Light of the Goddess, not the dark shadows where the one-eyed Balor roams."

"He must be stopped." Arthur's voice was emotionless. "I won't have my grandson wreck even more havoc than my son did."

"My soldiers are already preparing to march," Custennin said.

Arthur rose and Nimue knew he silently cursed the stiffness in his legs. "I go with you."

"It's not necessary, Arthur. I can handle this," Custennin replied.

Arthur drew himself up to his full, still-imposing height. "You think that my seventy years prevents me from fighting?"

"It's not that—"

"My sword arm is still strong," Arthur interrupted. "I have been given another chance to atone for the grievous sin of incest that I committed. I will go." He turned to Nimue. "Will you bring me Excalibur once more?"

"Dear Goddess, I cannot!"

A muscle twitched in Arthur's jaw. "You think me too weak as well, Nimue?"

"Never that!" She clutched at his arm, hoping he would understand. "When you asked me to go with you to Lèon, you left Excalibur with me. I gave it to our daughter, Argante, as part of the Lady's ceremony, for safe-keeping."

"Yes. Argante will surely let me use it."

"She would, if she had it."

"What? What are you talking about, Nimue? The sword was to rest at Avallach—"

"I know. But Astrala came to collect it. Argante could not deny her. It is with the Grail now, in Avalon."

Arthur closed his eyes and drew a deep breath. When he opened them, he took Nimue's hand. "I still must do this, my love."

Nimue bowed her head so he would not see the fear in her eyes.

Without Excalibur, would he return?

* * * *

"At least, they've acknowledged our request to parlay," Arthur said to Custennin as they were shown into the great hall of Cymen's near Venta.

"I still find it hard to trust Saxons," Custennin replied, "especially this son of Aelle's. He was the rebel when Aelle agreed to ally with you."

"Then his agreeing to parlay is even more important." Arthur turned as Cymen walked in accompanied by another man. "Is that him?"

"That's Melehan all right."

"He lookes nothing like Medraut." Arthur studied him as they came closer. It was hard to believe this youthful-looking man was a full score of years, yet he had to be. If not for his warrior's body with its broad shoulders and well-muscled arms and thighs, he might have even been taken for a woman, so fair was his face. His cheekbones were high, his nose straight and short, his mouth as full as any maiden's. Blond curls circled his head, but when Arthur saw his eyes, he knew this was no untried boy. His eyes were penetrating and the same grey color as Arthur's and Medraut's. They widened slightly as he met Arthur's gaze and then became hooded.

Cymen motioned them to sit near the hearth where a banked fire glowed, sending a bit of warmth to take the chill off of the damp, foggy autumn day. He glanced briefly at Arthur before addressing Custennin.

"What is it you wish to discuss?"

"We've heard rumors that there is unrest in your lands." Custennin's brown eyes hardened as he looked at Melehan and then back to Cymen.

"Rumors?" Cymen waved a hand. "There are always rumors."

"True. But when I sent scouts to investigate, the report came back that you are amassing men and training daily as if in preparation for war. What say you?"

Cymen shrugged. "It's wise to keep fighting men in shape, wouldn't you agree?"

Custennin narrowed his eyes. "Mayhap. The other report I received was that young Melehan here has ambitions."

"I admire ambitious men," Cymen replied.

"I'm not here to play with words," Custennin answered and turned his attention to Melehan. "Is it true or nay?"

This time, Melehan shrugged. "'Tis no secret that your priest found a scroll that belonged to my grandmother. 'Tis no secret, either, that Medraut was my father." He looked at Arthur and then back to Custennin. "I believe Medraut would have stood to inherit Camelot had he lived. Am I correct?"

36

"You are not." Custennin removed a parchment from his cloak. "Arthur appointed me his successor when he was taken away from the battlefield of Cam's Landing. This is Bedwyr's testament to the fact." He unfolded it and laid it on the small table in front of them.

Melehan left it there. "Blood counts far more than words on paper." He turned to Arthur and silver light flashed from his eyes. "Isn't that right, Grandfather?"

Arthur started. In the more than twenty years that he'd assumed the name and person of Armel, no one had recognized him. How could this total stranger know? Then he recalled Nimue's words. Melehan was an incubus.

"Armel is counsel to the king of Lèon," Custennin said quickly. "He is a holy man and has no heirs."

Melehan smiled angelically, but his eyes were like granite. "He may be counsel by whatever name he chooses, but he was King Arthur before his...em, *transformation.*"

Cymen straightened. "By Woden! He cannot be!"

"Certes, he's not." Custennin glared at Melehan. "Arthur lies buried with Gwenhwyfar at Ynys Gutrin. The inscription is on the headstone."

Melehan's eyes sparked silver once more and Arthur wondered if he *could* possibly know that it was Lancelot buried with Gwenhwyfar in the graveyard. Since they'd died of the plague, Nimue had put Arthur's name on the stone so they wouldn't be dug up and burned. And so Arthur could be free to live as Armel.

"I have visited the marker." Melehan turned to look at Arthur. "Arthur is not buried there."

Custennin leaned forward, outraged. "Have you desecrated holy ground?"

"I have done nothing." Melehan still looked at Arthur. "Blood calls to blood. I would have felt a kinship. You might say I inherited some of my mother's—grandmother's special skills."

Arthur gave no outward evidence of the shock that went through his system. How would Melehan know about the grave? What kind of hoax was he playing?

"I can assure you, Grandfather, it is no hoax. You aren't the one buried there."

Arthur felt the blood draining from his face. Melehan had not spoken aloud, yet Arthur heard him clearly. How could he have known what Arthur was thinking? He kept his face impassive. If what Nimue said was accurate, his grandson's mother would have had strong, other-worldly powers. Coupled with the inherent evil in Medraut as a result of the incest between Arthur and Morgana, who knows what this young man who looked so angelic was capable of doing?

Melehan smirked. "It might be wise to return to the subject of my inheriting my rightful land, don't you think?"

Custennin stood. "There will be no discussion! I was appointed heir."

"That might be so, when everyone thought King Arthur was dead. Dig up the grave. You'll find it empty. And, since the king obviously still lives, it is still his crown which I shall inherit. We don't need to go to war with this. Simply step down and return the throne to my grandfather."

"This is nonsense!" Custennin signaled to his guard to gather their horses and turned to Cymen. "I pray you will not be a party to the ramblings of someone who has *obviously* taken leave of his wits. I warn you. If you do, blood will soak this land once more and I will give no quarter."

Cymen frowned. "I dislike being threatened when I have committed no act of aggression."

"See that you don't." Custennin and Arthur turned and walked toward the door. "For if you do, I'll be ready."

They mounted their horses in the bailey and rode in silence until they were well out of sight of Cymen's fortress. Arthur brought his horse up alongside Custennin as they neared a pass, well out of earshot of the guard. "That boy is dangerous. I'm not sure you should have agitated Cymen. You don't need him as an enemy."

Custennin threw him a dark look. "I have not your skills for diplomacy. I have had to keep Briton safe—what hasn't already been taken by those yellow dogs—through use of threats and force. It is my way." He leaned back in his saddle. "I wonder how Melehan knew—"

A berserker war-cry rent the air and the guards wheeled to form a protective circle around their king as fully-armored

Saxons on horseback swarmed from the trees to the right, their round shields up in defense, axes at the ready.

Metal scraped leather as Custennin's warriors drew swords from their scabbards. Even in that little time, another band of Saxons closed in from boulders on the left, surrounding them.

Arthur reined in his horse. "At last, the Saxon fight mounted."

"A fine time to notice that point," Custennin muttered. "We're outnumbered three-to-one."

"We've had worse odds," Arthur replied, "but so far, no one has advanced on us." He scanned the waiting men, looking for Cymen or Melehan and wasn't surprised to find his grandson on the largest horse. It should have been nigh impossible for so large a party to be able to lie in wait, even if they rode at break-neck speeds. Arthur sighed. Melehan must have sent them ahead, even while they were still talking.

"Your atheling granted us safe passage," Custennin said. "Would you dishonor him by threatening our peace party?"

Melehan raised his visor. "These are not Cymen's men. They're mine. They've all stayed with me when Wehha was forced to retreat to Anglia."

Arthur scrutinized him. So Melehan gathered defectors just like Medraut had. Or turned them from their own athelings. Even if he hadn't inherited the basic evil that lived in both Morgana and her son, Melehan still wielded strong other-worldly power. Arthur wondered if he was aware of it.

"Even so, you stay on Cymen's land. You owe him your loyalty," Arthur said, "as a guest, if for no other reason."

"Being his *guest* is only temporary, Grandfather. Once you have taken the throne and named me your heir, I shall move to Camelot."

"Camelot is not mine to offer," Arthur replied.

"It will be," Melehan responded. "We have no quarrel with you, Grandfather. In fact, I have given specific orders that you not be harmed. I need you alive to declare me your heir. You are free to go. It is the imposter king, Custennin, that we want."

Custennin turned to Arthur. "Go. I will handle this."

Arthur's hand tightened on his sword grip. "I've never stood down from a fight."

"It isn't your fight," Custennin said under his breath. "Take advantage and go."

"I cannot." Arthur raised his sword. "I will fight."

Melehan drew his sword. "It is Custennin that I want."

"Then come and take him," Arthur replied.

His voice was drowned out by a melee of stamping hooves and clashing of ax upon shield and sword. The road became a swirling bowl of dust as horses reared and bodies engaged. Through it, Arthur fought at Custennin's side, his hand on his sword still steady, his horse responding to the pressure of his thighs. He hated to admit it, but doing battle after so long a time was accelerating.

From the corner of his eye, he saw Melehan lift a spear to let fly at Custennin. Reaching for his dirk, Arthur threw it at his grandson, the knife spinning blade over handle and finding its mark in his thigh between the byrnie's hem and the edge of the cuisse. Melehan roared in pain and his spear flew wide of Custennin.

As the blood gushed out of the wound, Melehan signaled his men to retreat and raised a fist. "I have not finished with you, Imposter. I shall return."

"Shall we follow them, my lord?" one of the guards asked Custennin.

"No. We are still guests on Cymen's lands. I will write a formal protest once we are home. Arthur is right. Sometimes, diplomacy pays. We don't need another war." He turned to Arthur. "Well done, once again."

Then he gaped. For Arthur was slouched across his horse's mane, blood flowing down its neck and the spear protruding from his side.

* * * *

"He still lives," Custennin told Nimue as the men carried an unconscious Arthur into the infirmary, a cloth tightly wound about his ribs.

"Barely." Nimue followed along, holding Arthur's hand and praying in the Old Tongue. "Mother of us all, I did not bring Arthur back to die at Camelot. Would that I had his scabbard back!" She turned to Custennin. "We must take him to the Lake. Argante will summon Morgan to take us through Faerie to Avalon."

"I'll have a travois prepared." He snapped his fingers and one of the warriors ran to do his bidding.

"Lord Armel has lost a great deal of blood." The medic unwound the cloth to look at the gaping wound and then quickly applied pressure as the blood began to flow once more. "What fool pulled the spear from him?"

"My squire," Custennin replied. "The lad acted before we could stop him."

Arthur's eyelids fluttered open. "Nimue?"

"I am here, my love. We're getting ready to take you to Avalon."

He attempted to smile, but it turned out to be a grimace. "I don't think I'll make it this time."

"I won't let you die!" Nimue's small hands made gestures of protection over his heart and she began to chant again.

Arthur drew a shuddered breath and looked dimly at Custennin. "Did Melehan die?"

Custennin shook his head. "He's wounded badly, but alive."

"Then you must finish it," Arthur whispered and struggled for breath. "He is worse than Medraut."

"Save your breath, old friend. I will take care of it."

"Hush, Arthur, please." Nimue brushed his hair back from his face. "You must conserve your strength."

He took her hand. "I love you. Always believe that."

A warrior burst through the doorway. "The horse and sling are ready, my lord."

"Good." Custennin motioned and six men lifted Arthur to carry him outside. He gestured feebly to Custennin and attempted a grin.

"It was good to fight one last time." He reached for Nimue's hand. "Good bye, my love."

Arthur closed his eyes to the mortal world for the final time.

* * * *

Nimue refused to give up, even when she could detect no breath or heartbeat. And no, she told Custennin, she was not going to let Arthur be buried in the cold earth. He would go to Avalon. She prayed to the Goddess the entire way to the Lake, hoping that the spell she was creating would last.

Argante awaited her on the shore with Barinthus, the boatman. "Father is dead?" she asked as she watched the warriors place Arthur on the barge and then quietly depart.

Nimue thrust her chin out. "You, of all people, should know better than that! As Lady of the Lake, summon Morgan. We must pass through Faerie."

"I am already here." A swirl of sea foam rose beside the boat and Morgan materialized, her gossamer gown swirling around her, dispersing droplets of water around her. "Once more, I will accompany the king." She put a hand on Arthur's forehead and then dropped it quickly. "He's so cold!" She looked at Nimue. "I cannot feel his spirit."

"That's because I hold it inside of me," Nimue replied as she stepped on board, "but doing so is taxing me greatly. I have not used my powers in far too long. We must go quickly."

Morgan nodded and the boat moved toward the mists that surrounded Avallach. "A spirit is free. How is it that you can hold his inside of you? "

Nimue paused in her chanting. "Love. Love binds us together." The corners of her lips rose at Morgan's frown. "It is a concept that a faerie would not understand."

Morgan's frown grew deeper. "Love. 'Tis the same answer I got from Lancelot when he refused me. 'Tis the same answer Cern received from Gwenhwyfar."

"Yes." Nimue attempted a smile. "Lancelot and Gwenhwyfar were destined for each other. They passed through death together and are now in the Otherworld, never to be separated again. Neither you nor Cernunnos could change that, even though you tried."

"And are trying still," Morgan muttered.

"What?"

"They aren't dead, Nimue. Cernunnos and I reached them just before the mortal death throes and gave them a choice. They now reside in the land of Faerie, young once more and immortal."

Nimue stared at her, hope flaring. Perhaps the Goddess had answered her prayers indeed. "Can you do the same for Arthur?"

Morgan shook her head. "I cannot bring him to life. I am sorry."

"Then I will plead my case with the priestesses of Avalon." Nimue looked down at Arthur. "I will not let him go to the Otherworld without me."

"Is love such a strong bond then?" Morgan asked wonderingly.

"Love is everything," Nimue answered. "To have love is to live. Without it, one only exists." She caressed Arthur's face gently with her hand. "I will not let him go."

* * * *

The High Priestess, Rhiannon, escort of souls passing to the Otherworld, waited on the shore as the barge broke through the faerie mist and scraped gently onto the white sand of Avalon. Her hair glistened as blue-black as the raven who sat on her shoulder, her obsidian eyes only a shade more opaque. Nimue's heart sank. "I had expected the Morrigan."

"Her work is on the battlefield, to gather the souls lost there and to bring them to me." Rhiannon watched as Avalon's manikins, chattering in childlike voices that were deceptive of the strength in their diminutive arms and legs, lifted Arthur's body from the barge and placed it on the hide of leather to carry him up the hill. She turned back to Nimue. "You have his soul. You must return it to him so I can take him to Janus."

Nimue lifted her chin. "I cannot do that."

The raven fluttered its wings and blinked a beady eye at her. Rhiannon soothed it with a single word of the Old Tongue. "You cannot or will not?"

Nimue drew a deep breath, knowing the high priestess had the power to make it her last. "I will not."

Rhiannon lifted a delicate, ebony brow. "If you refuse to yield it, your soul could accompany his."

Nimue bowed her head. "I am aware of that."

"You surprise me, Nimue. In all your years as Lady of the Lake, never once have you disobeyed the Goddess."

"And she is not disobeying now."

Startled, Nimue looked up as did Rhiannon. The sweet fragrance of apple blossoms drifted down the hill accompanied by soft strains of a harp that fell like a sigh upon the air. Ethereal music that Nimue knew had no human hand to it. They were surrounded by a phosphorescence of glowing white light, shimmering with translucent particles of gold and silver.

43

The light gathered itself in a swirling movement, taking form. A blonde figure stepped forth, the essence glowing around her.

Nimue went to her knees. "Astrala. Did you bring the scabbard that will save Arthur?"

"You dare to speak to the Grail Maiden without leave?" Rhiannon asked.

"Forgive me," Nimue said with downcast eyes. "I only—"

"I understand," Astrala said gently. "As a priestess once, you have earned the right. You may rise."

"Thank you." Nimue stood. "The scabbard?"

Astrala shook her head. "It will work only to save what is alive. Arthur has passed from the mortal world."

"Then I shall be about my business," Rhiannon said in a hollow voice. "Janus waits at the gates. Return his soul, Nimue, or prepare to accompany him."

"The time is not yet," Astrala said.

The high priestess looked irritated. "What nonsense is this? Arthur is either dead or he is not. You both know Arthur has a place in the Otherworld where he will be honored. Why do you fight this?"

Astrala's face lit. "Because *Arthur* will fight once more."

Nimue clasped her hands to her breast. "I knew he would live!" She looked up the hill to where the manikins had disappeared. "Will you take me to him?"

"I will, but he is not there." The Grail Maiden gave an enigmatic look. "Come."

Blinding white light swirled around Nimue and a swish of air lifted her, spinning her through some sort of tunnel that ended abruptly inside a dimly lit cavern. Thousands of crystals glowed in reflected light from a source that Nimue couldn't see. Then she gasped.

She was in a tomb. All around her were marble slabs on which lay fully armored knights. She squinted to read the names etched in the stone beneath each one. Cai, Arthur's foster brother. Gwalchmai, Gaheris, Garreth...Arthur's nephews. Bors and Lionel, Lancelot's cousins. Peredur and Galahad.

Nimue turned to Astrala. "The Knights of the Round Table?"

"They slumber." Astrala gestured toward a point of light. "Watch."

The point of light advanced, becoming brighter and bigger as it approached. Its luminous center hovered for a moment, then a figure emerged from its incandescence before the light faded. Nimue gasped again and felt something tug hard within her breast and then a golden thread left her body and made its way toward the figure.

Arthur's shade stood still as if to get his bearings. Nimue watched the thread be absorbed and knew Arthur's soul had returned to him. He began to slowly walk the circle of sleeping knights, pausing at each one as if remembering.

"Arthur!" Nimue called.

Astrala placed a hand on her arm. "He can't hear you or see you. We are not here in his time."

Nimue watched as the shade moved on. His eyes shone as he recognized his men. He stopped at the empty slab that had Bedwyr's name on it. Nimue looked questioningly at Astrala.

"He will join them soon," she said.

Arthur's spirit body frowned as he looked around, as if searching for someone. "What of Lancelot?" Nimue asked.

"Arthur looks for him."

"Lancelot has chosen to live in Faerie," Astrala replied.

So Morgan hadn't lied after all. "I wish I could tell him," Nimue whispered.

"He will know, one day." Astrala lifted her hand to sketch an element in the air. Another marble slab took shape in the middle of the circle.

Nimue read its inscription. *Arturius Rex: The Once and Future King.*

The tomb began to fade even as Nimue watched Arthur lie down upon his stone bed, armor forming over him and then she found herself standing on the shores of Avalon once more, alone with Rhiannon.

The Grail Maiden's voice came to her in the ethers. *"Know that he sleeps only to awaken when he is needed once again."*

Chapter Four

"I dreamt of you last night, my lord," the Saxon wench whispered as she kept her eyes demurely on the bandage she was wrapping around Melehan's thigh.

He almost smiled through the pain that was throbbing in his leg. He looked about the room that had been given him at Cymen's court. It was richly appointed, the walls hung with tapestries that were probably the spoils of war. A comfortable, stuffed chair with ottoman sat before the hearth and the floors, as well as the bed, were covered richly with soft, thick wolf pelts. If his leg would heal, he could enjoy his surroundings ...and the wench who tended him.

"Why does the wound not heal?" he asked. "You've been tending it these past three days."

Ilsie looked up, troubled. "Truly, my lord, I do not know. My skills are respected here—"

"I have no doubt of that." Melehan brushed the back of his hand along the side of her plump breast. "Mayhap you have not used all your skills on me?"

She blushed. "I meant to say, my *healing* skills are sought after."

"Hmmm. Did you not say you dreamed of me last night?"

Her fair face flushed deeper. "I should not have mentioned that, my lord."

"Why not? Tell me how you dreamed of me."

"I—"

The door opened abruptly and Melehan bit back a curse when he saw Cymen standing there. Could the man not have given him some time for a bit of sport? Then he remembered that the wench was a niece of Cymen's. The Saxons were even more protective of their clanswomen than the Britons were.

"I need to speak with Melehan, Ilsie," Cymen said.

"Certes." She gathered the basin and dirty bandages and scurried toward the door, chancing one look at Melehan before she left the room.

Melehan turned to Cymen. "What is it you wished to talk about?"

"Arthur is dead."

Melehan sat up in the bed, oblivious to the fresh burst of pain that shot through him. "What?"

"Your spear killed him."

"That cannot be. I aimed for Custennin. It flew wide when I was struck."

Cymen grimaced. "From the accounting I received, Arthur moved in front of Custennin to protect him."

Melehan felt the blood leave his face. Dimly, he remembered seeing his grandfather slouch, but he thought it had been part of the knife throw. "Why would anyone do something so foolish as to get in the way of a tossed spear?"

The Saxon's lips tightened into a thin line. "From the stories my father, Aelle, told me, Arthur always did the honorable thing. It was the reason Da allied with him, even when Aesc would not. It's the same reason Cynric would not fight for us."

"But Arthur was not at Camelot when Wehha and Ida laid siege," Melehan said bitterly. If only the Saxons had all stuck together, he might even now be sitting in a place of power.

"True. Custennin was and *is* at Camelot. I bear no love for the man, but neither do I wish to start a war. He will come for you to avenge Arthur's passing. You will need to leave."

The Saxon was right. Custennin would waste no time in marching here, once Arthur was laid to rest. And there was only one place Melehan knew he would be safe. There was one woman who could hide him from mortal eyes. Aoibhill. He would go to Eire.

Even as he struggled to get his trews on and pull on his boots, his thoughts turned to her. He had never told anyone that the old nurse who helped raise him was actually a beautiful, fire-haired faerie. Queen of Eire's faeries, no less. The one time he had brought up the subject of seeing a sprite in the forest, his foster mother had mumbled something about sin and swooned and then, for days, had made him stay on his knees in prayer to St. Patrick. After that, he did not share what the faerie queen taught him deep within the forest.

"I will go to Eire." He laced up his tunic and picked up his cloak from the chair. "Is my horse ready?"

"Saddled and waiting. You have provisions for several days as well."

"My thanks, then." Melehan limped to the door and then stopped. "I am still the rightful heir to Camelot. I will return."

"Don't be a fool," Cymen said sharply. "You resurrected King Arthur when, for years, everyone assumed him to be dead. That story is even now traveling from one bard to another. The man was a legend, even when he was king. And you were the one to take his life. Again. There is no place in Briton where you will be safe. Do not return."

"But—"

"My Atheling!" the fyrdman burst in, breathless.

Cymen turned to the soldier. "What news?"

"A churl arrived at the gate. King Custennin rides this way."

"How far out?"

The fyrdman gulped in air. "Anon. The churl was on foot, the Britons are not."

Melehan needed no further urging. Ignoring the stabbing pain that pierced his leg with every step, he ran into the bailey and leapt upon the waiting horse and headed south toward Portus Adurni where he could catch a ship to Eire.

He only hoped that Aoibhill would not be angry with him. He knew what her wrath could do. Then he shrugged. He was not the young lad who had left Eire as a squire five years ago. Fighting first with Medraut and Childebert and then later with Wehha, had made him a man. And, he *was* an incubus.

He would handle Aoibhill.

Chapter Four

"Arthur is *dead*? You stupid, little fool!" Aoibhill angrily swished her gossamer skirts as she turned away from Melehan. "Do you have any idea of the true amount of damage that you have done?"

The faerie sprite who attended him on the chaise in the queen's mystical castle began to fade as Aoibhill's wrath lashed out in bolts of lightening. He sighed, restraining the red glow fromhis eyes that would let Aoibhill know how angry he was.

"It was an accident. I had aimed true for Custennin." She looked ready to release more fire, so he changed the subject. "Why did you never tell me who my father was?"

"For your own protection," she hissed, barely restraining herself. "Morgana told me when Arthur was born, Uther Pendragon gave him into the keeping of that magus, Myrddin, so the babe would not be killed by those who sought to hold power. His foster parents, just as yours, had no idea of who he was."

"But why didn't you tell *me*? All those times you took me for walks into the forest to learn the dark arts...why didn't you tell *me*?"

Aoibhill eyed him more calmly. "Boys are wont to brag. It was safer that you didn't know."

"Medraut—my father—did *he* know I was his son when he came to Eire to recruit soldiers to join the Saxons against Custennin?"

Her lavender eyes showed real mirth for the first time since he'd arrived here. "No. Once I had talked to Morgana, we agreed it would be better Medraut not know, so I erased his memory of the conception."

"You were there when I was conceived?" Melehan tried to sit up and then winced from the pain of his infected thigh.

Aoibhill's mouth twitched and, had she been a cat, he would have sworn she'd lick her whiskers. "You might say that."

49

"Witnessing the act and enjoying it? You hold nothing sacred, do you?"

Her eyebrow rose. "Sacred? That seems a strange word coming from one who seduces women even as they sleep beside their husbands."

He felt himself flush, partly with pride and partly not. "It is who I am. You explained all that to me when I was barely in my manhood."

"Yes. Yours is a unique gift. I had to wait many years for the proper man who could create you."

"And I suppose you put some kind of spell on my real mother so she wouldn't remember any of this either?"

Her mouth twitched again. "Your mother remembers every detail."

This time, Melehan lifted a brow. "Is that a secret to keep me safe too, or will you grant me the privilege of knowing who she is?"

"Certainly. You're looking at her."

It took a moment for him to register what she had said. "You...you're my *mother*?"

"I am. Why do you suppose I took such an interest in you? Even to the extent of using the glamour so your foster parents would only see an old crone, eager to tutor you in exchange for coin?"

Some of it made sense now. When he was but a child, Aoibhill had come as his nurse. And, while she was clothed in plain homespun and her hair was brittle and grey, he had always seen an ether about her that sparkled in shades of reds and yellows. And then the day had come...

"Today you are ten-and-three," Rhia, his nurse said as she held out her hand. "Come, walk with me. We shall go into the forest."

Melehan scooted off the bench in the solar where he had been doing his numbers. He was always glad to be free of that boring task, but it was a real treat when Rhia took him into the forest. There, he learned things—dark things—that would have him praying on his knees for weeks if his foster mother ever found out. But those things were his secret with Rhia. He took her hand, wondering again why it felt so smooth when it looked so wrinkled.

She was unusually quiet until they reached the small clearing that was really more of a grassy bank for the bubbling brook that wound its way through the trees. The place always had an eerie fascination for him and today, the lone hawthorn that grew out of a small boulder nearby had a single blossom on it.

They sat down amidst a patch of primroses and Rhia tilted her head to look at him. "Tell me about your dreams. They have been unusual, lately, have they not?"

He blushed. How could she have known about those dreams? The ones where he woke up and his sheets were wet with a sticky substance? They'd only begun a fortnight ago, along with the girl... He couldn't tell Rhia about that. Melehan looked into his nurse's eyes and saw, not the normal faded blue, but an iridescent lavender instead. Her gaze was compelling and he found himself talking.

"I dream of a girl with long black hair and eyes as dark as night. She seems so much older than me and yet she's not."

"What does she do?" Rhia asked.

He felt his face turning redder. Yet, his nurse's eyes enthralled him. "She touches me...all over...and then my thing grows hard. My muscles tighten. My body feels like it's going to explode. And then...it does." He tore his gaze away from hers and looked down at the earth.

"It is nothing to be ashamed of, Melehan," Rhia said gently. "It means you have become a man. Would you like to meet the girl?"

He looked up, startled. "She's real?"

"Oh, yes. But perhaps not to this world." She gestured toward the hawthorn.

His eyes followed her hand and he blinked. The boulder wavered, blurring in some sort of mist that surrounded it. He blinked again. The rest of the air was clear, but the rock was barely visible for the denseness of the vapor around it. A woman's long, bare leg emerged, followed by the other. A filmy material barely covered the torso of the black-haired girl who now stood before him, smiling.

"Who are you?" he whispered.

"Her name is Ona," Rhia said, "and she is a succubus."

He could only stare at the girl whose dark eyes filled him with desire. "A what?"

"A succubus. A being who visits men as they sleep and brings them special dreams, such as yours."

He managed to look at his nurse, whose eyes were swirling pools of lavender now. "She came from that rock. How can that be?"

"Perhaps it was an illusion," Rhia said softly and motioned with her arm. "Look around you."

Small, transparent beings seemed to float in the air, flitting from one primrose to another. He thought he heard tinkling laughter. A shadow caught his eye and he turned, in time to see a black figure skittering behind a tree. And then he noticed the creature attached to the bark, studying him with lively brown eyes. Movement in the water attracted him and he saw what looked like a miniature female with flowing green hair and webbed feet.

"What are all these things?" he asked.

"Sylphs," Rhia answered as she pointed to the translucent beings playing among the flowers. "The one on the tree is a nymph and the water sprites are called Asrai. You also saw a gnome darting away. You have seen into the land of Faerie."

Melehan looked around him once more and then at the girl whose scant tunic was so sheer he could see the fullness of her breasts and tight nipples. He ached to reach for her but feared she was nothing but air. "Are you real?" he asked again.

Beside him, his nurse laughed. "As real as I am. Look at me, Melehan."

He managed to tear his eyes away from the luscious curves he could see beneath the filmy material that Ona wore. His mouth dropped open.

Instead of the bent, grey-haired crone who was his nurse stood a tall, majestic woman with flowing, coppery hair, resplendent in strips of bright silk that floated softly around her.

"You see me for the first time as I am," she said.

Melehan found his voice. "Who are you?"

"I am Aoihbill, queen of the faerie you see around you. Would you like to know about my world, Melehan?"

His eyes darted to Ona and back and he nodded. Aoihbill laughed, the sound rich and throaty.

"I can see where you want to start. Very well. Ona will teach you all you need to know. When she is finished, you will know what you really are."

"A man?" he asked, a little boastfully.

Aoibhill laughed again. "More than that. You are an incubus, born to seduce women in their sleep and turn their wills to you."

He hadn't really listened to that, intent only on what pleasures Ono would bring...and bring them she did.

Then had come lessons in magic and the dark arts; things Aoibhill said would be as useful to him one day as his warrior skills were.

"And I did all of that work for naught." Lightening flashed outside as Aoibhill grew angry again.

"I'm not sure I understand," he said. "Was your plan to capture Camelot? Even if Wehha had been successful in laying siege to it, Medraut had been killed in Armorica. I didn't know then that he was my father. How would I have inherited?"

"You are still the rightful heir," Aoibhill said. "Who do you suppose sent that young priest to the village?"

"You?"

"Certes. I kept in touch with Morgana as well."

"And you knew Arthur was alive?"

She narrowed her eyes and thrust her lower lip out. "No. Not at first. He had done a very good job of cloaking himself. It wasn't until the priestess, Nimue—the Lady of the Lake—went to him did I find out. My spies were punished for that."

He tried not to flinch. He knew what happened when Aoihbill was crossed. Faeries were stripped of their powers and left to the mercy of humans in the mortal world where they were thrown...if they survived the tortures that she devised and chose to inflict on them. Even his father's grisley death paled in comparison to what Aoibhill was capable of.

"I still don't think I understand," he said cautiously. "You are queen of all the faerie here in Eire. What use would you have of Camelot? Unless, Certes, you wanted to make your son a king?"

53

Cynthia Breeding

"You would be quite welcome to hold the lands, Melehan, but I had another purpose in mind. Mayhap, it *is* time you knew." She turned and walked toward a table at the back of the room and waved her hand. A wooden trunk appeared on top of it. With a flick of her finger, she removed the silver lock and lifted the lid. Aoibhill took out a scroll along with a small box and carried them back to him.

"Are you aware," she asked as she sat down beside him and began to unroll the scroll, "of how your father died?"

He hesitated and then nodded. "I was there. We had retreated behind fortress walls, save for Medraut. A Breton challenger called him out. Lancelot, Childebert said his name was."

"Ah, yes. Stories of his prowess on the battlefield—and elsewhere—reached even our shores. Go on."

"They fought well. Truthfully, I've not seen a better swordsman," Melehan admitted reluctantly. "But when Medraut—my father—was down, it seemed Lancelot was giving him some choice."

Aoibhill's hands stilled on the vellum. "How so?"

"We were too far away to hear, but Lancelot moved his sword from Medraut's throat and positioned it over his manhood." Melehan paused and tried not to wince. "Then he ran him through, staking him to the ground."

"Not a pleasant or glorious death then."

"But he wasn't dead."

The faerie's eyebrows lifted. "Lancelot did not kill cleanly?"

Melehan shook his head. "He turned and walked away. Somehow, my father managed to raise up enough to throw a dirk at him, but it was as if he *knew*...he dropped and rolled away from it."

"Niniane, his mother, had fey blood. I met the bitch once," Aoibhill said.

"I cannot say," Melehan replied, "but it was then that we all noticed the other man who had not retreated from the field."

"Another Breton?"

"No. He wore the armor of Camelot. He threw a blade so fast it was nothing but a silver flash. It found its way to Medraut's heart."

Aoibhill narrowed her eyes thoughtfully. "Arthur?"

54

"In hindsight, probably. He and the Breton fought side-by-side or back-to-back all day." He smiled suddenly. "If the man who threw the knife that killed Medraut was Arthur, then I'm glad he's dead by my hand. I just wish Lancelot were still alive, for his death would be by my hand as well."

"Foolish man," Aoibhill scolded. "There are far better revenges you could have had. I should have taken you into my confidence years ago and this could have been avoided." She sighed. "I must make do." She unrolled the scroll again.

"This is the story of Faerie, not only here in Eire but across the water in Briton as well." She turned to Melehan. "Do you remember my telling you of the Horned God, Cernunnos?"

"The antlered one who rides the Wild Hunt at full moon? He is known in Briton as well."

Aoibhill's face looked pinched. "Well, his home was once here."

"In Eire?"

"*Here.* In Faerie. He was my consort."

"Why is he not my father then?"

"Because," she snapped, "he was stolen from me."

"How can that be? You're the queen of Faerie."

"*This* faerie land. There are others."

"Ah." His diabolical grin widened. "Don't tell me some other faerie stole him from you?"

"Not some other faerie. Another queen." Her eyes flashed silver. "And you would be wise to stop smiling. If that had not happened, I would never have enchanted Medraut and you would not be seated here!"

He sobered. "My apologies. I just find it hard to believe that anyone—even another faerie queen—could have stolen your consort."

"Well," she said, somewhat mollified, "she had help. Have you heard of Myrddin?"

"The wizard? He disappeared two score years ago. Right after Cam's Landing, I think Medraut once said. Dead and buried someplace."

"He may have disappeared, but I doubt he's dead," Aoibhill huffed. "He came here once, centuries ago."

"Centuries? How old are—"

55

"Age and Time do not matter in Faerie," she interrupted. "He came for Eire's blue stones to build the Giant's Dance. He had the faerie queen, Morgan le Fey, with him to transport the stones." Her eyes flashed silver again. "She bewitched Cernunnos. I don't know how she did it. I didn't even realize they had met. But when she left, he was gone too."

Melehan watched her warily. "If he means so much to you, why haven't you gone over there and ensorcelled him back?"

"I wouldn't have to *ensorcel* him at all. He only needs to have the veil of enchantment lifted to see that I am his true consort." She sighed. "It's not that simple though. A faerie queen must be invited into another's domain or risk loss of her powers. The only other way I can gain entrance is for the king of the land to demand I be allowed to enter."

"I think I'm beginning to see why you wanted me on the throne." Melehan frowned. "Cymen told me I could not return."

Aoibhill sighed again. "While Custennin reigns, that is probably true. There is another way."

"Which is?"

"The isle of Iona lies between us and Briton. For centuries, the druids made their home there and some priestesses of the Goddess of Avalon as well. On Samhain, Iona functions as a bridge between the lands of Faerie. There is a spring, not far from a sacred grove whose doire is part fey. I have watched her through the mists, which is as far as I can go. She ages, but slowly. Her mortal half will be easy to seduce."

"All mortals are. What will you have me do once I enter Briton's Faerie?"

She leaned forward. "Seduce Morgan. Get her to leave Faerie, if only for a moment. Without her presence, I can slip in."

"I've never tried to seduce an immortal before," Melehan replied. "I'm rather fond of my head. I would not like to lose it if her temper equals yours."

Aoibhill opened the small box she had been holding and withdrew a silver chain with a strangely marked round pendant and slipped it over his neck. "This will protect you. I spelled it long ago to lure Morgan to it. Once you've gotten her away from her land, I will summon Cernunnos and be back here before that mouse will know what happened."

Melehan fingered the metal, cold to his touch. "I don't want to incur your wrath, but what if—just possibly—the Horned God doesn't want to go?"

Instead of the flash of fire he'd expected, she reached into the box again, bringing up a silver horn no larger that his fingernail. "The horn of Aphrodite. He will hear its call and be compelled to come to me."

"Another enchantment?"

"Something like that. You leave Cernunnos to me and do what you do best." Her smile widened. "You are an incubus, Melehan. Use your powers."

Chapter Five

Cernunnos studied Lancelot from across the small glade where they all had gathered to enjoy the warmth of the mid-day sun and Faerie wine with something Gwenhwyfar called cheese. He looked down at the soft, white substance he held in his fingers, not believing it really came from the goats that roamed the pasture. Then he looked back at Lancelot.

The man sat with his back against a birch tree, his dark hair a contrast to the white bark, his long legs stretched out in front of him. Gwenhwyfar lay contentedly on her back, her head in his lap. Certainly a scene for debauchery if ever Cernunnos had seen one. One slight tug at the tie on her shoulder and the silk gown would fall away, exposing the fullness of her breasts. Obliquely, he could see the faeries by the bracken. Ganus had already removed Sadi's dress and much giggling was going on. Yet, what did Lancelot do? His hand merely played with Gwnhwyfar's hair.

Cernunnos' gaze shifted to Morgan, perched on a flat rock not far away. She, too, was watching Lancelot and Gwenhwyfar. He fought back the urge to snarl. Such was their ritual these past days. Whenever he came upon Gwenhwyfar, Lancelot was with her and Morgan not far behind. They ignored her and she ignored *him*. He growled. Never in all their centuries together, had Morgan *ignored* him. They'd each taken pleasure from mortals, from time-to-time, but always, *always*, when he beckoned her, she came. And their lust knew no bounds. No mere man could satisfy her like he could. How oft had she told him that? And he ached for what she did to him. Faeries had few inhibitions, their insatiable curiosity being a basic trait, but Morgan had the gift of imagination as well. Cernunnos' recent couplings with each of the faerie maids had done little to slack his appetite. He growled again. Why was Morgan tormenting him? Because Lancelot and Gwenhwyfar were in *love*. That intrigued and fascinated Morgan. She decided she wanted *love*, too.

Cernunnos looked back to where Lancelot sat and sharpened his hearing so he could take in their conversation.

"The cheese was good, Gwen."

"Prince showed me where the goats were before he left. It felt good to do something human again like milk them. I did have a bit of a problem explaining to Morgan what a churn looked like."

"It was a rather odd-looking one that she created, but it worked."

"Tomorrow I'm going to explain to her what I need to make the bannocks you like so much."

"Then I will have to find a hive of bees," Lancelot replied, "since I know how you like honey." He trailed his finger down her cheek. "Do you remember the first time we had bannocks with honey?"

Gwenhwyfar's eyes turned dark. "Twas the time in the cottage."

"The first time we were together."

She turned her face to nuzzle against his hand. "I was so afraid it would be the last time as well. Elaine—"

"Shhh. She will never come between us again. No one will, Gwen."

Taking his hand, she held it in both of hers. "You are right. No one will ever come between us again. I love you, Lance."

He brushed a kiss over the tip of her nose. "I love you, too."

Love. There was that word again. Cernunnos snorted in disgust. *They talk about food? No wonder he does nothing but barely kiss the woman.* If this kind of lack of action was Morgan's new idea of passion, she needed a good, hard tupping. Not some silly talk about food. But she eluded him every time he came near.

He glanced her way again. She was sitting, enthralled, watching the two mortals. From the way her ears were pointed, he knew she'd heard their conversation as well. *Food.* He got up, shaking his head. He didn't understand what all this love idea was about, but apparently it had to do with feeding.

It was time Morgan came back to his bed he thought as he stomped off. If *food* was what Morgan wanted, then *food* was what she'd get.

* * * *

Cernunnos waited patiently the next day, lurking behind one tree and then another to the dismay of the gnomes who called them home. He didn't even pay attention to the alluring tree dryads that scooped down to sweep their long, brown tresses over his head. Instead, he watched from the shadows as Morgan conjured one ingredient after another for Gwenhwyfar. There was also an odd little box that appeared to be made of stone, now sitting in the middle of the glade where they'd had lunch yesterday. It sat atop what looked liked squares of muddy moss that were afire and smelled worst.

"You'll be surprised how these will taste by putting these soft balls of dough in this oven instead of directly on peat," Gwenhwyfar said to Morgan and looked approvingly at the box. "Camelot was one of the few places that had such a thing."

Morgan eyed it dubiously. "It seems like a lot of trouble."

"Lancelot loves fresh bannocks." Gwenhwyfar smiled. "And he's always...affectionate...when I keep them warm for him."

Morgan's eyes lit up. "Is there a special thing you put in them to get him to show affection? A potion?"

"Not a potion," Gwenhwyfar answered. "I make them with love from my heart."

Morgan sighed and Cernunnos watched as the two of them walked away, leaving the box unattended for the moment. He scrutinized the box, catching a whiff of the bannocks baking. It did smell good. And if there was *love* in one of those round pieces, then he'd give one to Morgan and they could settle this foolish nonsense.

He darted out and reached in the oven for a bannock and then soundly cursed as he pulled back his hand to suck a burnt finger. Did mortals do nothing easy? Who knew that fire would be hot? Faerie flames needed no such heat. More carefully this time, he managed to snag one and wrapped it in one of the pieces of cloth Gwenhwyfar had stacked nearby. It should be delivered warm, she'd said. That was what must make the *love* work. He could do that. He covered the cloth with both hands, making heat within his palms. Now he had to find Morgan. Quickly.

Thankfully, she was in her favorite spot near the scrying pool. Spying on some unsuspecting human, no doubt.

"I've brought you something, my queen."

She jumped a little and sidled a safe distance away from him. Then faerie curiosity got the better of her and she tilted her head. "A present?"

"Something better than that." Cernunnos held out the cloth. "Love."

"What?"

"I've brought you love," he said again and unwrapped the linen. "Here."

Morgan stared at the bannock and then at him. "You've brought me one of Lancelot's bannocks?"

"Yes," Cernunnos said proudly. "It has *love* in it. What you said you wanted. Take it."

Her eyes narrowed dangerously as the water in the pool began to swirl. "If you think to mock me, Cern, think again."

He frowned. "I don't think to mock you. I bring you this so you'll stop avoiding me and let me bed you."

The water formed small, choppy waves. "You expect me to lie down for you—when I know you've rutted with each of my faerie maids these past days—because you bring me food?"

"Yes." Cernunnos willed himself to be patient and not down a tree accidently. "Food is what Lancelot and Gwenhwyfar were talking about when they spoke of love. I know you heard it, too."

Morgan looked at him incredulously. "Food?"

"Yes. Food. Have your brains become addled that you don't hear?"

A sudden gust of wind splashed water over the edges of the pool and puddled around his feet. She lifted her arms and let the wind sweep her up and away from him. "Not my brains, Cern. Yours."

He watched as she disappeared and then he cursed, causing the earth to tremble and the water nymphs to dive deep beneath the surface.

He had done his best and this was the thanks he got? *What did that fool faerie woman want anyway?*

* * * *

Morgan materialized on the bank of the stream behind spiny gorse bushes and watched as Lancelot emerged from bathing. She took in his naked, lithe form, the muscles of his broad back flexing as he bent to retrieve a towel. He had the powerful arms of a warrior and heavily muscled thighs of a superb horseman. Not that Cernunnos was lacking in those qualities, for he was equally broad of shoulder and narrow at waist. Morgan tossed her head. Cernunnos brought her *a bannock* when she wanted to be treated like Gwenhwyfar was by Lancelot. He straightened suddenly and turned, as if he heard her thoughts. A dusting of dark hair spread across his chest and trailed in a line past his flat belly, ridged with layered muscle to... She sighed in disappointment as he wrapped the cloth around himself before she could get a good look at the very best part of him.

"You've no right to spy, Morgan," he said.

"I wasn't spying."

He lifted an eyebrow. "Lurking behind bushes while a man bathes isn't spying?"

"I'm not lurking. I just arrived." She stepped away from the gorse and moved toward him. "I do not know why you won't let me pleasure you, Lancelot. You don't know how good I am." She brushed her fingertips along his bicep. "Shall I show you?"

"No." Lancelot stepped back from her and shrugged into a tunic he'd left lying on the nearby rock.

She tilted her head and gave him a slanted look through her lashes. "I *could* bind you with a spell and take my pleasure."

"You could *try*," he replied, "but even if you succeeded, how much pleasure would you get from an unwilling man?"

Dark clouds began to gather and thunder rumbled.

Lancelot glanced up at the scudding clouds. "Is it not enough to know that you have Cernunnos?"

She thrust her lower lip out. "You would like the outcome."

"I would not dishonor Gwenhwyfar like that."

Morgan frowned. "Because you love her?" The look of relief on his face might have been comical if she weren't so frustrated with him.

"Yes. Because I love her. How many times have I said it? Gwen's fate and mine may be in Faerie, but our destiny lies with each other. Leave be, Morgan, and go back to Cernunnos. He wants you."

"But he does not love me."

Lancelot looked up from the belt he was tightening. "Since when did that matter to you? You each enjoy the game of making the other jealous, yet neither of you hesitates to lie with another. Or do *I* have to remind *you* how it was each time Gwen and I tried to visit using the scrying pool when I could not gain entrance to Faerie and she was trapped here?" He finished tying the belt and reached for his boots. "You like to play games, Morgan. 'Tis who you are."

She looked away. "Mayhap I am tired of playing games."

Lancelot put his boots back down. "What are you saying then?"

"Only that I wish he paid attention to me like you do to Gwenhwyfar."

"I would say that Cernunnos pays a great deal of attention to you, Morgan."

"Oh, yes," she said as she turned back to him, "he wants my body."

A corner of Lancelot's mouth quirked up. "Isn't that what you just asked of me?"

Thunder rumbled again. "Do not dare to make fun of me!"

He sobered. "I'm sorry. I did not intend to insult you. It seems to me that you and Cernunnos have always taken great pleasure in each other." He picked up his boots again and pulled one on.

"Oh, yes," Morgan said caustically, "we do. But, he takes pleasure with anybody that is female. Just ask any of my faerie maids this week."

"That is hardly a new trait of his." Lancelot tugged on the other boot.

"No, it's not!" Morgan rounded on him, eyes flashing. "Is it asking too much for him to restrain himself?"

"Have you asked him to?"

"I shouldn't have to ask him!"

Lancelot sighed. "It is a compliment that women seem to think men can read your thoughts and desires. We cannot. 'Tis a sad failing of ours. Talk to him."

"I already have!" Morgan hissed.

Lancelot frowned. "And he refused your request?"

"He did not understand it."

"How so?" Lancelot studied her. "What it is you really seek?"

She looked down, feeling her face heat. Faerie queens did not blush. *Ever.* Yet... "I wish him to love me like you do Gwenhwyfar," she whispered.

Silence met her remark. When she defiantly brought her chin up, Lancelot was nearly gaping at her in astonishment.

"I had no idea," he said quietly.

"There is something missing with Cernunnos and me. I didn't know what it was. But when I see you with Gwenhwyfar—even before, when she was trapped in Faerie—there was something special. And not only did you refuse me, Gwenhwyfar refused Cernunnos. He is a *demi-god*, one of the most powerful beings other than the goddess of Avalon. How did Gwenhwyfar have the strength to do that when not one single mortal ever has resisted his magic before?"

"Love is the strongest magic there is."

"Then tell me how to make him love me!"

Lancelot shook his head. "You can't *make* him love you."

"Then what must I do?"

He took a deep breath. "For one thing, stop trying to seduce me or anyone else. Love is built on trust and respect. Turn to him for your wants and needs. Let him know he can depend on you. That, together, you can face any problem and solve it."

"Was it that easy for you and Gwenhwyfar?"

"No, it was not." Lancelot looked into the distance as if bringing back memories and then he looked down at her. "There were lots of obstacles. People got hurt. There were times neither of us thought we'd see each other again. We risked death to be together. More than once."

Morgan felt her eyes grow round. "You were willing to give up your mortal lives for each other? Why? If you had died, you would have nothing."

"You're wrong, Morgan." He gathered up the rest of things and turned to leave. "If one of us had lived without the other, then we would have had nothing."

* * * *

Gwenhwyfar finished feeding the last chunk of apple to Prince when Lancelot appeared in the stable. She lifted her face for his kiss as he wrapped his arms around her.

"Ummm. You smell good." She noted the damp ends of his hair. "If the tub water is still hot maybe I should bathe too."

"No tub." He released her and moved over to pet the unicorn. "I took a dip in the stream instead."

Gwenhwyfar frowned. "Morgan just came back from there."

Lancelot grinned. "Jealous?"

"Always."

"That's nice to hear, even if you don't mean it."

"How do you know I don't? A handsome, strong, virile man and a beautiful woman who just happens to be a faerie—"

"And not half as beautiful as you." Lancelot swept her back into his arms and gave her a deep, long kiss. "Would you like me to prove whom I prefer?"

"Very much," she said and then reluctantly pushed back. "But Prince was just about to tell me what news he's brought from Avalon."

"Later then." Lancelot let his fingers trail over her clothed breast before dropping his hand. "What's the news?"

Gwenhwyfar turned to the unicorn and began their silent communication. Her eyes filled with tears as she twined her fingers in his silky mane.

"What is it, Gwen? What's wrong?" Lancelot put his hand on her arm. "What's he saying?"

She shook her head and put her hand over his and continued her silent conversation. At last, she gave a tremulous smile and looked at Lancelot. "Prince spoke with Nimue. Arthur passed over. There was no time to heal him."

Lancelot drew a deep breath. "What happened?"

"Nimue said that Arthur returned to Briton to aid Custennin. Apparently, some young rebel who fought with Wehha was trying to rally the Saxons into fighting again." Gwenhwyfar shook her head. "Why Arthur would think, at three-score-and-ten, that he should engage in battle—"

"He was *king*, Gwen. Have you ever known Arthur to stand down?"

She stared at him. "You're right. I never did understand—"

"I'd have joined him."

"And possibly have been killed too? Oh, Lance, for once I'm glad we're in Faerie where you'll never have to fight again."

Lancelot's eyes turned to slate. "It would have felt good to fight beside him once more." Then he sighed. "Did Nimue bring him to Avalon?"

"Yes. If there is any good to this story, Arthur rests with the other knights of his round table."

Lancelot lifted a brow. "After Cam's Landing, they were taken to the crystal cave on Avallach. I helped Barinthus ferry them across the Lake myself."

"There is a portal on the top of the hill, is there not? I remember Nimue telling me that is how Myrddin brought Arthur back."

"Yes. Did Myrddin return to Avalon, too?"

Gwenhwyfar looked at Prince and then back at Lancelot. "He doesn't know. Nimue only said that she was able to glimpse the tomb where they all lay and that Arthur's shade joined them."

"I wish we could pay our respects."

"I don't think that's possible," Gwenhwyfar answered. "I sent Prince to Avalon to ask the priestesses for sanctuary there, but it seems the only way mortals can leave Faerie is by permission or absence of its queen."

"Perhaps if I ask her—"

"No!" Gwenhwyfar said sharply. "Do you remember what price she exacts for that kind of favor?"

"Mayhap this time she won't demand my body for her pleasure," Lancelot replied. "We had a talk today—"

Gwenhwyfar went still. "By the stream?"

"Yes, but—"

"Were you naked?"

"Gwen—"

"Were you naked?"

"Yes, but let me—"

"You don't need to say more, Lance. The woman—damn faerie—follows you endlessly. Then she spies on you bathing and you stand there, naked, talking to her?" A hysterical bubble of laughter rose in her throat. "Oh, I don't think she's just going to give us her blessing. She wants you, Lance. She always has."

"Shhh!" Lancelot pulled Gwenhwyfar to him and slanted his mouth over hers, his hands kneading and massaging her back, pressing her against him, holding her tight, deepening his kiss until her arms came around his neck and clung to him.

"I'm sorry, Lancelot. I have no reason to be such a jealous shrew." She nestled her face into his shoulder and tried not to cry.

"It's all right." Lancelot smoothed her hair with his hand. "You're upset with the news of Arthur. We'll find a way to leave here. We will."

Gwenhwyfar only wrapped her arms around his waist more tightly, thankful that Lancelot had always been her champion. Had always had the ability to console her. She wouldn't let him know that this time it wasn't working. There was no way to leave here. Cernunnos would continue to stalk her and Morgan would pursue Lancelot for eternity.

Time meant nothing in the land of Faerie.

* * * *

Morgan paced in front of the heatless flame that burned in the hearth, trying not to give in to the vulgar human habit of biting her fingernails, even though she could magically restore them to whatever length she wished. Still, there was some odd sort of comfort in it, she thought, as she nibbled one.

She couldn't *make* Cernunnos love her, Lancelot had said. That remark didn't set well with her, since she was used to having her own way in everything, especially here in her own realm. She was *queen* of Faerie!

Still...what had withholding the pleasure of sport that she also enjoyed gotten her? Cern only had to look at a faerie maiden; lustful as they all were, there was no need for him to even mesmerize.

Morgan paused. She was almost sure he'd tried to mesmerize Gwenhwyfar when she had come upon them in the cave. How had she resisted him? Was this love magic really as strong as Lancelot said? What else had he said? Something about trust and respect. She began pacing again.

Did she respect Cernunnos? *Yes.* He rode the Wild Hunt every full moon, but he took only those souls who poached his forests of birds and beasts for sport, not need. He granted boons for those who still worshipped the old gods. Even in her domain, her creatures deferred to him as he strode through glade and glen, stream and fields.

Did he respect her? He never used his power against her. He pleasured her well. Was that respect? She didn't know.

Trust. Morgan almost laughed, nearly biting her finger and quickly slapped her hand down. *Only when he's in my sight. Even now...*

Turn to him for your wants and needs. Morgan stopped. By all the gods, what had she been doing? She wanted him. He needed her. Or he did before he decided to bed a different faerie each night. She whirled, knowing what she would do.

She would seduce Cernunnos into loving her. After all, seduction was one of the things she did best. She'd take him a bannock to show she appreciated his gift after all. She giggled. This would work.

* * * *

Cernunnos hid his amusement as Gwenhwyfar kept at least one piece of furniture between them in the living area of the huge, hollowed tree that served as his home in the forest. He did enjoy toying with her, herding her slowly toward the one corner of the room from where there would be no escape. She knew it too, for she kept maneuvering away from it. His mouth twitched. Frankly, he was surprised she had come to him at all.

"You know the price I will exact for escorting you to Avalon," he said.

Gwenhwyfar stepped behind a chair as he moved closer. "For once, can you think about something other than ravaging me against my will?"

"No." His hazel eyes were sultry. "It would not be against your will either."

"Mesmerizing someone is the same thing!" She darted behind a table. "And will you stand still!"

"Certes." He halted and lifted a hand. Immediately, items in the room began to waver. The table slid to the side and Gwenhwyfar grasped for it.

"Stop this. You're making me dizzy."

He lowered his hand and the furniture fell back into place. "See how I wish to accomodate you, Gwenhwyfar? I would do so in bed as well."

She gave an exasperated sigh and tried to sidle toward the door. "I should have known it was a mistake to come here. But it's important to Lancelot—and to me—that we visit the tomb where Arthur lies. We didn't even know the other knights were there. It would ease Lancelot's mind and heart if could see them once again."

"Lancelot's problems are not my concern." Cernunnos moved to block the entry.

"If you were a gentleman—"

"I think we've already established that I am not," he said. "Over the centuries, I've found that if there is one thing mortal women do *not* want in bed it is a prim and proper 'gentleman.' I'm sure you don't find Lancelot as such, do you?"

"Leave Lance out of this!"

"I thought he was the reason you were here, my lady?"

"Don't twist my words," Gwenhwyfar said hotly. "I'll leave since you obviously do not have a heart to do the right thing."

He frowned, antlers beginning to form in the ether above his head. "I can be generous when I choose to be."

"I haven't seen it." She looked at the door. "Would you step aside?"

"In a minute. Perhaps there is something else you can do in return for my escorting you."

She eyed him skeptically. "What?"

"Explain to me the significance of bannocks in your world."

"Bannocks? We eat them."

"Do they always have *love* in them?"

Gwenhwyfar looked confused. "I'm not sure—"

A strange, lilting melody filled the air, stopping her in mid-sentence and causing Cernunnos to whirl around in the doorway, totally blocking it.

"Hello, Cern." Morgan's voice was low and seductive. "I've come to make amends." The faerie giggled, the sound floating softly on the air. "You know how well I can do that."

Cernunnos leaned against the bark frame. "I'll meet you at the waterfall."

"I can't wait that long," Morgan responded in a throaty, beguiling tone. "Let's just go inside."

Gwenhwyfar peered over Cernunnos shoulder. "I was just leaving."

Morgan froze in the midst of loosening the thin straps that held her filmy, gossamer gown up. Her eyes darted from Cernunnos to Gwenhwyfar. "What's she doing here?"

"It's not what you think, Morgan." Gwenhwyfar pushed past Cernunnos into the open. "I had a favor to ask."

The wind whipped the grass flat where Morgan stood as she narrowed her eyes. "I know what payment Cern always asks. Did you pay it?"

"He hasn't granted the favor," Gwenhwyfar said.

"Yet. Because I arrived."

"True, but—"

The trees began to bend as the wind strengthened. Morgan's eyes flashed. "Don't let me interrupt then." She flung something on the ground, turned and ran into the forest.

"Wait!" Gwenhwyfar called after her as she ran after her. "It isn't what you think! Let me explain—"

Cernunnos watched as both women disappeared in the dense foliage and shook his head. For once, he had actually been innocent. Gwenhwyfar could explain that to Morgan a lot better than he could.

He looked down to see what Morgan had thrown and then bent over to pick it up. A bannock. She had brought him a bannock when she'd rejected his gift earlier.

Morgan was no doubt playing one of her games, but he wasn't sure what the outcome was. He grunted. In all his centuries, he had yet to understand that faerie. He looked down at the bannock again.

And for the immortal life of him, he didn't understand *bannocks*.

Chapter Six

Why he couldn't have just appeared on Iona, instead of being forced to cross the turbulent, cold, wet St. George's Channel on a boat, Melehan didn't understand. It was Samhain, after all. Strange occurrences were supposed to happen.

But Aoibhill had insisted the druids would sense his magic, dark as it was in contrast to their light, so he had to travel as a mortal man. Further, to provide him a reason for traveling to the holy isle, he posed as a knight who had displeased the Irish king, Diarmait mac Cerbaill, and was in need of sanctuary. The descendants of the few druids who escaped Roman persecution years before hadn't taken a liking to the Irish kings' approval of St. Patrick either, so Melehan was welcomed to their isle.

He looked up at the night sky. A full moon had risen, shedding its silver light across the emerald hills of Eire, casting dark shadows among craggy boulders. From afar, he could hear the druids chanting in the grove of young oak trees. They would stay there until dawn, welcoming the new year.

Mist was forming, rolling in from the sea, as he made his way northward toward the well at the crossroads. Beyond it, a single, blue menhir stood, embraced by a hawthorn on its left and a rowan on its right.

As he moved toward the distant stone, he felt the doire of the well watching him, but he couldn't see her, which was fine with him. Keepers of wells were beings of light and she would, no doubt, sense his incubus status, even if he tried to neutralize his power.

He approached the faerie mound upon which the menhir stood. The hour was near midnight. Even as the mist thickened, he could feel the veil between the mortal and immortal world thinning. The portal should be here.

Melehan felt soft, tiny hands playing with his hair even before the faerie gathered form from the mist. Her fingers grazed his cheek as she gazedat him with eyes as green as the Eire hills he'd left behind.

"Why does a stranger approach my home?" she asked in a beguiling voice.

She was beautiful. Her moon-pale hair cascaded about her shoulders and the wispy tunic of finely spun cobwebs did little to hide her generous breasts and luscious curves. Aoibhill had warned him that it would be an illusion. The fae who guarded the portal was one of Morgan's oldest and wisest. Right now, it was hard to believe.

"I displeased the Christian king across the sea and seek sanctuary here."

The faerie raised a delicate eyebrow. "Then you should be with yon druids."

Melehan lidded his eyes and gave her the special look that worked on all mortals. "I fear they cannot protect me."

"And you seek entrance into Faerie?" she asked, unfazed.

The look hadn't worked. Melehan allowed his eyes to begin glowing as he silently began the words to mesmerize.

The faerie's smile widened, revealing very white teeth with sharp fangs. For a moment, her glamour faded and he thought he saw a white wolf shimmer in the air, but when he blinked, there was only the lovely faerie looking up at him with golden eyes. Was she a shape-shifter or was it Samhain?

"Scotti warriors cannot find me in Faerie unless you allow them passage," he said.

"Quite true." She appeared thoughtful. "But you won't be able to return either."

Little did she know that when Aoibhill conquered, the rules would change. "I will be content to live in Faerie if all its creatures are as beautiful as you."

"Tis no need to flatter me," she said as she stroked his arm and stepped closer. "You are a handsome mortal and I grow weary of guarding this portal without company. Mayhap you would allow me to pleasure you?"

Melehan bit his cheek to keep his response in check. The mesmerizing effect on faeries was strong and fast. He'd expected to have to do the seducing. "I would like nothing better—" he began and then her mouth silenced him.

If all faeries were as lusty as this one, he would enjoy his mission in Faerie, he thought as, moments later, she had divested him of his clothes and was making sensuous love to every place on his body. He groaned as she straddled him. She leaned forward, her tongue licking his throat as he bucked hard beneath her. He felt a sudden sharp sting and then pure ecstasy as her womanhood clutched at him, squeezing more strongly than any mortal woman ever had. With a shudder, his body reacted and he felt his seed shoot powerfully into her.

Oh, yes, if this is how faeries played, he'd take his time in exiling Morgan. *After* he'd experienced the queen of Faerie for himself. *Many* times.

She rolled off of him and he suddenly found himself dressed. Melehan frowned. Surely what had just happened hadn't been an illusion? He looked around. He was still in the mortal world, for the moon was directly overhead, bathing the menhir in pale light.

The faerie gestured toward the stone where a crack now appeared. "Go quickly. The portal doesn't stay open for long."

A practical faerie. He liked that. She didn't seem to expect any soft words or compliments, either. Melehan *really* going to like Faerie. Still, to be polite, as he stepped through the widening crack he asked, "Do you have a name?"

From far away, he heard her reply.

"Lupiana."

The stone closed behind him, leaving a white wolf at its entrance. She licked the fang that had his blood on it and snarled. "I have marked him for you, Cernunnos. The incubus is up to no good." Then she turned and loped off to the forest.

* * * *

Melehan shook the water off himself as he stepped out of the scrying pool and was surprised to find his clothes were dry. Toward his right lay a meadow and what appeared to be a steep hill, shrouded in fog. He took several steps in that direction only to bump into an invisible barrier of some sort. Not that way then.

He turned to his left where a hawthorn grew close to a rowan with a cluster of primroses between them. An incandescent shimmer hovered between the two trees. Faerie? He took a deep breath and stepped through.

Immediately, he felt the change. The air tingled. And the colors! The sky was a deeper blue and the grass a brighter green than anywhere he had seen. The trees seemed to move, even though they were standing still. Melehan rubbed his eyes and looked again. The bark *was* moving, only this time he could see mischievous brown eyes blinking at him and small brown bodies with tiny, delicate hands and feet slithering along the bark. *Dryads.* His gaze moved upward at a soft humming sound and spotted little golden bodies with glassy wings flittering through the leaves. *Wind-singers.* He caught a dark shadow moving from tree to tree. *A gnome.*

A clustering of sparkling, pastel colors floated toward him and as he watched, it formed itself into the shape of a woman. A very beautiful woman. *Faerie*, he corrected himself. *Morgan?*

The faerie tilted her head, her bright red hair swinging down as she studied him with lively, cinnamon eyes. "Who are you?" she asked in a sultry voice.

"My name is Melehan," he answered and bowed. "And whom do I have the honor of addressing, my lady?"

She giggled and stepped closer, extending her hand. "I am Branda."

He brushed his lips over her hand, lingering a little longer than he should, but she didn't seem to mind. Her skin was like white satin, but surprisingly, she felt human. He straightened.

Branda lowered her lashes and lifted her face. "Would you like to kiss me, handsome Melehan?"

Stroking her cheek gently with the side of his hand, he said, "I've heard that when a mortal man kisses a faerie, she enthralls him."

She slanted a look at him that was pure seduction. "I wish only to pleasure you."

And I you. Little did she know that an incubus was immune from any permanent enchantments. But, until he met Morgan and had her in his control with the pennant, it would be better not to play with her faeries, lovely as this one was.

"I would make sure that pleasure is mutual." He let his hand drift across the upper swell of her breast before he dropped it to his side and sighed. "But you should know, I come seeking sanctuary from the outside world."

"Sanctuary? I do not know the word."

"Protection," he answered. "In the mortal world, I displeased a king. Your guardian on Iona allowed me to pass through."

Branda's mouth formed a pout. "Brina would not let you through without payment. If you kissed her, then you are hers."

"Brina?"

"Our guardian at the stone."

"I didn't meet anyone named Brina."

Branda frowned. "Brina takes her duty very seriously. She is one of the old ones among us."

Melehan shook his head. "The lady said her name was Lupiana."

The faerie's eyes widened and she stepped back. "It cannot be," she whispered.

"I'm sure that was her name."

"Then you are in great danger," she said in the same whisper. "You must go back at once."

"Why?"

"Because..." She became agitated, tiny silver sparks flashing from her. "I cannot tell you and I cannot send you back. But my queen can. I will take you to her."

Melehan considered her. He knew he wasn't in danger. An incubus was hard to kill, even though he wasn't immortal. Still, if she led him to Morgan, his work here might be swift. Once he'd shown her the pennant, her will would be bent to his and he would ask that she accompany him to Briton and protect him while he made his apologies to King Custennin. This would be child's play.

He inclined his head. "I do not wish to distress you, Lady Branda. Take me to your queen."

She nodded and looked up at the sky. He followed her look thinking the moon glowed pure silver in Faerie.

"We must hurry," she said. "Soon it will be dawn."

Probably something about the portal not opening after the sun rose, he thought as he followed her along the twisted paths deeper into the forest. He was nearly out of breath when she stopped by a stone cottage surrounded by gardens everywhere.

She knocked once and he heard a velvety-soft voice bid them enter. It seemed faeries in Briton spoke in seductive, sultry voices. He didn't mind.

But he wasn't prepared for Morgan. Aoibhill had said she was a mouse, all brown like the earth. Her hair was brown, it was true, but it reflected every shade and hue of brown and gold he'd ever seen as she swung herself to a sitting position from her chaise, long, slender, bare legs exposed as the silky saffron gown slipped up. Her slanted eyes glowed like emeralds, fringed in heavy black lashes and her full, wide mouth was as rosy as an apple. This was no mouse.

"Who have we here, Branda? How came he to my lands?"

"His name is Melehan, my lady," the faerie replied in a shaky voice. "The wo—Lupiana sent him."

One of Morgan's shapely eyebrows went up. "How interesting." She turned her full attention to Melehan. "And why did you wish to come to Faerie?"

He explained his circumstances, substituting King Custennin for Dairmait mac Cerbaill. At least that part was true. Custennin didn't like him. "And so, I came here for protection," he concluded and reached into his tunic. "I brought you a gift, certes."

She clapped her hands in delight. "I love presents!"

He bowed and lifted the necklace, the strange silver etchings catching the reflected flames from the hearth. "This is for you, my queen."

Morgan le Fey stared at the pendant, fascinated.

Just as he'd hoped.

* * * *

Cernunnos would have laughed at the glowering looks he was receiving from Lancelot, but in truth, the Wild Hunt had taken its toll this night. Things were changing as the mortal world advanced and evil was found in too many places. He'd had to travel far to find a coven celebrating what Samhain was truly about.

But Gwenhwyfar and Lancelot had been waiting near the pool when he returned and so here he was, standing in the cool, dimly-lit tomb that housed the knights of the Round Table. Lancelot clearly didn't trust that Cernunnos hadn't demanded his usual payment for such a favor as leaving Faerie for Avalon.

Cernunnos could hardly believe it himself. Gwenhwyfar had actually returned after not being able to find Morgan and explained about bannocks. Apparently, they were only food, but something about her making them because Lancelot liked them had to do with *love*. He wasn't really sure he understood it, but a bargain had been struck and he had to honor his end. He just didn't have to let Lancelot know that the payment had been an explanation of bannocks. Let the warrior squirm for once. Cernunnos perked his ears so he could hear the conversation taking place where Arthur lay.

"Old friend," Lancelot said as he gazed down at the stone-like effigy, "I wish I had been with you to fight that final time."

Gwenhwyfar ran her hand softly over the hardened face. "I remember how upset I was when he left for battle right after we were married. I didn't understand then that Briton meant more to him than I ever could."

"Do you wish it had been different?" Lancelot's dark eyes remained on her.

"No. Myrddin was right. We weren't meant for each other." She slid an arm around Lancelot's waist and leaned into him. "But, if that marriage had not been arranged, you would not have come for me. If Arthur hadn't spent so much time gone, he wouldn't have appointed you my champion. If—"

Lancelot hushed her with a kiss. "Our fate always rested in the hands of the Goddess. Come, let's visit the others."

They moved slowly around the room, taking time to acknowledge each knight's effigy. Lancelot stopped at Galahad's.

"His life was so short. I wish we had made peace with each other earlier than we did."

"Galahad had to learn tolerance," Gwenhwyfar said as she stroked Lancelot's back. "He didn't have an easy beginning."

"No. Thanks to Elaine's lies."

"He learned the truth of those. And he did have Dindrane in his life, if only for a little while. He had love."

Cernunnos lifted his head and narrowed his eyes. There was that word again.

"And Peredur as well." Lancelot pointed to the slab with Peredur's name on it. "He may have been the only complete fool I've ever known, but he never gave up on Blanchefleur."

"And don't forget how Gwalchmai trailed after Ragnell until she finally agreed to marry him."

"And he was the source of many a jest for putting up with her shrewish mouth," Lancelot said, "but a man in love will suffer any indignity."

Cernunnos snorted. Why should a man have to be subject to humiliation because of a woman? If Morgan ever sought to belittle him to prove himself... His antlers began to grow and he stopped the thought. This *love* could hardly be worth such a blow to his pride. A lusty mate, willing to show a woman how much he wanted her, should settle the matter. After all, both the man and woman derived pleasure from the act.

"And don't forget Tristan," Gwenhwyfar said, gesturing. "When he was injured, Iseult flew to him with white sails up."

"They always did have their secret codes," Lancelot agreed. "And Isolde was nearly the death of him, telling Tristan the boat sailed with black sails instead."

"It just proves that love will survive." Gwenhwyfar placed her arms around Lancelot's neck and he drew her close. "Doesn't it?"

Cernunnos felt himself grow hard watching as Lancelot deepened the kiss and his hands slid down to grasp Gwenhwyfar's rounded bottom and pull her against him. Now *that* might be love, he thought and wished they could return to Faerie. He had his own mating to do with Morgan. She was always ready for him when he returned from the Hunt. He sighed. Nimue had told them a feast would be prepared and even a god didn't refuse the priestesses of Avalon. It would be awhile before he could slake his need.

But Morgan would grow frustrated too. And a frustrated Morgan was one very passionate, wild faerie.

Yes, he could wait. He could only imagine what bedding her would entail.

* * * *

"The jonquils become you, my lady," Melehan said with a deep bow as he presented the flowers to Morgan.

She looked at the yellow bouquet. Had she ever seen more exquisite blossoms? She chose one. Each petal was velvet soft as she brushed it against her skin.

"They lack next to your beauty," Melehan whispered as he sat down beside her on the bench in her garden, "but I hope you like my humble gift."

Morgan gave him a lingering look. Such a handsome young man with his golden curls framing a face almost too handsome for a male. The chiseled cheekbones, straight nose and full, wide mouth were perfection. Only the squared jaw saved him from being called beautiful. That, and his eyes. Clear and grey, like the sea on an overcast day. They reminded her of someone.

"They're lovely," she murmured. Had Cernunnos ever given her flowers? She couldn't remember. Her eyes focused on the pennant she wore. The gift Melehan had given her yesterday. When was the last time Cernunnos had gifted her?

And where was he? She had waited until well past dawn for him. No doubt he was enjoying some rollicking sport with a mortal and lost track of time.

Melehan reached for her hand. Morgan let him take it, aware of how strong his long fingers were and how gently he held hers. Was Cernunnos this gentle? Or was he even now touching some other woman like this? She pushed the thought away. "If you treat all ladies this way, you must have been a very gallant knight."

He smiled angelically. "Certes, I have been taught to treat women well, but I didn't know what it was to cherish one until I met you."

Cherish? Was that like love? Morgan looked into his eyes to see if he was jesting, but he met her look innocently enough. Her fae senses could detect no deceit. She frowned slightly, remembering an earlier conversation with Branda.

"My lady," the red-haired faerie said as they sat in the solar, sipping primrose wine early this morning, "remember who sent him. The wolf."

"Lupiana is one of Cernunnos' subjects," Morgan replied, "and since Cern has not seen fit to get himself here after the Hunt, he no doubt had her send Melehan to keep me occupied until he returns." She flicked an imaginary piece of lint from her silk gown. "Not that I won't still be angry with him."

Branda shook her head. "When has Cernunnos ever sent you another man for your pleasure? And one who looks like this—"

"Are you interested in him, Branda?" Morgan asked. "Are you trying to warn me away from him because you want him?

You know I've always been generous with mortals. You may play with him if you want."

Her face turned nearly as red as her hair. "No, my lady, that is not my intention. But think of how Cernunnos guards you from Lancelot...and it's plain to see that Lancelot is faithful to Gwenhwyfar."

Thunder rumbled in the clear sky outside and Branda drew back, her eyes wide. "I did not mean to insult you, my lady."

Morgan made an effort to still her temper. It wasn't Branda's fault that Morgan was in a foul mood. She had been ready to forgive Cernunnos for that little episode with Gwenhwyfar and the man didn't show up. She shrugged. "Lancelot is an interesting diversion. I rather enjoy making Cern jealous. Perhaps I should do the same with Melehan when Cern returns."

Branda cast her eyes down. "As you wish, my lady, but be careful."

"What troubles you, my lady?" Melehan asked as he stroked up her arm.

She closed her eyes briefly to relish his touch. It was so light and yet so promising. But...the stirrings that she usually felt at the beginning of a seduction weren't there. Melehan was young and handsome, his muscular body most pleasing to look at. Yet, her own body didn't heat in reaction.

"Just a small problem that I need to work out." She closed her hand around the pendant. "I want to thank you for this again. It's beautiful."

Melehan let his gaze drift down. "If only I could take you home with me, I would shower you with jewels of every color." He sighed once more. "But without immortal protection, I do not see how I would live long enough to right the wrong that has been done me."

"What wrong has been done you?"

He paused. "It seems a shame to waste such a fine afternoon with my troubles."

Morgan laid her hand on his arm. "You are my guest here. I would not ask if I did not want to know."

Still he looked hesitant. "Are you sure, my lady?"

"Quite."

"My men and I were riding toward Camelot to pay homage to King Custennin," he began, "and I had the strangest sensation that we were being followed. I don't claim to have fae powers, but I'm sure you know the feeling?"

Morgan nodded. "Go on."

"Well, I sent scouts back to check our trail. It wasn't long before they returned and confirmed my suspicions. There were near a score of men behind us, no standard unfurled, nothing to identify who they were. We could only assume they were Saxon rebels in search of bounty."

"What did you do?" Morgan asked softly when he grew quiet in thought.

"We took cover and waited for them," he said at last. "If they didn't notice us, we would let them pass unharmed. Unfortunately, one of our horses neighed, alerting them. The next thing I knew, we were fully engaged in battle."

Morgan creased her brow. "Why would that anger Custennin?"

Melehan took a deep breath. "They were Custennin's men, traveling incognito because King Arthur rode with them."

"*King Arthur?* Are you sure?"

"Yes, my lady. He had been living in Armorica under another name. I didn't know that he and King Custennin would be on that road. I swear it."

She patted his hand. "I'm sure that can be explained. Arthur is a reasonable man, even if Custennin isn't."

He looked down at the ground. "Perhaps under other circumstances. I wounded him. Certes, it was an accident. And his mage was there to heal him—"

Morgan gripped his arm. "*Myrddin* was there? I thought he had lost his—well, no matter. *Myrddin* lives? You're quite certain?"

Melehan nodded. "So, you see, even if I could get an audience with Custennin, the wizard would cloak everything I have to say and twist it about—"

"No, he won't." Morgan stood suddenly. "I know how to tweak Myrddin's ear. I will take you back to court myself. This can all be cleared up quite easily."

"Would you do that for me, my lady?" Melehand grabbed her hand and kissed it. "I don't deserve to be treated so well."

"Oh, but you do." Morgan absently fingered the pennant. "You've given me a gift worth far more than you know." Myrddin lived. Myrddin, with whom she had struck a bargain long ago that brought Arthur into this world. The wizard owed her. And he was just what she needed to reinforce her magic and make Cernunnos love her.

She was so engrossed in that thought that she didn't notice Melehan's sly look as he turned away.

* * * *

As they slipped through the fine veil that separated Avalon from Faerie, Cernunnos felt the hair at his nape rise. He lifted his head, scenting the air. Something wasn't right.

Lancelot stopped beside him. "What is it?"

"There is a stranger here." His antlers began to form in the ether.

"A human?" Gwenhwyfar asked.

He used both his animal and demi-god senses to scent once more. "Possibly. But there is something else...it smells of dark magic."

"How could dark magic enter?" Lancelot inquired. "The earthly portals are well-guarded. It took me years to be able to break through."

For a moment, Cernunnos broke his concentration and glanced at Lancelot. "That was the Grail Maiden's magic. I'd have kept you locked out for eternity."

Lancelot's eyes darkened. "I know. You stole Gwen—"

"Stop it, you two," Gwenhwyfar interrupted. "If there's dark magic here, Astrala would have had no part in it." She turned to Cernunnos. "Are there earthly portals that can be breached by a human?"

"There shouldn't be. Morgan has them well-protected."

Lancelot looked dubious. "If they're guarded by faeries, anything could happen."

Cernunnos grunted an assent. "I have my own creatures that stand guard as well." He stilled suddenly, closed his eyes, and tilted his antlered head.

"I have marked him for you, Cernunnos. The incubus is up to no good."

Cernunnos' eyes flew open. "Lupiana!"

"Who?" Gwenhwyfar asked.

"No time to explain. Somehow an incubus has gotten into Faerie. We must hurry." He sprinted off, not waiting to see if they followed.

Lancelot paced him easily, Gwenhwyfar farther behind. As they drew closer to the scrying pool, Cernunnos could see two figures through the swirling mist. One was Morgan, the other a blond man. Getting near, he could smell the enchantment that had been placed on Morgan. He just didn't know what it was.

He stopped abruptly, a few feet from the pool. Beside him, Lancelot pulled his sword, ready to fight.

The blond man looked up, a twisted grimace on his lips. "You'll hardly need that."

"Yes, put that away." Morgan glanced at Gwenhwyfar before looking at Cernunnos. "I don't know where you've been, but we'll speak of that when I return."

He could see the two, tiny red marks Lupiana's fangs had made on the incubus. "You're not going anywhere," he said to Morgan.

She raised a brow even as the water began to stir in the pool. "May I remind you that I am queen here? This young man is in need of my protection. There has been a misunderstanding at Camelot that I should be able to fix." She smiled at Melehan and then addressed Cernunnos. "*When I return*, we will talk."

"Listen to me, Morgan. This man is an incubus."

"Don't be ridiculous! He's a very gallant young man with excellent manners. Something you might take note of, Cern."

"You've been ensorcelled."

Her eyes widened and then she began to laugh. "Ensorcelled? *Me?*"

"Step away from the pool, Morgan. Let us talk."

"No." She slanted a look at Melehan. "Are you ready?"

He bowed and gestured. "After you, my lady."

She giggled. "I do so like being at court. This is going to be fun." Without looking at the others she stepped into the water and disappeared in its swirling depths.

"*No!*" Cernunnos shouted and leapt after her.

Melehan was about to follow when the point of a sword at his throat stopped him.

"We're going to talk." Lancelot pricked Melehan's neck just enough to draw blood. "Starting with, who in the Christian hell are you?"

Chapter Seven

Nimue awoke with a start. Something was wrong. She swung out of bed, as she had so many years ago when Medraut captured Camelot, not questioning her instincts. Slipping into a robe, she quickly made her way outside toward the House of Healing. In the pre-dawn, she could see the mists that generally lay like a blanket between Avalon and Faerie swirling in restless agitation.

The other priestesses were already gathered behind the building in the copse of oak trees where their strongest magic lay. The twin healers, Sulis and Isis, whispered together while Brighid softly strummed her harp, calling forth the windsingers, messengers of the air. Rhiannon, escort to the Otherworld, and Morrigan, collector of souls dying in battle, were holding their own conversation, both of them looking confused.

"What is it?" Nimue asked. "What's happened?"

Arianrhod, the tall, black-haired spinner of the Wheel of Fate, answered her. "It seems someone has breached the portal of Faerie. Morgan and Cernunnos are gone."

Nimue furrowed her brow. "Cernunnos was just here. Morgan likes to play in the mortal world—"

"Their essence is gone," Arianrhod replied.

"But how can that be? What kind of being is powerful enough to enter Faerie and not succumb to it? Let alone, abduct its queen and a demi-god?"

"Those are excellent questions," Hetaira, the initiator of relationships, replied as she swept her long, blonde hair back. "No one seems to have any answers and I have lost two who were about to discover real love."

Nimue looked at Rhiannon and Morrigan. "You would be able to detect if they were lost in-between worlds?"

Rhiannon nodded. "I have already spoken to Janus, the keeper. No one has approached his gates. They do not wander in the in-between."

"There will be a battle,"—Morrigan's black eyes flashed in her ageless face—, "but it is yet to come."

"All I can detect is the presence of something dark and evil in Faerie," Arianrhod said, "but whatever it is, it is shielded well." She turned to Inanna, the gentle protector of human culture. "Were you able to find their threads of life anywhere?"

She shook her head. "I have spread my senses over all of Briton. Cernunnos and Morgan are not there."

Even as the first rays of sunrise lightened the eastern sky, a shimmering of soft light began to radiate from the middle of the circle. An ethereal form took shape as the scent of apple blossoms suddenly filled the air. The light became brighter until, at last, Astrala emerged. The priestesses bowed their heads.

"You look for Cernunnos and Morgan, not in the wrong place, but in the wrong Time," she said.

The priestesses looked up then, but it was Nimue who stepped forward to ask, "What Time do you speak of, Grail Maiden?"

"The entity that got through the portal had the means to send them far into the Future. A future that even I cannot see clearly."

"That would change Destiny!" Arianrhod exclaimed. "That is my sacred responsibility, no one else's."

The blue of the morning sky reflected in Astrala's eyes as she turned to her. "Indeed, it seems that Destiny will be changed because of this. For the first time since Galahad returned the Grail to me, it glows."

She placed a hand on Nimue's shoulder. "You, Daughter, must be prepared."

"I?" Nimue asked in surprise. "How will I make a difference?"

Astrala's smile was enigmatic as her form began to fade. "You will know."

Nimue reflected on her words as the priestesses disbanded, each to seek solitude to ponder what might be done. The mists surrounding Faerie looked more like angry storm clouds now, dark grey and scudding over the forest and causing Avalon's serene lake shore to whip into its own frenzy. Whoever—or whatever—had invaded Faerie clearly was not a harmonious presence.

She made her way down the hill to the entrance that led to the tomb where Arthur and his knights lay. Usually, she felt peaceful and calm there, where she could sit by Arthur and recall the pleasant memories of their last years together. But today, peace did not come. "I fear trouble," she said as she looked down on the slab where Arthur lay. "Evil lurks near. I can feel it." She reached out to run her fingers over the cold stone. "Would that you were alive to help me combat it."

Beneath her fingers, the stone warmed and a small sound like a groan vibrated through the tomb. It seemed to her that Arthur stirred, as if awakening from a deep sleep, but when she blinked and looked again, the effigy was still and the room silent.

* * * *

Lancelot prodded the tip of his sword against Melehan's neck again. "As I said, who in the Christian's hell are you?"

Before he could answer, the water in the pool began to swirl again, splashing over the edges as a form rose from its midst. Lancelot spun, sword at the ready, while he pulled Gwenhwyfar protectively behind him.

Aoibhill stepped from the pool daintily and gave Lancelot an amused look. "You can put that thing away," she said in a sultry voice, "and stop threatening my son."

Lancelot didn't move. "And you are?"

"Aoibhill. Queen of Eire Faerie." She arched a delicate eyebrow. "Morgan didn't tell you I was coming?"

"Morgan isn't here," Gwenhwyfar said as she stepped out from behind Lancelot.

"Really? That's such a disappointment. I'd so looked forward to seeing her again after so many years. Do you know when she might return?"

"I imagine at any time,"Gwenhwyfar answered. "She went to Camelot to speak in defense of Melehan—something about a misunderstanding—but since he's still here, I'm sure she'll come back for him."

"Then I believe I'll wait for her." She looked at Lancelot who still held his sword. "That is, if I'm welcome?"

Gwenhwyfar gave Lancelot an uneasy look and he shrugged and reluctantly sheathed the sword, but kept his hand on the hilt. He trusted this faerie even less than he did Morgan, but he couldn't very well run her through.

"I don't know that it's my place to offer you hospitality—"

"Certes, it is, if you are Lady Gwenhwyfar," Melehan said smoothly. "You were queen at Camelot, were you not? If Morgan is...absent...then who else would take her place?"

Aoibhill turned her lavender eyes on Gwenhwyfar. "Gwenhwyfar. Even in my remote world, I have heard of you."

Gwenhwyfar looked startled. "How so?"

The Eire queen seemed amused again. "Our worlds are not so far apart. Briton warriors have visited my lands before." She smiled, revealing small, white teeth. "I have even entertained one of them, though he'll probably have no recollection of it." Aoibhill paused as if remembering. "I recall that he was quite smitten with you." She studied Gwenwyfar as if she were a strange specimen not seen before. "I suppose I can see why."

Lancelot put a protective arm around Gwenhwyfar's shoulders. "As befits a queen, my lady drew many admirers."

Aoibhill tilted her head and slanted a glanced upward. "Let me guess. You must be the champion. Lancelot, I think I heard you called?"

Melehan drew himself up, his grey eyes glittering. "Lancelot?"

"Yes." His hand tightened on the hilt of his sword as he looked from one to the other. "How did you get here?"

"Through the pool, as I'm sure you did," Aoibhill answered, "although I must say, I certainly didn't expect to see either of you here. Morgan must be very generous to allow mortals to roam so freely in her domain."

"We have an agreement," he said.

She let her lashes sweep down on her cheeks before she slowly looked back up at him. "Knowing Morgan, I'm sure that you do," she said demurely.

Beside him, Lancelot felt Gwenhwyfar tense and he squeezed her shoulder. "She's been most kind," he said.

Aoibhill laughed. "Kind? That's a new description for how she lures a man to her bed."

Before Lancelot could stop her, Gwenhwyfar bristled. "Morgan loves Cernunnos and he loves her."

The air suddenly turned chill. "What makes you say that?" Aoibhill asked, her voice brittle.

"They..." Gwenhwyfar looked up at Lancelot and then wrapped her arms over his. "They see that Lance and I love each other and they ask what love means."

"Oh." The coldness of the air lessened a bit. "Immortals are always amused by mortal behavior. No doubt they study you for nothing other than entertainment." She looked to Melehan. "Where is Cernunnos, by the way? It has been a bit since I've seen him as well."

"He has not returned from the Wild Hunt yet," Melehan said.

Lancelot cast him a sharp look, but said nothing. They all knew Cernunnos had followed Morgan to the mortal world, but why did Melehan want to hide it? Lancelot sensed something else was in play here, but he didn't know what. For once, he wished Nimue were here, or even Myrddin. With the Sight, he could soon put-to-rights what was wrong. For now, he would support Melehan's contention.

"That is true," he said easily. "Cernunnos mentioned something about having to escort someone to Avalon after the Hunt. That may be where he is."

Aoibhill pouted. "Well, then, I'll just have to wait for his return as well." She looked at Melehan. "Will you take me to my quarters?"

He nearly leapt at the chance. "Certes, come with me."

Lancelot watched as they walked away. "Something is amiss."

"I feel it too," Gwenhwyfar replied.

"Do you think Prince might be able to slip through to Avalon once more and speak with Nimue?"

"I don't know." She pointed at the low, dark clouds that continued to hover just past the barrier and blocked mystic Avalon from view. "I'm not sure he can get through."

Gwenhwyfar bumped into him and Lancelot turned to see that the unicorn had silently appeared. She gave his shiny coat a pat. "How long have you been here?"

Long enough. He stamped a hoof. *Much is wrong here.*

"We know," Gwenhwyfar said gently and Lancelot wished again that he could communicate with the fey creature.

The unicorn looked up at him then, with those silver-blue eyes that nearly matched his coat, and it looked to Lancelot as though the animal were amused. It nodded its head once, took the leap over the pool and disappeared into the heavy fog that enclosed them.

* * * *

"I thought Lancelot was dead!" Melehan said as soon as he'd shut the door to the room Aoibhill would be staying in.

She shrugged. "I thought he was too."

Melehan paced as his mother settled on the chaise by the window. "This gives me an opportunity to avenge my father. How would you like for me to kill him?"

She carefully arranged the folds of her silk gown and then brushed her hand along the velvety cushion before running her fingers over the smooth, waxed mahogany of the side table. "At least, Morgan has good taste," she said.

"Did you not hear me?" Melehan stopped in front of her. "How do you want me to kill Lancelot?"

"I'm not sure that I do."

"What? You don't want to avenge the man who was my father? Your...lover?"

She looked unperturbed. "I carefully chose Medraut over many others to sire you. He served his purpose, nothing more."

He stared at her. "Surely, you don't expect me to do nothing?"

Aoibhill arched her eyebrow. "I didn't say that."

"What then?"

"Sit, dear boy. You always were a restless child." She swung her long legs to one side gracefully and patted the seat beside her. "And do get your emotions in check. Your eyes are turning red."

With an effort, he calmed himself and sat down. His mother was right. He needed to keep the glamour of a handsome, blond man about him. One never knew when one of Morgan's faeries might be spying. "What then?"

"I didn't tell you the whole story of Camelot," she said, "or at least what I've learned of it from Arthur's sister, Morgana." Aoibhill gave a smug look. "Now there was a mortal I could respect...did you know she wrecked havoc throughout Briton by bringing the plague there? Quite a feat, no?"

"I suppose. So how is she important to my getting revenge on Lancelot?"

"Patience, Melehan. You know I don't like to hurry a story." She looked around. "Do you suppose Morgan has some primrose wine?"

He sighed. There was no use rushing her when she would not be rushed. He got up to rummage through a cabinet, found a skin, and poured her a glass. Handing it to her, he sat back down. "Tell me."

Aoibhill took a sip of wine. "It's actually quite good. Won't you have some?"

"Mother, please. Tell me what I need to know."

"Oh, very well." She put the drink down. "Well, first, you need to know that Gwenhwyfar is nothing more than a whore."

Melehan refrained from rolling his eyes. "I've heard the rumors, Mother. I fought with Medraut. I know that her marriage to Arthur was arranged and that he was fool enough to trust her to that Armorican bastard, Lancelot. I know, too, that Arthur didn't want to acknowledge his own son, but Gwenhwyfar treated Medraut well—"

"Medraut was besotted by her."

Melehan stopped, surprised at the trace of bitterness in his mother's voice. Surely she wasn't jealous when she'd just admitted she'd used his father for her own purposes?

"Did you care for him?"

'Certes not. At least, not any more than I did any other mortal lover. Besides, Medraut was half-mad. But there was a time when I had a love..." She stopped. "Never mind. What you need to know is that throughout their whole, sordid lives, Lancelot and Gwenhwyfar always felt tremendous guilt over their love for each other." Aoibhill laughed. "The delightful irony of the whole thing is that Arthur loved the priestess, Nimue, although she remained out of his reach for years."

He waited for her to stop laughing. "And how is this helpful?"

She looked at him as though he were quite daft. "We can *use* that love."

"How?"

Aoibhill sighed. "Men. Think, dear. If Lancelot loves Gwenhwyfar, what would be the worst thing you could do?"

"Kill her?"

She sighed again. "No. Take her from him. Make her yours."

"How...? Oh," he said as understanding flashed through his mind. "You want me to invade her dreams." He frowned. "But Lancelot won't know that. I've lain with women many times with their husbands snoring soundly beside them."

Aoihbill shook her head as though she truly felt sorry for his dim-wittedness. "I'll make sure he wakes up."

Melehan felt his eyes widen. "But he'll see me in my real form."

"Exactly. No one can compete with an incubus. He'll know he's lost and he won't be able to do a thing about it." She patted Melehan's thigh. "That's revenge, son. And sweeter to the taste than this wine." She lifted the glass to her lips and took a sip.

Melehan watched her. Gwenhwyfar was a beautiful woman, with lush curves in all the right places. Revenge would be sweet indeed. And tonight, he would begin.

* * * *

"I wonder why they haven't returned," Gwenhwyfar said as she and Lancelot stood near the scrying pool watching the still-threatening clouds roil past the barrier of Faerie.

Lancelot put his arm around Gwenhwyfar's shoulders. "Do you miss them?"

She leaned against him. "I never thought I would. Keeping Cernunnos at a distance and hoping Morgan doesn't seduce you when my back is turned isn't exactly easy." She looked thoughtful. "But lately... Well, Cernunnos actually had a conversation with me that wasn't about getting me into his bed."

"That's an improvement." Lancelot brushed his lips across her forehead. "What did you talk about?"

"That was the strangest part. He wanted to know about love."

Lancelot raised his eyebrows. "Are you sure that wasn't just another attempt to disarm you?"

She shook her head. "I don't think so. He seemed to really want to know." She looked up at Lancelot, her eyes alight with glee. "He thought it had to do with bannocks."

"Bannocks?"

"I tried to explain that when someone loves someone they do things for each other without being asked. Things that please the other person...like you liking warm bannocks with honey."

Lancelot bent down to nip her ear. "You know *why* I like that."

She tilted her head, inviting his kiss to her nape and sighed with pleasure as his warm tongue slid across her neck. "We *did* sort of start a tradition that day at the cottage, didn't we?"

"Ummm," he answered as he nibbled a path down her throat. "Perhaps we should go back and—"

"Lance, I'm serious!" She giggled when he tickled her. "I'm worried. Why wouldn't Morgan come back if Melehan is still here?"

Lancelot slid his arms down around Gwenhwyfar's waist and pulled her back against him, resting his chin on the top of her head. "I don't know."

"And why would Aoibhill—the *Eire* queen of faerie—so conveniently show up just now? Morgan has never mentioned her. They can't be friends. And Melehan...how did he get here in the first place?"

"Too many questions, Gwen. I don't have the answers."

"Well, maybe Prince will." She eyed the scudding clouds again. "If he made it through. Lance, what if he doesn't return?"

"Shhh, Gwen. Your unicorn is a magical creature. He'll return." Lancelot turned Gwenhwyfar around and gave her a sound kiss. "Now why don't you go and get some of those bannocks ready for me?"

Her green eyes twinkled. "You go get the honey then and I'll meet you in a little while. I'm going to take a bath first, though."

"Don't bother to put your clothes back on," he called after her and then laughed as she gave him a backward wave.

Lancelot turned in the other direction. Morgan kept hives on a hill not far away. He moved through the forest as silently as any four-footed creature might, enjoying the sound of birds chirping and water bubbling from the brook that ran through Faerie. He was almost upon the small glade when he heard them. He stepped behind an ancient oak and peered out.

Aoibhill stood in the middle of a patch of bluebells, a tiny silver horn in her hand.

"Why does Cernunnos not come?" she asked Melehan who leaned against a nearby rowan.

"I'm sure I don't know."

She looked down at the horn in her hand. "This has never failed before. *Never*. Even if Morgan had somehow managed to enchant him, the magic in this horn would overcome it." She looked at Melehan thoughtfully. "The Hunt is tiring. Cernunnos should have returned by now. Are you sure he didn't follow Morgan?"

Melehan looked uneasy. "I don't think—"

"You don't *think*?" Aoibhill's eyes narrowed and the forest stilled suddenly. "Did he or didn't he?"

He straightened. "What difference would it make? You told me to get Morgan away from here so you could enter—"

"What difference?" she shrieked and the forest suddenly came alive with the sounds of creatures, large and small, scuttling away as fast as they could. "What difference? *Did he follow Morgan?*"

Melehan began to back away. "He *might* have."

"You fool!" Aoibhill flung the tiny horn to the ground. "Do you know what you've done? You're as stupid as your father!"

"Leave my father out of this!"

"Why should I? Even Arthur didn't want to recognize his son! I should have known better when I chose him to sire you!" She turned and stomped off, the ground trembling in her wake.

Melehan started after her. "Wait! I don't understand..."

Lancelot waited until they both had disappeared before he entered the small clearing and retrieved the little silver horn. Even to his unpracticed hand, it felt warm and tingled with magic. He tucked it into his tunic and narrowed his eyes as he looked at the grass path, now brown from where the Eire queen had singed it with her wrath. What had she said about Melehan's father? That Arthur wouldn't acknowledge his son? Then he felt his blood run cold.

Medraut was Melehan's father. The evil lived on.

* * * *

"Mmmm," Gwenhwyfar murmured as Lancelot nuzzled her neck. She rolled over in the soft bed to burrow into him. Moving his lips along her throat, his hand untied the silk strap on her shoulder and slid her gown down to expose a breast. His mouth covered her nipple and she arched her back to allow him better access. She groaned as the suckling at her breast became more forceful, followed by a whimper of pain as the sudden sharpness of a bite.

"You're hurting me," Gwenhwyfar gasped, but he didn't stop. She pushed against his hard chest with her hands...a chest that felt different from Lancelot's.

She opened her eyes, but before she could scream, a claw clamped itself over her mouth. Hovering in the darkness above her was a form of something that was only half-man. The thing had red, glowing eyes and an elongated muzzle, with sharp fangs. Frantic, she pushed harder, but the thing made a bestial sound that almost sounded like a laugh.

"You woke too soon," it whispered to her, "but never fear. I'll be back." A gust of cold air blew suddenly across the bed and the beast was gone.

Gwenhwyfar sat up in bed, grasping the sheets to her and looked around wildly. The open, flapping shutter left in enough light to see Lancelot's side of the bed was empty. Then she remembered he'd said he was standing watch over the cottage where Aoihbill and Melehan were staying. She slipped out of bed and, with shaking legs, went to secure the shutter. It must have sprung open and let that cold draft in that woke her up.

She sat back down on the bed. *Sweet Mary, what just happened?* She hadn't had a nightmare since right after Medraut had abducted and tried to rape her, years ago. That was *over*. Medraut was dead. When Lancelot had brought her the news earlier that Melehan was Medraut's son, she'd felt a shock. She gave herself a little shake. The sins of the father weren't always visited on the child. And Melehan had been the epitome of good manners in the short while she'd known him. It was silly of her to react so strongly to the fact that Medraut had fathered a son. And to conjure up a beast with eyes like glowing coals and a face that was almost lupine... She gave a small shudder. She hadn't once seen anything in Faerie that looked so hideous. When Cernunnos returned, she would ask him about it, but really, it must just have been a dream.

She lay slowly down, only to bounce up quickly. "Ouch!" She moved her hand over the side of her breast and felt something sticky. Holding her hand out, she squinted in the near darkness.

Blood.

* * * *

Bel's Fires! Lancelot held a nearly hysterical Gwenhwyfar to him, smoothing her hair and trying to sooth her. "It's all right," he said softly. "I'm here. I won't leave you alone at night anymore." When she just clung harder to him, he cursed again. While he stood guard over a cottage that remained dark all night, Gwen was having nightmares. The news that Medraut had a son evidently was more of a shock than he'd realized and he felt like kicking himself for not remembering the after-effects of Medraut's near rape of her.

The first rays of the morning sun slanted in the window before her trembling finally stopped and she slipped from his lap to sit on the edge of the bed. "The beast—or whatever it was—was real, Lance," she finally said. "Look."

He clenched his jaw when he saw the bite mark with the dark, bruised mottling around it. "How..." He stopped himself. The door had been bolted from the inside. He'd had to bang on it to get Gwenhwyfar to open up. He set his mouth in a hard line. He'd put that bolt on the door to keep Cernunnos out, yet something had gotten in. "You said the window was open? Do you think whatever it was came in that way?"

Gwenhwyfar shrugged. "I don't know. I'm not even sure what I saw. Red, glowing eyes, fangs..."

"Cernunnos' hounds have red eyes and fangs. Do you think one of them was loose last night?"

"The hounds have never harmed me before." She began to tremble again.

"All right." Lancelot pulled her to him again. "Let's not talk about it right now. How about going to the scrying pool and trying to see if we can discover anything there?"

It didn't take them long to dress and be on their way. Gwenhwyfar knelt by the water and moved her hands over it. "I don't have the skill that either the fey or the priestesses have," she said when all she could produce was a milky swirling. She sat back dejectedly in the grass. "Mayhap we could ask Branda or Sadi to try?"

"If we could find them," Lancelot replied. "They've been elusive since we've been back."

"No doubt leery of the Eire queen," Gwenhwyfar answered, "especially with Morgan gone." She sighed and looked out to the billowing fog that kept Avalon from sight. Then she squinted. "I think Prince is out there!"

Lancelot turned, even as the silvery-blue coat of the unicorn took shape in the dense, swirling mists. A moment later, it made the leap over the pool and landed beside them.

Gwenhwyfar threw her arms around him. "Did you get through?" she asked as he rubbed his horn along her arm in affection.

The unicorn nodded his head and shook his mane. A piece of parchment dropped out. Gwenhwyfar reached down to pick it up.

"It's from Nimue," she said as she opened it and then frowned. With a shaking hand, she gave it to Lancelot.

He read it quickly. "Dark and evil...so Aoibhill is not what she seems." He paused, not sure if he should continue that line of thought when Gwenhwyfar finished it for him.

"And neither is Melehan probably."

"We will watch them, Gwen, and be careful." He looked back at the letter. "Morgan and Cernunnos are somewhere in the future. As strange as things can be in Faerie and even with the powers of Avalon, I have never heard of such a thing."

"Nimue said even Astrala cannot see it," Gwenhwyfar said in a small voice. "They won't be coming back then."

Lancelot reached for her hand, unwilling to voice what he was feeling. "There must be a way for us to get them back. We need to go to Avalon."

She shook her head. "Mortals can only leave Faerie if escorted. That's why Cernunnos went with us. We are trapped, Lance." She swallowed hard. "Trapped with an evil queen, Medraut's son, and some hideous phantom beast that threatens to visit me each night."

Lancelot drew her into the crook of his arm, the other hand on his sword hilt. "I'll protect you from that damn beast, Gwen, but we've got to get to Nimue. There must be a way to bring Morgan and Cernunnos back." He grimaced. Who would ever have thought he'd welcome the sight of the horned god?

She nestled against him and sighed. "But what if there isn't, Lance? What if there isn't?"

Chapter Eight

In the dusky twilight, Cernunnos picked himself off the floor and reached down to lift Morgan up as well. He brushed his doeskin trews as he looked around.

"What is this place?" Morgan asked.

"It sure isn't Camelot," Cernunnos answered as he moved away from her and began to study the strange architecture. Lining the wall past the entrance was a long stone bench. Another such bench lined the wall opposite it. Cernunnos looked to his right at what looked like a tombstone with strange lettering. To its side, another stone slab bore a carving of a sword and a chalice.

"Look!" Morgan pointed to the window next to the entrance to his left and giggled. "Two lovers in stone and a man with horns."

Cernunnos touched his head. "My horns don't look like that."

"Certes not." Morgan flounced toward the far end of the stone building and then stopped by a railing separating a slightly raised area. Her eyes grew round and she motioned for Cernunnos to hurry. "This is some kind of shrine."

Cernunnos stepped up. Across from him were four altars. To his right was yet another one in front of a pillar that depicted a woman and child. "Is this not the Christian virgin?" he asked.

Morgan gazed up at it and then back to the other altars and pointed to a death mask centered on the wall between them. "That is not Christian," she said.

"No," Cernunnos answered, his attention focused on yet another carving to the right of the mask. "Nor is this." He tilted his head and studied it. "This is a likeness of me!"

Morgan came to his side. "Your face is covered in leaves and you have sprouts coming out of your mouth. It's not exactly how most people would describe you."

He glowered. "Have you forgotten the other side of the god? The Green Man who is protector of the forest?"

"Oh, stop pouting, Cern." Morgan cast a slow glance in his direction. "I haven't forgotten. I just like you better in your...er, animal form."

Somewhat pacified, he stopped frowning and looked up at the main window. "A cross inside a square inside a circle. Isn't that a pattern that Myrddin used?"

Morgan shrugged. "Mayhap. I didn't pay much attention to Mryddin's spells." She gazed up at it. "It looks like something Nimue might use."

Cernunnos turned and surveyed the three pillars opposite him. "These are interesting," he said as he moved to the one on his left. Eight dragons lay at its base, with double sprigs of foliage leading upward from their mouths, winding around the pillar like four ropes. "A tree," he said thoughtfully the more he studied it. "My symbol."

"If it's a tree," Morgan replied as she pointed once again to the mother and child engraving, "it could also be the Christian Tree of Life."

Cernunnos gave her a surprised look. "I didn't know you knew anything about the Christos."

Morgan shrugged. "All those years I spent tweaking Myrddin's ear, I had to listen to Gwenhwyfar sprouting her beliefs to both Nimue and Lancelot. This tree could also be Yggdrasil, the Saxon tree that binds earth with heaven." A sly glint came into her eyes. "I spent time listening to Cynric as well."

"I'm quite aware of your fondness for the smooth-talking, blond warlord," Cernunnos said with more force than he intended.

"He did have the most penetrating—" Morgan smiled innocently—"blue eyes."

"And he was besotted with Gwenhwyfar," Cernunnos snapped.

Morgan ignored him, moving a few feet away to read a Latin inscription on a lintel near the pillar. Then she laughed. "Here is the secret to this place, Cern. Listen: '*Wine is strong, the king is stronger, women are even stronger...*' I believe this may be a shrine to the Goddess after all."

"Finish the inscription, my dear," Cernunnos said as he came up behind her. "*...but truth conquers all.*" We still don't know where we are." He peered down some steps leading to a crypt. "Would you like to go down there?"

"Not yet." Morgan said and gestured. "Have you noticed the ceiling?"

Cernunnos looked up. The roof was barrel-vaulted and divided into what looked like five sections, the first section carved with daisies, the second with lilies, the third with sunflowers, the fourth with roses and the last, he noticed as he walked along, was covered with stars, the sun, a crescent moon. "Tis a pagan place," he said and then added, with smug satisfaction, "Did you see the many faces of the Green Man along these walls? Tis a shrine to me."

Morgan retraced her steps, stopping to pay attention to the various green men. "Did you notice they seem to age as you walk along?" she asked teasingly.

"I do not age," he nearly bellowed. Obviously, Morgan was still displeased with him for being late from the Hunt and he had yet to explain to her that he'd taken Lancelot and Gwenhwyfar to Avalon. "The fact is, we still don't know where we are."

A worried look crossed her face. "That is true. I had thought when I stepped through the pool that I would appear in Custennin's court. These surroundings have more the element of Avallach. Mayhap we are on the isle."

"Hardly likely that the Lady of the Lake would allow a shrine to *me* on the isle. Even Myrddin went by invitation only," Cernunnos answered.

Morgan glanced outside with an uneasy look. "Well, wherever we are, it has grown dark. What do you suggest we do?"

Cernunnos pulled her toward him. "I know what we're going to *do.* Let's find out if those steps lead to someplace with a bed, shall we?"

Morgan gave what she hoped was her best seductive gaze and wrapped her arms around his neck. "For once, you won't get an argument from me. Lead on."

* * * *

Morgan awakened the next morning to the sound of voices. Uncurling from the warmth of Cernunnos' chest, she sat up on the hard floor. Beside her, Cern slumbered away. She shook her head. He always slept like the entombed after a night of romping wildly. It *had* been a good night. Mayhap this was love after all.

The voices grew louder and she grabbed her clothes and shook Cernunnos awake. "People are coming," she exclaimed as she got dressed.

Cernunnos blinked at her sleepily and then, with instant animal-alertness, he sprang to his feet, pulling his trews on and donning his tunic.

"At least, we'll find out where we are," Morgan said as she started up the steps.

A hand on her arm made her stop.

"We don't know if they're friend or foe," Cernunnos said and let his antlers grow in the ether above his head. "Let me deal with them."

Morgan refrained from rolling her eyes. "I can create a glamour that will hide us from sight. Have you forgotten?"

Cernunnos studied her for a moment and nodded. "Do it then."

They proceeded up the stairs and emerged by the tree pillar just as the door to the building opened and a woman with a warm Scottish burr intoned, "Welcome ye are to Rosslyn Chapel."

A flock of people followed her in, chattering in strangely-accented Briton. Morgan stared. They were the most strangely dressed people she had ever seen. Most of the men wore short leggings that bagged at the knees and sandals that were reminiscent of Roman times. Their tunics were strange affairs that either fit snugly with strange lettering and pictures on the chest or were looser-fitting material in a variety of colors and plaids. But the women! Morgan nearly gaped. Even in Faerie, such copious amounts of skin were not seen. Bare midriffs and skirts that barely covered anything. Others wore tight leggings with tops that stretched thinly over ample figures.

Beside her, Cernunnos' eyes took on a lusty gleam. Morgan elbowed him. *Hard.* "What kind of people are these?" she whispered.

Before he had time to answer, one of the group pointed at them. "Look!" the woman cried, "the guides are wearing costumes!"

Morgan looked behind her. There was no one there.

"I thought you had us glamoured," Cernunnos said.

"I did!" *How could that woman see them?* "Maybe she's Sidhe?"

"If she is, then they all are," Cernunnos replied. "They're coming this way."

Morgan turned back to see the whole group descending on them. "What do we do?"

"Be ourselves." Cernunnos drew himself up and let his antlers show. "This should intimidate them."

The group halted, jaws dropping.

The plump Scottish woman hastened up, a pleasant smile on her face. "I wasn't aware special arrangements had been made for these tourists," she said.

Morgan tilted her head curiously. *What was a tourist?* These people seemed friendly enough, so she benevolently said, "Sometimes we grant an audience with mortals."

A puzzled look crossed the woman's face. "If ye'll pardon me, lass, but did ye say 'mortal?'"

Morgan reminded herself that mortals were slower in their thinking skills. "Yes."

Someone in the back of the group called, "Who are you then?" while a couple of the younger women twittered.

Cernunnos gazed down at them, his hazel eyes glowing preternaturally. The two girls stopped, their own eyes glazing over.

"Stop that!" Morgan hissed.

He acted like he didn't hear her. Instead, he fixed his seductive look on the lady who seemed to be in charge and bowed slightly. "I am Cernunnos," he said in a deeply vibrating voice, "God of the forest."

The woman nodded faintly. "Certainly you are."

Cernunnos frowned and Morgan nearly giggled. The look he had given the woman should have reduced her to a quivering mass of passionate desire.

He arched an eyebrow. "If you don't believe me, look around. My image is everywhere."

One of the older ladies in the group nodded her head sagely. "He's talking about the Green Man," she said. "I've been here before. That image can be found over one hundred times in this building."

A teen-ager took several steps closer. "Cool hologram, man," he said as he looked at Cernunnos' antlers, transparently visible.

"Okay, so the guy is great in costume," said a young man whose well-muscled biceps were displayed with a shirt that lacked sleeves. "Who's the girl?"

"Not Mother Mary," his friend said.

Morgan glared at him. How dare anyone compare her to a *mother*? Instead of shriveling before her eyes, though, he merely gazed at her. He was either very brave or her powers weren't working. She lifted her chin. "I am Morgan le Fey, Queen of Faerie."

The man who had dared to compare her to a mother looked her over appraisingly. "Like in King Arthur's wicked sister?"

Wicked? She raised a hand to cast a lightening bolt at the impudent boar, but nothing happened. "Certes, not," she said with a forced smile. "You are referring to Morgana, the mortal."

"Oh, yeah," he said.

"Have you seen King Arthur?" Morgan asked. She would forgive this man's rudeness if he knew of the king's whereabouts. King Arthur would help them.

"The movie?"

Morgan frowned. *What was a movie?* "The person."

For the first time, the young man's confidence began to waver. He looked at one of them and then the other. "You mean the guy who's been dead for, like, fifteen hundred years?"

She gasped. "How long?"

Before the man could reply, Cernunnos intervened. "It is true that Arthur is not in this world. I saw his tomb not long ago."

"Yeah...right," the man said.

"Well," the Scottish woman said brightly, "let's proceed with our tour, shall we?"

There were murmurings in the group as they began to move toward the Lady Chapel, Cernunnos and Morgan following behind. Cernunnos pointed out every Green Man he'd found to the ladies of the group, much to Morgan's chagrin. Whether his powers were working she didn't know, but the ladies were all straining to be near him.

She peered at the man with the well-muscled arms. "Would you like to see the crypt?" she asked as she swept her lashes down and then up.

"Just you and me?"

"Certes," she replied and held out her hand.

Cernunnos took it. How he had moved so quickly, she didn't know, but the look of irritation on his face was quite satisfying.

"We'll *all* go look at the crypt," he said.

She allowed him to lead her demurely while the rest of the group followed. It was crowded as they all gathered around the two stones along the north wall. The Scottish woman explained that the figure carved on one of the stones was a thirteenth century Knight Templar and the other a figure called a berserker.

Morgan had no idea of what a Templar was, but she knew about berserkers. "Lancelot would fight like a berserker," she said and ignored Cernunnos angry glower. "I enjoyed watching him on the battlefield."

The man with the sleeveless shirt gazed at her. "You actors stay in character, I'll give you that."

There was a murmuring of general assent and suddenly people were pulling pieces of leather out of their pockets, taking out paper slips, and handing them to her.

"Yes, definitely," the Scottish woman said as she added her own money to the amount. "You've both done quite well. You deserve these tips."

What was a tip? Morgan didn't know, but she decided it was some sort of gift so she accepted the paper graciously.

It wasn't long after that the group left the building, waving their good-byes and thanks. Morgan watched from the door as they all walked toward some odd, silver thing sitting on black wheels. It made a horrible noise as the people got closer and black smoke belched out the back of the thing. Then, one by one, the people disappeared into it. Horrified, she started after them, but Cernunnos drew her back.

"That monster is eating them!" she exclaimed. "They've done nothing to deserve to die! Let me go."

He shook his head. "We don't know what that thing is and we don't know if we have the powers to fight it. Look. It's leaving and you can see the people waving from inside. They're not dead."

"Well, what is that thing and where are we?"

Cernunnos sighed and shut the door. "I don't know, Morgan, but it seems like we've been sent to a different world."

She sank down on the bench. "How could that happen? I've been through the pool hundreds of times and so have you. We always appear exactly where we expect to."

He looked at the pendant that she wore and his eyes narrowed. "Where did you get that?"

Morgan looked down at it. "Melehan—the young, blond man that you saw—gave it to me. I was so intrigued with it." She fingered it for a moment. The metal scorched her and Morgan felt her blood chill. Dark magic. She hadn't noticed it before which meant that the sorcerer—Melehan?—had to be powerful indeed. She tore it from her neck and threw it on the ground.

"By the Goddess of Avalon, what have I done?"

* * * *

Cernunnos paced the floor of the chapel, trying to make sense of what happened. Morgan sat on the stone bench near the carving of the lovers and the devil, as the Scottish woman had explained it. His faerie queen hadn't moved for over an hour. He looked up at the relief again. How appropriate that Morgan sat next to it, for he now knew who the devil was.

"An incubus," he said again as he stopped by a window and looked out at the sun disappearing behind the nearby forest. "Lupiana warned me. If only I had arrived a few minutes sooner."

Morgan looked up, her face tear-streaked. "It was my fault, Cern. You told me to wait and I was angry with you. I should have listened."

He masked his surprise. Morgan rarely admitted that she was wrong about anything and he didn't think, in all the centuries they'd been together, that she *ever* admitted that *he* was *right*. Some of his annoyance with her eased. "You were under the spell of that pendant," he said in a gentler voice.

"Still, I should have recognized his power. Branda had a bad feeling about it. I should have trusted—"

Cernunnos drew her up and wrapped his arms around her. "Tis done, Morgan. We need to find a way to get back." He glanced out the window over her shoulder and then quickly took her hand to lead her away from the door. "Someone comes."

Not having time to get to the crypt, they ducked behind two pillars.

The door opened with a slight creak and an elderly man bearing an oil lamp and accompianed by a boy of perhaps eight years, stepped inside.

"Check the crypt," the old man said to the boy. "We need to make sure there aren't any of them tourists hiding about before we lock up."

Cernunnos held his breath as the child scampered by. If only Morgan's glamour at making them inivisible were working. He almost gave an audible sigh. Who knew which of their powers were intact? It seemed an eternity before he heard the boy's boots coming up the steps again. The footsteps slowed as they neared the pillars that Morgan and he were crouched behind and Cernunnos shifted slightly to stay in the shadows. The boy moved on.

"All clear, Grandda."

"Good. Yer mother will be waitin' with a fine pot of venison stew when we get back," the old man said and closed the door behind them.

Cernunnos let out a sigh of relief and Morgan stepped away from her pillar. "We can't stay here." He peered into the near darkness outside. "The forest is not far. We'll see if I can summon the creatures to help me."

They walked down the hill and through an old cemetery. Looking up, Cernunnos could see the ruins of a castle. Morgan noticed it too.

"Do you suppose someone still lives there?" she asked.

"Doubtful," Cernunnos answered as they approached it and he could see shells of walls. "I think it wise we avoid humans for the present." He looked around and noticed steps leading downward. "Come." He held out his hand. Again, he masked his surprise when Morgan complied without resistance. They walked along the riverbank and crossed a small bridge, then followed a small path that led toward the sound of a waterfall. They continued to walk amid large boulders until they came to a wall of stone where the river dashed against it, almost reversing itself. Cernunnos squinted.

"Can you see any of your people?" he asked.

Morgan moved closer to the edge. After a few moments she looked up at him, concern on her face. "I see no asrai or undines. Not even naiads." Tears began to glitter in her eyes. "I've lost my powers, haven't I?"

"They may not be a part of this world." Cernunnos put his arm around her. "Let's walk into the forest and see what luck I have." They turned and then both of them froze in their tracks.

Standing not ten feet away from them was the small boy from the chapel.

"Who are you?" Morgan asked.

"My name is Seth." He tilted his head of red curls and looked up at them. "I seen ye earlier."

Cernunnos cursed silently. "Did you tell anyone?"

"Nah. Grandda tells me I make too much up. I wanted to see if you was real."

Morgan slanted a look at Cernunnos and then looked at the boy. "Why do you think we're not real?"

The child shrugged and lowered his eyes. "Tis sometimes I see things that others don't. My mum don't like me to speak of it because I get teased." He glanced back up. "Never seen a man with horns before."

Cernunnos was glad he'd retracted them earlier. "It's a little trick I use when I'm in...costume."

Seth stared at him gravely. "I doona think ye be in costume."

Cernunnos returned the stare. *Does this child have powers?* In his side vision, he saw Morgan's ears grow pointed. She must be thinking the same thing he was. *Can this boy help us?*

"Can you keep a secret?" he asked.

Seth's brown eyes lit up. "Aye."

"We are from a place far away. My name is Cernunnos. I'm a...a guardian of forests and animals."

"Like a parks warden?"

"Something like that. And this is Morgan, my friend."

She shot him a daggered look before turning to the boy. "My *full* name is Morgan le Fey. I'm queen of Faerie."

The child's eyes grew round. "Ye mean like in them stories about King Arthur and his knights?"

Morgan pursed her lips. "*Exactly* like that. And we seem to be lost. Can you tell us how to get back to Camelot?"

Cernunnos groaned inwardly. He would have gotten around to bringing that up. They weren't *lost*. Exactly.

Seth frowned slightly. "Doona know where Camelot is. That was a long time ago. No one has ever found it." Then he brightened. "But, come morning, ye can see Arthur's Seat from here."

"Arthur's Seat?"

"Aye. 'Tis a mountain. People say Arthur had a hill fort there. And," he continued importantly since he had their undivided attention, "Queen Gwenhwyfar is buried not far away."

Morgan looked at Cernunnos and he read her silent question. They had left the mortal Gwenhwyfar near Ynys Gutrin. He shook his head slightly. This terrain didn't look right.

She turned back to the child. "Where?"

"Meigle. Tis north of here."

"And where might *here* be?" she asked.

Cernunnos winced. Did Morgan have to make it sound like they didn't know *anything*? He could figure out where they were, come morning when it was light.

The child looked at them a bit oddly. "Edinburgh," he said and then, to clarify as if they didn't know, "Scotland."

Din Eidyn. Pictland. Yes, there had been a battle there. Invaders from across the North Sea. He didn't know why Morgan and he had arrived here, but at least they were still in Briton. That was a relief. One of those people called *American tourists* had mentioned something about King Arthur having died fourteen hundred years ago. That was impossible. Yet... It was something he would find out tomorrow, when there was light. He would then take charge of this situation.

"What year is it?" Morgan asked the child.

"2005." He cocked his head again and looked hopeful. "You really are from another Time, aren't you?"

Morgan spoke before Cernunnos could stop her. "Remember that secret Cernunnos asked you to keep?"

The boy nodded eagerly.

"Well, it seems someone has magically moved us into your Time and we...um, don't quite have all of powers back yet. We need a place to stay and something to eat. Could you help us with that?"

Cernunnos glared at her. Did Morgan think he couldn't find a shelter for them? Or food? When the forest was *his*? She should really allow him to take charge.

"Aye," Seth said. "Ye can follow me home and I can finally prove to Grandda that I doona make things up."

"We can't do that, lad," Cernunnos said somewhat sharply. "No one must know who we are."

The boy looked disappointed and Morgan patted his arm. "It's important, Seth. We must get back to our own time." She winked at him. "But you'll know we're real."

Slowly, he nodded. "I'll keep yer secret," he said, "but ye can still follow me home and sleep in Grandda's barn. I'll fetch ye some clothes and I can pilfer a bit of bread and cheese without anyone knowing."

"Good lad," Cernunnos said and let his antlers grow. The boy's eyes widened at the sight. "We're trusting you."

The child swallowed hard but didn't look away. "Ye can trust me."

Surprisingly, he did. What an odd thing. He'd never trusted a mortal before. As they followed the child home, Cernunnos wondered if, mayhap, the boy wasn't fey.

It didn't really matter, he supposed. Tomorrow, he would take Morgan and head south. He'd ridden the Hunt over this country thousands of times.

How hard could it be to find Camelot?

Chapter Nine

They headed north instead. Cernunnos looked over at Morgan, walking beside him on the road to Edinburgh in the pre-dawn. How he had let her talk him into this nonsense, he didn't know, but here they were.

"Stop glaring at me," she said as she brushed her hair behind her shoulder. "I remember Myrddin helping Arthur in some northern battle defend the Picts. And the Picts allowed the sidhe to move freely. It's quite possible there is a portal here somewhere that may let us go back." Then she tweaked Cernunnos' ear and did a little pirouette in front of him. "I rather like these new clothes."

He grunted. "Women shouldn't be wearing leggings."

Morgan ran her hands down her denim-covered thighs. "I don't know. They allow for a lot of freedom to move. *You* wear leggings."

He glanced down at his new trews. *Jeans*, Seth had called them. The soft, form-fitting top that clung to him was called a *T-shirt*. He had to admit the clothes were as comfortable as his tunic and doeskin, but he didn't much like the fact that Morgan was wearing the same kind of top and that it showed the outline of her generous breasts to all who would look. He drew his brows together in a deeper frown. So far, he hadn't needed to slay anyone who did look.

"For pity's sake, Cern, why are you glowering so?"

"I prefer you in your gown."

"We wanted to blend in with these people. A silk gossamer gown that shimmers with Faerie lights would hardly have done that." She adjusted the straps of the backpack she wore. "I still have it though." She swept a glance upward through her lashes. "Mayhap I'll put it on later so that you can remove it?"

In spite of himself, Cernunnos began to grin. Morgan hadn't lost the power to captivate him. He wondered if they could find a spot in a lush green field... He felt himself grow hard at the thought. At least he hadn't lost *that* ability.

He grabbed her arm suddenly as two lights appeared on the road and a roar could be heard. Seth had explained about *cars* and that big silver thing yesterday had been a *bus*. Still, Cernunnos didn't trust anything that sounded like a dragon and moved faster than his flying horse. He sneered at it comptemptously as it sped past. "Stupid beast without a brain," he said.

More and more of the noisy things moved along on the road as the sun rose and he was tempted to swing a fist at every one of them. And then, one pulled over and stopped.

"Do ye need a lift?" a cheerful woman's voice rang out from the passenger side of the car.

"A what?" Cernunnos asked suspiciously.

"A lift. A ride. 'Tis a fair walk to Edinburgh, if that's where ye be headed."

"I don't—" Cernunnos began and then realized Morgan was headed for the car. "Wait, Morgan!"

She turned to him, her eyes glittering with excitement. It was a look he knew well. His faerie queen saw this as an adventure. She tended to leap into a situation without giving thought to the outcome. And he didn't trust *cars*.

But the gray-haired male driver had gotten out and was holding the back door open. Morgan smiled at him before disappearing into the depths of that contraption. Cernunnos had no choice but to follow her. He didn't much like the sound of the door closing either. It reminded him of a mortal gaol.

"Where are ye headed?" the woman asked as the car eased back onto the road.

"Arthur's Seat," Morgan replied.

"Aye. Ye can see it to the east there," the woman said and pointed. "Ye have a strange accent. Are ye tourists?"

Tourist. That was a word from yesterday as well. *American tourists.* "Yes, we are," Cernunnos replied. "From America."

"Ye don't sound like a Yank," she said, looking puzzled. "No matter. My husband, Henry, here,"—she patted the driver's shoulder affectionately—"tells me I blether on too much. Well, then, we'll give ye a bit of a tour along the way. I'm Janet."

Cernunnos nodded, not liking the way the countryside was streaking past his window. Would the beast belch fire? And how could Morgan look so calm, like she was enjoying herself? Then he felt her nudge him, none too gently.

"I'm Morgan," she said to Janet. "And this is...Cern."

"Ken? A fine Scottish name," Henry said.

Morgan giggled and started to correct him, but Cernunnos gave her arm a squeeze. She looked at him surprised, but for once was still.

"Now you two just relax," Janet said, "and we'll show you a bit of the town."

"Assumin' ye want us to," Henry said dourly, although he favored his wife with a smile.

"That would be wonderful." Morgan leaned forward eagerly to look out the window.

Morgan had always had a childlike fascination with mortals, Cernunnos thought as he watched her turning her head this way and that. Any other woman—faerie or not—would show fear at being bounced into this world. But not Morgan. If he weren't there to watch over her, who knows what pit of danger she would fall into. His hand reached for the knife he normally kept strapped to his thigh, only to remember that he was unarmed. He growled.

"What did you say?" the woman turned to him,

"Nothing," he replied as the car merged with the heavier traffic of the city. What a noisy racket this city made. The first thing he was going to do, when they returned to Faerie, was gather his red-eyed hounds and ride his horse across a quiet night sky. He looked at Morgan again. Her eyes glittered with excitement.

"This be Princes Street," their chatty hostess informed them as the car made a right turn. "Over to the left is what we call New Town."

"If you remember the fact that it was built in the seventeen and eighteen hundreds," her husband chimed in wryly.

Cernunnos looked to his right. Ah. Something that resembled a glen at last. Grass and...his gaze followed a craggy hill and he nearly gaped. Atop the hill stood the most massive structure he had ever seen. Turrets and towers loomed everywhere.

Janet beamed at his reaction. "Aye. That would be our castle. 'Tis something ye need to tour before ye leave."

Cernunnos doubted that such a fortification would just allow anyone inside. "Who is the king that resides there?"

"We've not had a king since James brought England and Scotland together," Henry answered and then chuckled. "Though there's them that still wish we were fighting for the Bruce."

Morgan opened her mouth, but Cernunnos gave her hand a warning squeeze. Ask too many questions and these people would get suspicious. Bruce had probably been some warrior. They could find out later.

She slanted him a look and then turned back to Henry. "Arthur united Briton, didn't he?"

"Tis said that he did," Henry replied as he turned the car right on The Mound.

"Don't forget to show them Holyroodhouse," Janet reminded Henry.

"Headed there now," her husband answered as he turned left on High Street. In a few minutes they neared another castle with what seemed like even more turrets.

"Tis where the queen stays when she visits," Janet said proudly, "and tis where Mary spent most of her days, poor lass."

Cernunnos squeezed Morgan's hand again and she smiled sweetly at him just before she raked her nails across his palm. He tried not to wince. At least she wasn't hurling lightening bolts.

"There's a ruined abbey inside too," Janet chirped on. "Ye'll not want to miss looking at it either."

"Do you think the queen will let us in if she doesn't know who we are?" Morgan asked before Cernunnos could stop her.

"The queen's not in residence," Janet answered, "but the castle is open to tourists."

Tourists again. Who were these people? Some kind of wandering nomads? Cernunnos remembered he had said he was one. What really caught his eye, though, was the vast amount of parkland. Mayhap he could communicate with some of his creatures in it once they were alone.

"The park is open to tourists, too," Janet continued as Henry stopped the car. She pointed to the large hill east of the castle. "Just go past the crags there and ye'll find the easiest way to climb Arthur's Seat be from the other side. Once ye get to the top, ye'll be able to see the lochs as well as some old ruins of forts and such."

As Morgan thanked them and climbed out of the car, Cernunnos withdrew some of the paper slips that the *tourists* had given them yesterday. Seth had explained this was called *money* and that it paid for things like rides in *cars* and *buses*.

"How much do I pay you?" he asked.

The couple looked startled and then Henry waved the money away. "Ye owe us nothing. My wife is never happier than when she's nattering away with new people. Isn't that right, *mo cridhe?*"

Janet blushed like a school-girl in spite of her silver hair. "Ye do run on, *bodach.*"

"Take this then," Morgan said as she stepped to Janet's window and handed her a strip of gossamer silk.

Cernunnos felt his eyes widen. It was one of the scarves that attached to Morgan's gown. And it shimmered with faerie dust.

"Oh, it's beautiful," Janet said as she turned it to catch the sparkles that shone from it, "but ye doona need to do this—"

"I want to," Morgan said. "It's just a little gift."

Cernunnos arched a brow. It might be a little gift in Morgan's eyes, but anything that held faerie enchantment could be potently dangerous in a mortal's hands. Before he could say anything, however, Morgan gave him a falsely sweet look as she took his hand. If he spoke now, Morgan's talons wouldn't be far away.

"Thank ye, then," Janet said as Henry put the car into gear. "God bless ye."

Cernunnos wondered if the couple wouldn't need the blessings of their god more than he and Morgan did. Translucent bolts of light arched over their car as they drove away.

* * * *

Morgan took a deep breath when they reached the summit. The climb hadn't been that steep, but without her powers, she had to use real muscles. She set down her backpack and lifted her hair, allowing the cool breeze to blow it gently back from her face. The sun warmed her face as she looked out over the vast park.

The view was amazing. Three lochs, their clear waters reflecting the blueness of the sky, sparkled like sapphires amidst the emerald green of the lawns. Across the expanse, the city rose up, a strange mix of buildings. Morgan turned toward the north and lifted her head to sniff.

"Tis the sea you're smelling," Cernunnos said at her side. "I doubt a mortal would take notice."

"Mayhap not all of my powers are gone then," she said hopefully.

Cernunnos cupped her chin in his hand and then let his fingers trail down her throat and across her breast. "You still have to the power to captivate me. Why don't we find a spot well-hidden and—"

She removed his hand. "There are people around."

He arched an eyebrow. "When has that ever stopped you? You haven't forgotten the time we spied on Gwenhwyfar and Lancelot in the meadow?" He reached for her again, a teasing grin on his face. "Or the time when—"

"No, I haven't forgotten." She stepped away. "It's just..."

"What?" he asked with barely-concealed impatience.

"I don't know." Morgan looked off into the distance and then back at him. "Did you notice how much that couple seemed to care for each?"

"The ones who brought us here?" When she nodded, he shrugged. "What of it? They're old in mortal years. Probably not capable of anything else."

She didn't return the smile. "He called her 'my heart.'"

"And she called him 'old man,'" Cernunnos replied drily.

Morgan remained thoughtful. "I think she meant it in a nice way though. Did you notice how often she reached over to touch him and how he looked at her when she did? Lancelot and Gwenhwyfar do that too. I wonder if that's love."

Cernunnos grimaced. "Will you stop thinking about love? What we have is better than that."

She tilted her head and eyed him. "Is it?"

The earth trembled just slightly beneath them. "Are you saying satisfying our lust—and the many, many different ways we do it—does not please you?"

"Certes it pleases me!" Morgan flared back and the wind rose a bit. "It's just—I don't know—just that something seems to be missing from the rest of our lives."

"I think you are looking for an excuse why Lancelot refused you," Cernunnos said between clenched teeth as the ground trembled once more.

Morgan wanted nothing more than to hurl a lightening bolt at the dolt, but, even though she could feel the power build, she couldn't release it. She stamped her foot in frustration. "I don't want Lancelot."

"When did *that* happen?" Cernunnos asked.

When *did* it happen? Morgan didn't know; she just realized, suddenly, that it was so. "It's true, I thought I did, but we talked—"

"When was this?"

Morgan felt herself blush. "Well, he was bathing—"

"Ah. So the bastard was naked and you were just casually talking?"

"Will you let me finish?" Oh, what she wouldn't give for a nice jolt of lightening. "I'll admit, I went to watch Lancelot with the intent of... Well, it didn't happen. What he did say was that he loved Gwenhwyfar and no one or nothing could change that."

Cernunnos rolled his eyes. "And I suppose you're going to tell me she feels the same?"

"You weren't successful in your seduction either," Morgan spit out.

His antlers began to grow. "Mayhap I haven't finished yet."

Morgan managed to discharge a few sparks from her fingertips, singing some of the golden hair on Cernunnos' strong forearms. "*This* is what I'm talking about! All you think about is whether a female will succumb to your charms."

He rubbed his arm. "I don't see what is wrong with that."

Morgan sighed, her temper somewhat mollified by the fact that she had actually singed him. "Cern, Lancelot said that if he lost Gwenhwyfar, his life wouldn't be worth living. That they risked death for each other. Would you do that for me?"

"We're immortal, Morgan."

"Are we?" She looked around. "This is not our world. Most of our power doesn't work. What if we can't go back?"

"We'll get back."

"What if we don't? Would you risk mortal death for me?"

He frowned. "Instead of wasting time considering our fate as mortals, why don't we start looking for that portal you thought was here?"

Morgan looked down at the ground, not wanting him to see her hurt. He had avoided answering her question. That could only mean he wouldn't risk death. He didn't love her. She swallowed hard, feeling hot tears well up. Faeries never cried. Did that mean she was human now? No. She would find that portal. She had to. Strengthening her resolve she lifted her face, jutting her jaw out.

"I'll find that portal, my lord." Without another word, she turned and started down the hill.

* * * *

Cernunnos had the very unpleasant feeling that Morgan was upset with him as he followed her down the summit, but he couldn't discern why. He had, after all, made a practical suggestion. He knew Morgan wanted to return to Faerie. All he was trying to do was make that happen as soon as possible by focusing on finding a portal. Yet, Morgan seemed to be fixated on how men and women *looked* at each other. She hadn't even noticed that he, Cernunnos, god of the Wild Hunt, hadn't *looked* at a mortal female since they'd arrived in this strange time and it had been a whole day. She could at least appreciate that.

Morgan stopped in front of a small cave, the tips of her ears growing slightly pointed.

"What is it?" Cernunnos asked. "Do you sense something?"

"I'm not sure. I can feel a faint strand of magic, mayhap from long ago. Something happened here."

"You are quite right."

Cernunnos turned to see a portly gentleman, dressed more formally than the tourists wandering about, beam at them from a round face somewhat flushed with exertion from the climb. It was strange, though, that Cernunnos hadn't heard him approach. He wondered if that was one of his powers that no longer worked.

"Do you know what happened?" Morgan asked the man.

"No one knows for sure," he answered, "but in 1836, seventeen small wooden coffins were found in this cave. Each contained a carved figure." He gave a sheepish look. "I'm a bit of an amateur historian."

"Do you know where they came from?"

"That seems to be quite the mystery," the rotund man replied. "Some say witchcraft might have been involved."

Morgan looked thoughtful. "Or faerie magic?"

His eyes twinkled. "Your wife has quite the imagination," he said to Cernunnos.

"He's not my husband," Morgan said, her tone clipped.

The man looked puzzled. "Forgive me. I just assumed—well, to go on then. Faeries are mythical, certainly, although there are some superstitious types still about that might believe in the sidhe. The Inquisitions of the fifteen and sixteen hundreds were quite real though. While it's doubtful that any of the poor souls were truly witches, they were certainly killed."

While Morgan questioned the man further, Cernunnos thought about her quick denial that he was her husband. He *was* her consort. She should have made that clear. So, she was still angry with him. He knew of only one way to cure that. His faerie queen was an extremely passionate woman whose lust wouldn't be held-in-check for long. And he knew each and every one of her most sensitive spots... He slanted a glance at her.

She stood with her hands on her hips, an annoyed expression on her face. The elderly man had moved off.

"Have you heard anything I've said?" she asked.

Certes, he hadn't. Accounts of witch trials didn't interest him. He was thinking of the best way to bed her. Her scowl didn't bode well.

"I didn't want to interfere with your ability to sense a portal." He took her hand and turned it over, kissing her palm slowly. For a moment, desire flashed in her slanted, green eyes and then she removed her hand.

"If there was a portal here, it's been closed. That nice man did tell me about several other places on this hill. *Ruins*, I think he called them."

"Let us proceed then. I'd like to be back in Faerie by nightfall." He knew just the spot where he would seduce Morgan and make her forget this silliness about love.

Morgan gave him a hesitant look and he refrained from smirking. That small kiss had ignited something in her. He would feed that spark with little attentions this afternoon, he decided, and by evening...

"This way." She started down another small path. He followed her along two stony banks that showed evidence of cultivated terraces that might have once been used for farming and remnants of building foundations. She examined some of them, shaking her head each time and then continuing on. She stopped when they came to a cluster of numerous ruins.

"This was a fort." Morgan reached down and touched one of the rocks. "A very old one, I think."

"Arthur's?"

She sank down into the grass, her hand still on the rock, and closed her eyes. Cernunnos sat beside her. It seemed a long time before she opened her eyes again.

"Well?"

"I think mayhap Arthur did fight here. I felt Myrddin's presence."

Cernunnos remained quiet, remembering how the wizard had asked Morgan to produce enough glamour that Uther Pendragon could sire Arthur on an unsuspecting Ygraine. Always fascinated by the ways of mortals, Morgan had attached herself to Myrddin during much of Arthur's reign.

"Is Myrddin's magic strong enough to take us home?"

She shook her head. "There is no passage here. What I felt was the past. In our time, Myrddin slumbers in his crystal cave."

"Then we need to find it and awaken him. Camelot lies far south of here." Cernunnos stood and helped Morgan up. "Tomorrow, we will get tickets for the *train* that Seth told us about and head there. Tonight—" Cernunnos leaned down and kissed Morgan's cheek while allowing his hand to brush across her breast—"we'll find out if Seth's father's *credit card* will buy us a bed with soft feathers. Will you like that?"

"Mmmm. And a hot bath?" Morgan asked.

"Anything you wish, my faerie queen." Cernunnos hid his smile of triumph as she sighed blissfully and allowed him to lead the way down the hill.

* * * *

Disgruntled, Cernunnos decided the best part of valor was remaining quiet as, the next morning, they once more headed north. He looked glumly over at their new traveling companion.

The rotund historian from the cave had reappeared as Cernunnos and Morgan passed by the Salisbury Crags and offered them a lift to a hotel. Lord Tithswell, or 'Tillie' as he preferred to be called, had been only too delighted to accept Morgan's invitation to dinner and then he had managed to keep them up until all hours of the night, talking about King Arthur. As if they needed to know!

Yet, Morgan had been intrigued by the modern accounts of what had happened and Tillie, equally mesmerized by Morgan's faerie charms, had suggested they go to Meigle to see a Pictish gravestone from Arthur's time. When Morgan asked if he would accompany them, he had beamed like a beacon and puffed up like a peacock.

Cernunnos wished he could make peacock soup of the man. Not only had his plans for seducing Morgan with all those foolish, mortal ideas of *gifts*—he did have that credit card, after all—go awry, but everything else had too. After telling Tillie that afternoon that he wasn't her husband, Morgan had insisted on having her own room. When he'd tried the door later, it was locked and there had been no response. Cernunnos considered breaking down the door, but he had no intentions of begging for her attention. He was a demi-god, after all.

He didn't much like traveling in these strange things called cars and more than once, as Tillie drove toward Dundee, he spotted horses grazing in pastures and wished they would stop so he could purchase one. He probably couldn't make one fly since his powers were limited in this time, but for certes, he trusted an animal more than he did this thing he was sitting in. That they weren't struck by these metal objects hurling themselves at him from the opposite direction was nothing short of an Avalon miracle.

Maybe it would be better if he just closed his eyes and slept in his corner of the back seat. Morgan was nattering away enough for both of them.

Sometime later, he awoke, surprised that he had actually been able to sleep.

"We've taken a bit of a detour," Tillie said as they all piled out and Cernunnos stared up at yet another castle that had a big central tower surrounded by many smaller ones with turrets.

"What is this place?" he asked.

"Glamis," Tillie replied. "Childhood home of the Queen Mother, the Earls of Strathmore, and, Shakespeare's "MacBeth.""

Morgan looked puzzled but Cernunnos slanted a look at her and she didn't ask the obvious question.

"I see," Cernunnos said sagely. "Very interesting."

"Ah, yes. But there is a more interesting fact, which is the reason I diverted our course through Dundee," Tillie responded with a gleam in his eye. "About five hundred years before the infamous MacBeth killed Duncan, another MacBeth ancestor lived here." He paused for dramatic effect and watched them closely. "That laird had a wife named Guanhumara."

Cernunnos saw Morgan's eyebrows arch up.

"That was Gwenhwyfar's mother's name," she said.

"Precisely. I can see you do know your history," Tillie replied.

History. If only that man knew the real history. Cernunnos yawned and wished he could sprint across the lawn. Sitting in that car had cramped him.

Morgan glanced over to him and then back to Tillie. "I think we'd appreciate a chance to walk around. Could we?"

Bless you, Cernunnos said silently.

"Of course," Tillie responded. "There's a nature trail over there that takes you by the burn. I believe I'll stay here and rest in the shade, though."

Cernunnos didn't wait for him to change his mind. He took Morgan's arm and hurried her toward the trail.

He closed his eyes and inhaled the fresh scent of running water. When he opened them, Morgan's mouth trembled and her eyes were bright with unshed tears. "What's wrong?" he asked.

She shook her head. "No asrai or naiads in the water here either." Tears welled up. "Do you suppose they've been banished from this world?"

Cernunnos put an arm around her shoulder. "Mayhap they are here; we just can't see them."

Morgan leaned against him. Cernunnos laid his head atop hers and gathered her closer. He had never seen his faerie queen even come close to tears. For once, he wasn't feeling lustful with her body pressed against his. He felt more of a need to provide comfort instead. How strange.

"We passed some gardens and trees earlier," she said as she lifted her head. "Mayhap there's wildlife there and you could communicate?"

"Good idea." Cernunnos held her hand as they headed toward the area. They entered the Pineteum quietly and once again, Cernunnos took a deep breath of the heady smell of earth and pine. A hare darted out from a bush and Cernunnos held out a hand, but the rabbit hopped away.

They moved deeper into the shadows. Cernunnos could hear the soft rustling of undergrowth as other small creatures scurried away. A fox slid into the hallowed out trunk of a fallen tree. Cernunnos made his way over to it.

"Come out, brother," he said as he crouched down. The fox snarled and Cernunnos frowned. "I mean you no harm."

The fox emitted a sound between a whine and a bark and Cernunnos stood. "He wants to be left alone."

"He told you that?" Morgan asked wistfully.

Cernunnos shook his head. "No. I didn't understand what he said, but I know that look. He fears me."

They walked further. Suddenly, Cernunnos stopped. "There," he whispered.

A deer raised its antlered head and regarded him. He approached it slowly, hoping it wouldn't run away. Though the hart remained wary, he stood his ground.

"There's a good fellow," Cernunnos said softly. "You recognize me, don't you?"

He allowed his antlers to grow. "I am your king. Come to me."

For a moment, the animal's eyes widened and then it snorted and pawed the ground. Then the hart lowered its head and began to charge.

A flash of white light struck the animal and it stumbled and fell. Cernunnos stared at it and then looked at Morgan. She was rubbing her hand.

"It's not dead, is it?" she asked.

"No. Just stunned." He retracted his antlers. "How did you do that?"

"I can't hurl lightening bolts, but it seems I can gather something if I'm frightened enough."

"You were frightened? For me?"

"He wanted to kill you." She gave a rueful sigh. "I don't know how mortal you are. I had to do something."

"And I'm glad you did." Cernunnos stared down at the unconscious animal. "It seems I don't have the ability to command the animals that were once mine." A shudder went through his body at the thought. "Without our magic, what are we going to do?"

Morgan put her arms around his waist and tilted her head upward. "We have each other, Cern. We'll just have to survive."

He pulled her close to him. For the second time that day, he felt content that she was in his arms.

* * * *

Morgan looked back at Cernunnos as Tillie once more had them in the car and was headed toward Meigle. Cern had been so quiet on the walk back and Morgan didn't know what more to say to him. Never had she seen him without his powers.

Luckily, Lord Tithswell didn't seem to notice, for he made a running commentary on the Picts who had settled the area north of the Forth and held it against Roman invasion. He was still talking when they drove into the small town of Meigle and stopped in front of an old church.

Tillie pointed. "Just past the graveyard is a museum you will most definitely want to see,"

As they walked to it, Morgan glanced again at Cernunnos. Jaw set, his full, sensual lips could have been carved out of bronze. Only his eyes, a darker whiskey-color than usual, gave any sign that he was troubled. And she was probably the only one who would notice that. Then, as they stepped inside the small building, she gaped. Beside her, Cernunnos took a deep breath.

The stones were beautiful. Three huge slabs stood upright while others lay flat. All of them were carved with ancient symbols. Symbols from the time Morgan and Cernunnos had come from. Morgan walked toward the tallest stone, admiring its rose-hued tone. She craned her neck to look up at its almost dizzying height. A square cross inside a circle covered the top portion. Underneath that, pairs of beasts faced each other. To the left was a climbing figure, aided by a smaller, kneeling woman who seemed to be rescuing the climber from the coiled beasts to the right. Morgan moved around to the other side as Cernunnos joined her.

"I see you have already found the most interesting stone here," Tillie said as he walked over to them. "It's called Vanora's Stone. You probably know her better as Queen Guenevere. She was buried in the churchyard."

Morgan felt her eyes widen. "Gwenhwyfar? Buried here?"

"Ah, you pronounce it like a true Celt," Tillie said. "Shall I explain?"

Cernunnos arched an eyebrow and crossed his muscled arms in front of him. "Please do."

Tillie didn't notice the skeptical tone, but launched directly into his lecture mode.

"The man on horseback at the top is obviously King Arthur. These"—he pointed to three horseman riding abreast directly below the king—"are his nephews, Gawain, Gaheris and Gareth. Behind them rides Modred."

Morgan studied the next set of figures. "Is the woman Gwehwyfar? And why is she surrounded by four beasts?"

"That story is a bit squeamish, I'm afraid," Tillie answered.

"Tell it," Cernunnos said.

Tillie cleared his throat. "Well, then. The story is while King Arthur was fighting the Picts, Modred abducted Guenevere and imprisoned her at Barry Hill, not far from here. By the time Arthur arranged for her rescue, she had formed an alliance with Modred, who turned out to be a traitor." He gestured toward the carving. "Arthur ordered her to be torn apart by wild beasts."

Morgan gasped. "Arthur would never do that!"

Cernunnos gave her a warning look, then turned to study the carvings. "It seems to me that the lady looks in control of the beasts. Each is holding up a paw in submission."

Morgan heard the pain in Cernunnos' voice and knew he was thinking about the hart that had nearly attacked him. Quickly, she pointed to the next figure. "A man who is half beast?"

"Yes. A centaur." Tillie warmed back up to his subject. "From here, it gets a bit more pagan, if you don't find that offensive."

Morgan stifled a giggle and saw that even Cernunnos quirked up a corner of his mouth. If their guide only *knew.* "I don't think we'll be offended," she managed to say. "Please continue."

"Centaurs are creatures of wisdom," Tillie said. "They have knowledge of both man and beast. Arthur's teacher was Merlin. The centaur represents him. Texts refer to him as other-worldly, sometimes good, sometimes not. The serpent at the bottom was a symbol of priestess power. Theirs was an earth-bound religion, hence the carving of the bull."

Morgan tilted her head to view the bottom. "What an interesting story."

"It is." He moved his hand toward the stone. "We begin at the top with Arthur, a Christian king, fighting to unite Briton, yet we end with symbols of a pagan religion the Romans thought they had squelched. Guenevere is in the middle. Is she about to be torn apart or does she, indeed, rule the wild creatures?" Tillie stepped back to view the whole monument. "Perhaps a better question would be, was she Arthur's Christian queen, wrongfully accused, or did she yield more power as a priestess of the old ways?"

Gwenhwyfar a priestess? Morgan choked back a laugh.

"It would be hard to say," Cernunnos replied drily. "She managed to charm at least three men—Arthur, Medraut, and Lancelot—into being willing to die for her. Maybe there were more."

Morgan looked sharply at him, her sense of humor disappearing. Was Cern admitting he was besotted by the woman too? He had pursued Gwenhwyfar in Faerie *and* he never had answered the question of whether he would die for *her*, Morgan.

"You used the Celtic name for Modred just as Morgan did earlier for Guenevere," Tillie said approvingly. "I can see you are both scholars of Arthurian legends."

It's just that we know them. Morgan looked at the stone again, wondering how this story had come about. Lancelot and Gwenhwyfar had been rescued from Camelot far in the south. According to Nimue, she had prepared graves for them there. "How long has this stone been here?"

"Probably from the sixth century," Tillie replied. "The Picts were Christianized following a visit by St.Columba." He gestured toward the stone. "It wasn't until the eighteen hundreds that Guenevere was revered again. Before that, the local girls would avoid walking near her grave for fear of being barren as the queen was."

"That's not true!" Morgan blurted. "She had a child with Lancelot, but it died."

Lord Tithswell stared at her. "Fascinating. There is a theory that Guenevere did indeed birth a child, but Arthur insisted on taking the young boy to battle, swearing he would be protected under guard. Only the child was murdered. I had not thought that it might be Lancleot's." He paused thoughtfully. "They say it's the father's genes...perhaps Arthur was, in a way of speaking, the barren one."

Morgan looked down at the denim *jeans* she wore. She guessed they could keep someone from having a child if they weren't removed before a tumble to the ground...but in defense of Arthur, this historian should know he had a daughter. And a priestess one, at that. Morgan started to giggle at the thought.

Tillie smiled. "I see you caught the irony of my little jest."

She had no idea what he was talking about, but the look Cernunnos sent her told her clearly she needed to keep her ideas to herself. She sent him a look back. Really, they were going to need to talk about this...control thing of his. Soon. She tossed her long brown hair back.

"I've always been fascinated with Lancelot," she said and ignored Cernunnos' glower. "What can you tell me about him?"

"Ah!" Tillie exclaimed and waved his hands. "Part of the land you've been driving through was his. In fact, a small town a few kilometers down the road is still named for him: Coupar Angus." Noting her puzzled look, he added, "Angus—or Anguselus if you prefer the Latin—was king of Albania during that time. The name 'Lancelot' is actually a mistranslation from the French."

Morgan blinked. How could anyone have gotten their facts so completely wrong? His *real* name was Galahad and he had been called Lancer by the soldiers because... She opened her mouth to correct him when Cernunnos growled. She slanted a glance in his direction. They were definitely going to need to talk.

"I thought Lancelot lived at Din Guyardi," she said instead.

"Joyous Garde." Tillie nodded. "That was one of his strongholds. It lies to the southeast of here. Would you like to see it?"

She heard Cernunnos moan. Obviously, he didn't want any more historical lessons, but Morgan found herself fascinated. Who knew what misconceptions this world had of Lancelot. Besides, Cernunnos had practically admitted he was still besotted with Gwenhwyfar, so Morgan could express an interest in Lancelot, if she wanted to. And she did.

"I would love to see it." She purposely didn't look at Cernunnos.

* * * *

It was a good thing he didn't have all of his powers, Cernunnos decided the next morning as they set out once again with their self-appointed historian leading them. He would gladly have banished Lord Tithswell to the Otherworld.

Again, last night Morgan had chosen to have her own room. Somehow, Cernunnos needed to get that damn credit card away from her. If he had it, there would be only *one* room. He looked at the pesky little man chattering away as they drove through the small village of Bamburgh. Today would be the *last* day of this 'tour,' no matter what he had to do to get rid of their companion. And tonight...*one* room.

Morgan shaded her eyes with her hand as she looked up the incline that led to the castle. Even Cernunnos had to admit its position was strategic. Situated on a long, narrow outcrop of rock overlooking the sea, it was nearly impregnable.

"This isn't the original castle," Tillie said as they neared the entrance, "but you can see how easily defensible even a wooden hill fort would have been."

"And Lancelot was Arthur's strongest warrior," Morgan said with a purr in her voice. "He would have needed only a small number of men to hold off a legion."

Cernunnos refrained from commenting. Yesterday, he had felt so oddly protective of Morgan and she had yielded to him, but then something changed. Now, she was clearly reminding him of her attraction to Lancelot. She was retaliating for something, but what? They were going to have a long talk. Tonight. Right after he'd bedded her thoroughly.

Morgan walked down the drive and stopped to gaze around. "I can just imagine what this looked like nearly fifteen hundred years ago."

She should. We've both been there. Cernunnos watched uneasily as a speculative look crossed her face. He didn't dare give her another warning look to be quiet; he'd been getting too many glares back and another one wouldn't bode well for his evening plans. He just hoped she wasn't about to get into Faerie mischief.

"Tell me, my dear," Tillie urged.

Cernunnos almost groaned aloud. With that gleam in her eye, Morgan didn't need encouragement.

"This incline would have been fortified with earthworks,"— she pointed to the way they had just come—"with maybe a stone palisade?" She waved a hand to indicate the top of the castle. "The usual guards would have been posted on the battlements with the stables safely inside the enclosure." She paused, closing her eyes for a moment before opening them. "But the gardens—which the original name means—are beautiful." She glanced sideways at Cernunnos as if daring him to stop her. "I envision them laid out in precise triangles, so they form a wheel, with rocks lining the beds as spokes. Mayhap benches in the middle, surrounding a central fountain?" She shorty a wicked look at Cernunnos. "What do you think?"

He thought she was playing with fire. She had described exactly how Din Guyardi looked. In their time. What was the little minx up to? He sighed. Better to have her angry than rattling on about something that might expose who they were.

"It sounds like a spot Gwenhwyfar would no doubt enjoy," he said. A gust of wind came from nowhere, swirling leaves around them as Morgan bared her teeth in what might look, to some people, like a smile. Cernunnos knew better.

"Yes, I'm sure she did," she said sweetly, "since she lived there."

Tillie looked confused. "I haven't heard that before."

Cernunnos shrugged. "Morgan has an active imagination—"

She gave him a black look. "You know very well that Lancelot took her there after he rescued her from the stake. Don't you remember Arthur arranging it?"

Tillie gave her a quizzical look. "You make it sound as though you were there."

"I was!" she blundered and then, too late, covered her mouth with her hands as Lord Tithswell frowned. "What I mean is... certes, I wasn't *there*...I, uh..." She cast Cernunnos a desperate look.

He thought quickly, remembering how they'd been mistaken at Rosslyn. Seth had explained that people thought they were *actors*. Something like a bard. "As I said, Morgan has an active mind. She's been...writing a scene for us to use. We're actors."

Tillie's smile returned. "You're actors?"

"Yes, we are. Traveling ones."

"Then you must go to London!" he exclaimed, "and try your hand at Little Theatre. I know several directors. I will give you a reference."

"That would be wonderful!" Morgan chimed in and hooked her hand into the crook of Cernunnos' arm. "You did want to go south, didn't you?"

"That was my general idea." Cernunnos placed his hand over hers. "Is that what you want?"

She nodded demurely, her eyes wide and innocent, but the breast she deliberately pressed against his bicep told a different story. It seemed he had been forgiven.

Their mating was even more enjoyable after an argument. Tonight would be fantastic.

Chapter Ten

"Mmmm," Gwenhwyfar stretched lazily in bed as Lancelot's warm hand slid up her ribcage and his fingers began to knead a breast. She came fully awake as his thumb flicked across a nipple, hardening it immediately. "What a nice way to—Ah!" She arched her back as he closed his mouth over her other breast and began to suckle, gently at first, then drawing deep as she moaned her desire.

Lancelot's hand slid down her side, lifting her thigh to drape over his hip as she turned toward him, twining her arms around his neck. With practiced ease, he slipped inside her and Gwenhwyfar met his thrusts, falling into the ancient rhythm that soon had both of them panting with frenzied need. She felt him push against her womb and her toes curled, even as her inner muscles contracted tightly. Her body shuddered and ripples of pure pleasure washed over her as she felt the warm gush of Lancelot's seed deep inside.

She lay gasping for breath against the silken sheen of sweat on his broad chest. He tucked her closer and placed a kiss atop her head. "No matter how many times we do this, Gwen, it only gets better."

"You say that every time." She nestled against him, an arm around his waist.

"I mean it every time," he answered as he played with her hair. "And in Faerie, 'time' can be forever."

Reluctantly, Gwenhwyfar rose up on an elbow and looked at him. "Are we happy here in Faerie?"

Lancelot linked both arms behind him to cradle his head and eyed her. "You know what the alternative would have been."

"I don't mean that. We had to come here or we would have died. I'm not ungrateful for what Cernunnos and Morgan did for us. It's just that..."

"Just what? Are you still worried that we can't withstand their efforts at seduction?"

"No, it's not that either. I think—at least, I hope—that they both understood what we told them about love. That nothing they can do will change our feelings for each other."

"Good. You haven't had any more of those nightmares, have you?"

Surprisingly, she hadn't. The beast with the red eyes and fangs hadn't returned. With Cernunnos and Morgan missing, she had hardly given it a thought. "No more nightmares."

"Then what's the problem?"

"I'm not sure I can explain." Gwenhwyfar sat up and shifted herself against the headboard. "When I was here the first time, as a captive, I was not ill-treated. Except for Cernunnos' attempts to lure me away from you and Morgan's ever being present when I tried to talk with you through the scrying pool, life here was pleasant. Mayhap too pleasant." She glanced down at him. "Do you know what I mean?"

Lancelot moved to sit beside her. "I don't know that I do."

"I guess Sadi described it best. She couldn't understand why I was so obsessed with time and wanting to return to you. She said the faeries eat when they're hungry, play until they're tired, take their pleasure of each other when they will... I was sitting under a shade tree. It was a perfect day, like all of them are here. Blue skies, sunshine, a warm breeze..." Gwenhwyfar shook her head. "Nothing ever changed."

"Well, things may be about to." Lancelot took her hand and intertwined their fingers.

Gwenhwyfar frowned. "You don't think Cernunnos and Morgan are coming back?"

"I don't know. They've been gone nearly a sennight—or at least I think they have, it's hard to tell in Faerie—but it seems to me, if they had the means of returning, they would have done so."

"Do you think they've lost their powers?"

"Can you imagine either Cernunnos or Morgan staying away this long deliberately?" Lancelot's dark eyes searched Gwenhwyfar's face.

"You're right." Then she remembered something else. "Lance, I tried to send Prince to Avalon again and he couldn't get through the barrier at the pool. Mayhap something is keeping Cernunnos and Morgan out. Could it be Aoibhill?"

A muscle ticked in Lancelot's jaw. "That bitch rutted with Medraut. No good can come of that union and Melehan is living proof. He lured Morgan into that pool but didn't follow."

Gwenhwyfar grew thoughtful. "I suspected foul play with both of them, too, but so far, neither of them has done anything but walk about being pleasant."

Lancelot grimaced. "They're learning the lay of the land. Arthur always sent the least-threatening looking scouts to blend in with the locals and gather information before a battle. It helped him win."

Gwenhwyfar worried her bottom lip. "Well, there's a reason they're here and Morgan and Cernunnos are not. What can we do?"

"We wait. We watch. I will take Melehan out at the slightest hint of danger."

"If he's mortal, Lance."

"His mother claims to be faerie. His father was an evil bastard, but he was human." Lancelot glanced over at Gwenhwyfar. "You don't doubt that I can do it?"

"Certes, not." She leaned over and nibbled his ear. "You bested Cernunnos. Melehan will be no problem."

"At least not for now." He proceeded to turn her onto her back. "At least not for now."

* * * *

Melehan watched Gwenhwyfar from behind a thicket of gorse as she paced beside the small brook, the packed picnic basket on a boulder behind her. Lancelot would be late in meeting her, thanks to an injury Melehan arranged for one of the horses. He smirked. Lancelot's love for horses was well-known at Camelot. His attending the animal gave Melehan the time he needed to carry out his plan.

He eyed his prey. Long, red-gold hair flowed in silky waves framing a face with expressive green eyes, high cheekbones, a pert nose and lusciously full lips. He could see why his father had been so besotted with her. He, Melehan, would be more successful with Briton's Great Whore than his father had been.

By Lucifer's own fires, Gwenhwyfar had almost become a legend in her own time. From Medraut, he learned that hers had been an arranged marriage to an older Arthur. An Arthur who had little time for a wife and no time for a bastard son. From Aoibhill, he found out that Medraut had worshiped Gwenhwyfar from the time he met her as a lad of twelve years. No doubt, his mother had gotten that information at the crucial time when the man's lust had been well-sated and he didn't watch his words.

And then there was his nemesis, Lancelot. The queen's champion, appointed by the fool, Arthur, himself. Granting Lancelot permission to be constantly by her side—and even in her bed, if Medraut's tirades could be believed—yet, Lancelot was clever. He had honed himself into a fighting, killing machine on the battlefield and thus, became Arthur's strongest and best knight. It was brilliant strategy on the Breton's part. Making himself irreplaceable to the king, while having his fill of the queen. Melehan wouldn't make the mistake his father had. He wouldn't underestimate his enemy, but he would avenge his father.

He put on his most angelic expression and stepped away from the shrubbery.

Gwenhwyfar spun on her heels. "I wondered where... Oh, hello."

Melehan bowed slightly and gestured to the picnic basket. "I'm afraid Lancelot has been delayed."

"Why would he be delayed?"

Melehan gave a graceful shrug. "A horse went lame. Quite badly. The faerie lad wasn't sure they could save it. Lancelot's attending to it."

Her expression changed into one of concern. "I'll go to the stables at once."

He held back a triumphant smirk. How many times had he heard about the horsewoman that Gwenhwyfar was? Certes, she'd help. He'd counted on it.

"The horse is in the far pasture, past the forest. I'll escort you there."

"That won't be necessary." Gwenhwyfar bent to pick up the basket. "I can find my way."

Melehan kept his face impassive. He'd almost forgotten the tales about her stubborn independence. And...somewhere he'd heard, she handled a sword well. He quickly perused her form.

She harbored no sword under the fine silk gown she wore, but perhaps a knife? He would be careful.

"I'm sure you could find your way," he said with a gaze that had charmed hundreds of women before her, "but it is a long walk. So, if you'll allow me to do the chivalrous thing and escort you, we can talk as well. You've been rather elusive."

Gwenhwyfar didn't smile back. Instead she studied him as though he a specimen that might be used for a potion of some sort. "Were you really in trouble at Camelot?"

"I assure you I was." Lucifer's horns, the woman was direct. And she looked skeptical enough that it might be harder to get her to walk with him than he thought. "I foolishly mistook Custennin's troops for rebels that still roamed the countryside after Wehha's withdrawal." He gave her a sheepish look that usually endeared him to anything female. "Since I had originally fought for Wehha, I knew I would have a difficult time convincing Custennin that I had made a mistake."

The corner of her mouth lifted slightly before disappearing. "Custennin can be pig-headed, I grant you that."

He had no doubt of that. Custennin had little use for women, other than bed-sport. "I've become quite accustomed to having my head attached to my shoulders and didn't want them separated." Melehan gave her a look that made him appear as a little boy in need of a hug. "I knew that Morgan le Fey was powerful enough to convince Custennin to hear me out. That's why I came here."

Gwenhwyfar regarded him with a level look. "Why didn't you follow her then?"

He tried not to squirm. This woman had the tenaciousness of a terrier with a rat caught in a hole. "I was about to, but my mother arrived unexpectedly."

Gwenhwyfar arched an eyebrow.

"Yes, well. I regard my mother with the highest respect, but if left to her own devices, she can get into a bit of mischief." Melehan gazed at Gwenhwyfar engagingly. "You've been in Faerie long enough to understand what I'm saying?"

She sighed. "Well, they do sometimes act without considering the consequences."

"Exactly. When Morgan returns, I'm sure she'll expect everything to be as she left it. She hasn't seen my mother in some time, so I wouldn't want Aoibhill making any changes Morgan might object to." There would be full-fledged magical war when they did meet, but Gwenhwyfar didn't need to know that.

"When do you think she'll return?"

For some reason, Melehan got the feeling that Gwenhwyfar was testing him. He widened his eyes innocently. "As soon as she's convinced Custennin, I would think." He shrugged. "Kings hold court in their own time. She might have to wait for an audience."

Gwenhwyfar considered him. "Mayhap that is exactly what has happened. But Morgan won't be happy kept waiting. Is your mother impatient also?"

Melehan laughed. "Why don't I tell you some stories about my mother while we walk?" He saw the hesitation in her eyes. "Truly. I would not forgive myself if you didn't get to your destination safely."

She looked at him for another minute and then slowly nodded. "Mayhap we'll need another pair of hands to help with the horse at that."

"Certes." He took the basket from her to carry. "Allow me."

As they started down the trail, he kept his face impassive and his voice conversational. Gwenhwyfar didn't need to know about the cave his mother had found hidden behind boulders en route to the pasture. Or that Aoibhill had magicked it to be invisible. Or what his *hands* would do once he had Gwenhwyfar *safely* secured in that dungeon.

* * * *

Aoibhill stood in the doorway of the stables and watched Lancelot tend to the lame horse. The mortal was a handsome specimen. He had taken off his shirt to work in the warmth of the stall and she liked the way the muscles of his back and shoulders stretched and contracted with each movement. That broad back narrowed to a slender waist and, hunched down as he was, his thigh muscles bulged. Ah, yes. A handsome specimen indeed. No doubt, Morgan had found her way into his bed the minute Cernunnos' own back was turned.

Now it would be Aoibhill's turn.

"Will the animal be all right?" She walked inside to lean against the stall's entry, making sure the slit on her nearly transparent gown showed a great deal of her leg.

Lancelot didn't glance up as he finished wrapping an herb-soaked linen around the horse's foreleg. "She should be." He gathered up the basin and cloths he had used and ran a hand along the mare's flank.

She nickered contentedly and Aoibhill felt an urge to have Lancelot's hand sliding along her naked body as well. *Soon.*

"I'm glad." She didn't move when Lancelot approached to leave. "I certainly wouldn't want anything to happen to Morgan's creatures while I'm here."

"Why would that make a difference?"

She shrugged. "There was an incident, a long time ago, when I accused Morgan of taking something of mine. Well, actually, *misusing* it. I wouldn't want her to think I am retaliating." *Damn Cernunnos, anyway, for letting himself be taken by that little brown-haired mouse.*

"You can hardly be blamed because a horse went lame." Lancelot took a step toward her. "If you'll move aside, so I can pass?"

She tossed her head so her bright curls swung out and then settled over her shoulders. "Feel free to pass."

"These rags are bloodied and dirty. I wouldn't want you to ruin your gown."

She glanced down at it, letting her lashes sweep her cheeks before she slanted her gaze slowly upward at him. "I could take it off."

His eyebrow lifted. "Why would you want to do that?"

Aoibhill laughed. "Surely, you don't need an answer to that." She moved closer and ran her fingers along his shoulder and down his bare bicep. "I want you." When he didn't answer immediately, she added, "Morgan and I have shared lovers before." She leaned forward slightly so he could get an excellent view of her breasts. *Bigger and softer than the brown mouse's. When Cernunnos saw them again, he would remember!* She slipped her hand to Lancleot's tautly-ridged belly. "Mmmm. So hard. Are you hard elsewhere?" Her fingers trailed to the lacings of his trews.

Lancelot caught her hand and moved it aside. "I am not Morgan's lover."

Aoibhill arched a delicate brow. "Morgan would not have brought you to Faerie if you weren't an *extremely* good lover. I'm sure she won't mind if I share you." She moved closer.

He shook his head. "I don't share my body. It belongs to Gwen."

"How very noble of you. Didn't your mortal queen share *her* body though? With your friend, Arthur? How is this any different?"

A muscle clenched in Lancelot's jaw as he reached to take Aoibhill by the shoulders and set her aside. "That was a long time ago and we all paid the price." Turning, he stomped out of the stall.

Lancelot turned his back on her! No one did that. No one. Furious, she hurled a ball of magic at him. "Stop!"

He froze as the magic settled over him.

Aoibhill walked around to face him. "Ah, that's better." She poked at his arm. "You can't move, can you?"

His eyes glittered darkly.

"No one walks away from me, Lancelot." She ran her hands over his chest again and down his stomach and then lower. "Ah. Very nice. You will feel everything I do, my stubborn knight, and you will like it." Aoibhill began to chant in the Old Tongue and slowly, a dark mist began to rise, encircling them. "It is a wall of enchantment," she whispered, "a barrier you will not be able to break." She stepped back to slowly untie the straps of her gown, then let it slide along her curves to puddle around her feet and stood before him, naked.

"Do you like what you see, Sir Knight?" she asked seductively.

Lancelot's eyes turned to slate.

She put her arms around his neck and stood on tip-toe to kiss him and then frowned when he didn't return the kiss. Her lower lip thrust out. "I suppose I will have to release you from your spell if I want you to participate." She raised her arms and the mist thickened about them. "That should hold you in." She sketched a sign in the air in front of Lancelot, freeing his movements. "Now then,"—she reached for his trews once more—"I'm looking forward to having you sheath that very fine sword of yours inside me. No need to be gentle either. I like it hard and fast."

The next moment she landed with a hard, fast thud on the ground. Surprised, she looked up, but Lancelot was gone. She screamed her rage and started after him, only to be bounced off of her own barrier mist. "How did you do this?" she shrieked when she couldn't break through.

A hollow chuckle assailed her as, from far away, Lancelot's voice answered. "You forgot that I am half-fey, witch."

* * * *

Lancelot cursed as he pushed open the door to the cottage he and Gwen shared. He had thought Morgan irksome with her persistent flirtations, but never had she ensorcelled him. Even Cernunnos' mesmerizing ability hadn't totally captivated Gwen, although he had come close enough one time to drive Lancelot to near madness on the mortal plane. Aoibhill had power. Dark power. Lancelot didn't need to see the black mist she conjured to know her kind of power was evil. He had understood the incantation she made, for he spoke the Old Tongue as well, a gift from the Lady of the Lake when he was a child. A counter-command to it·had allowed him to pass through and to keep the witch imprisoned. He hadn't known if it would work, for he hadn't paid tribute to the Goddess in a long while. He did so now, fervently.

He didn't know how long he could bind Aoibhill within her own spell. And Melehan. Who knew what power resided in him?

Lancelot swore again. He and Gwen had to leave. *Now.* Even if it meant being lost in the mists that roiled around Faerie. Eventually they would lift. Everything shifted in Faerie, given time. He almost laughed at that irony. Time in Faerie could mean centuries on earth.

"Gwen!" When there was no answer, he opened the bedroom door and then the one to the small room that held a wooden tub for bathing. Gwen wasn't there. He frowned. When he'd learned of the lame horse, he'd sent a lad to let her know. Could she have gone to the clearing to await him anyhow?

He strode out of the cottage and along the well-trod path. About half-way there, he noticed trampled ferns and then broken branches of gorse. The hair on his nape rose as his hand went for the hilt of his sword. It encountered air. Muttering an oath, he remembered it wasn't needed in Faerie. Cautiously, he moved forward and then spied a small boot poking out from under the shrubbery. Pushing it aside, he looked down and saw the lad he'd sent with the message for Gwen. Kneeling quickly, he determined the child was still alive and didn't seem to be wounded, just unconscious. There were no beasts in Faerie who would have attacked the lad. And he was well-liked by the adult faeries as well. Who then? Lancelot felt his blood chill.

Melehan.

Lancelot shot upright and bolted for the clearing. It was empty. No trace of Gwen or the picnic basket. He scoured the area. To the right, some grass had been trampled. He moved toward it. A small boot imprint was visible in the dirt. He crouched down, noting some broken branches. Someone had taken the narrow path not long ago. He went a few more feet and then he sw it.

A much larger and heavier footprint in the soft loam. A man's footprint, alongside the woman's. Lancelot straightened, his eyes nearly black.

Melehan was with Gwenhwyfar. But where?

Chapter Eleven

Cernunnos noted the amazed expression on Morgan's face as the train—horrible, noisy, metal beast that it was—pulled into King's Cross and tried not to let his own uneasiness show. This world that they had been thrust into was an unnerving place. Everyone moved so fast and there were far too many of these metal cars scrabbling everywhere like a confused army of ants. And people talked into other little boxes that they held to their ears. Yet Morgan couldn't scent any magic from any of these.

"This cannot be Londinium," she said as peered out the window. "It was a Roman settlement on the banks of a river. I don't see any water."

"You said almost the same thing when we passed through Eboracum." Cernunnos gathered their backpacks and they descended from the train.

"Only it's called York now." Morgan twisted her head to look at other great, chugging machines on tracks. "I do not think I like this change."

He didn't either, but what could be done? He sighed. "We have to try and find Camelot. It's our only hope."

"Or another portal," Morgan replied. "There used to be plenty of Sidhe mounds in this area."

He took her arm to keep from losing her in the crowd of people pressing around them. By Mithras himself, where were all these people hurrying to? "I don't think we'll find any patches of primrose or even sacred oaks here."

Morgan took a deep breath once they were outside and then nearly choked. "Even the air is foul. We must get away from this...city? Is that what Tillie called it? Mayhap in the country you can speak with your creatures and find the way back."

"I would like nothing better." He tried to keep the bitterness out of his voice. "But when we tried to use this credit card in

Ebor...York, the man said it had been denied. We have only a few coins. Not enough to go farther."

Morgan widened her eyes. "We cannot stay here. What will we do?"

If the situation hadn't been so depressing, Cernunnos would have chuckled. He couldn't remember when—if ever—Morgan had asked for help or depended on him. As the Queen of Faerie, she had always been coyishly flirtatious, but never had she actually *needed* him. He found himself rather liking the idea.

"We do have the letter Tillie gave us," he said.

Her eyes rounded even more. "The one that says he recommends us as actors? You know you just said that so he wouldn't think I was serious about—"

"I know," Cernunnos replied, "but we have to do something. From what I've observed, all the people where we've stopped—the inns, the eateries, even that man who walked through the train to look at our tickets, want coin for their services. We need coin if we want to travel on. We must do something, I think, to earn it."

Morgan furrowed her brow. "I suppose we could pretend to be someone else. It seemed to work at that place called Roslyn."

"Yes. It was fair easy, as well." Cernunnos took out the paper Tillie had given them and looked at it. He had no idea what it said, since it wasn't in Latin, but he had memorized what Tillie told them. "There is a small *theatre*,"—he was actually quite proud of his knowledge of these new words—"called The Royal Sword. It's on Upper Street, not that far from here." Morgan looked impressed and Cernunnos hid his smile.

"You've learned to read this language?" she asked.

Cernunnos shrugged. "A bit, mayhap. Tillie did say we should take a bus to it."

Getting on another of those metal things that belched smoke out of its tail was the last thing he wanted to do, but for Morgan's sake, he would act like it didn't matter. "Come."

Surprisingly, they found it with little difficulty. A three-story stone building—Cernunnos looked closer. The 'stones' were all of the same size and spaced evenly—it had square windows in front and the main entrance was supported with two pillars. The place was adjoined, it seemed, to buildings on either side. He looked up and down the street. There was no space between the different designs of the buildings and he wondered if, at one time, it had been used as some sort of fortification, much like the stone curtain walls of Camelot.

Before they could knock on the door, they heard a loud rumbling and turned back to the street. A man, riding astride a two-wheeled machine, headed straight toward them. Cernunnos grabbed Morgan and pulled her behind him and brought his fists up.

The young man riding the machine widened his eyes and came to a halt beside them. "Relax! I've not hit a bloke yet!" he said as he climbed off.

Cernunnos studied the man. He had long, black hair and a goatee. A black t-shirt hung loosely over blue jeans on his rail-thin frame. Behind black-framed glasses, a lively set of vivid-blue eyes regarded them. Sensing no danger, Cernunnos lowered his arms and turned his attention to the contraption the man had been riding.

"I've not seen a horse quite like this before," he said.

"Do you mean hog?"

Cernunnos furrowed his brow. 'Hog' was another term for boar, he thought and then wondered why anyone would call a machine that. He walked slowly around it, admiring the polished chrome and gleaming black paint. It didn't really look like a horse, either, but the way the man rode it... "What do you call it?"

With obvious pride, its owner gave it an affectionate pat. "It's a Harley Road Glide," he said. "Top of the line, too."

"Hmmm." Cernunnos leaned over the handlebars to look at various gadgets. Truthfully, it was much more complex than a horse with its simple bridle. The leather seat, though, was somewhat like a Roman saddle. "How does it work?" he asked.

The young man was apparently eager to talk about his pet. "This is a clutch." He indicated a handle on the left of the bike. "You use it to shift gears." He pointed to a pedal on the left side. "Here's where your foot actually does the shifting." Gesturing to the right handlebar, he added, "Throttle here. Front brake too. Rear brake on the other side."

"Hmmm." Cernunnos stroked his chin as though he understood. "Fascinating."

"She rides like you were floating about the clouds, too."

The machine could *fly*? Cernunnos looked at it with new respect. Obviously, he had seen that it was powerful when it came down the street. But *fly*?

Beside him, Morgan cleared her throat. It seemed to bring both men out of their mutual admiration for the bike.

"Well, then, what is it that brings you here? The pubs and theatre won't open for several hours."

"We've come to be actors here," Cernunnos said.

The young man's brows arched over his frames. "Indeed? Well, I'm the director. What kind of experience do you have?"

Morgan smiled prettily at him. "We've just come from doing a...from acting at Roslyn Chapel."

"I wasn't aware they were allowing that," he said.

"It was a special performance," Cernunnos said quickly and produced the letter. "This is from Lord Smythe Tithswell."

The young man's face lit up. "Tillie? Why didn't you say so? Please come in."

Cernunnos exchanged a glance with Morgan. Mayhap their 'friend' would prove to be more helpful than he thought.

"I'm Andy Hollister." The man led them into a small office off to one side. The desk was littered with thick piles of papers and books were strewn everywhere. "Have a seat." He nodded. "You might have to clear some of that stuff off first though."

They sat on a lumpy sofa as Andy finished reading the letter. He took off his glasses and laid them on the table. "Tillie says you're interested in the King Arthur period." When they nodded, he continued, "You've come to the right place then. The Royal Sword was named after Excalibur. We concentrate on medieval plays."

Cernunnos nodded knowingly. He could only hope that 'medieval' meant something to do with Arthur. "We're ready to start work."

Andy pursed his lips. "Well, you certainly seem eager enough. We're getting ready to cast a script called *The Once and Future Camelot*—the story of the past Camelot and how the knights of the Round Table would fare in today's world. There may be parts for you. You'll have to audition, of course."

Morgan tilted her head and slanted a look at Andy. "Audition?"

Andy blinked, his eyes glazing, and Cernunnos glanced over at Morgan, surprised to see a soft glow surrounding her. Faerie glamour.

"I suppose you wouldn't have to," Andy finally said, his voice somewhat slurred as he gazed at Morgan. "I mean...with Tillie's recommendation..."

"Thank you," she said sweetly.

"Yes, well. Now then. The pay is not much. Do you have a place to stay?"

"We've just come into town," Cernunnos said.

"Well," Andy said again, the glazed look on his face not quite gone, "there are some rooms upstairs. If you're willing to work as stage hands, too, perhaps we could work out something."

"That would be fine." Cernunnos wasn't quite sure how a stage would need someone's hand on it, but this was a strange world. Morgan turned her gaze on him and, although he was immune to her glamour, he saw something else in her eyes. Something that looked like...respect, mayhap? Was she actually letting him make the decision? An odd tingle went through him. Usually, Morgan fought him over things like this. What was happening?

Whatever it was, he rather liked it.

* * * *

Morgan decided she rather liked acting. The 'cast' as Andy called the other actors who had come to audition, included some very good-looking and well-built men and, if she really wanted to admit it, the female actors were beautiful, too. Morgan had more than once glanced at Cernunnos to see which one would catch his eye, but strangely enough, he looked impassive. She tucked that thought away as Andy called for two actors to read parts. She stifled a giggle at the one who would be Lancelot.

"What's so funny?" Andy asked, still somewhat caught in the web of glamour Morgan had been able to maintain around him.

"That one is all wrong for Lancelot." She looked at the young, slender man with sandy hair and brown eyes as sad as a scolded puppy.

"Why?" Andy looked at the actor too. "Lancelot is a tragic hero. Every time he tries to do what's right, he makes things worse. He's blamed for much, yet his heart is pure."

Morgan almost choked. *Pure?* "I think you have him mixed up with Galahad."

"Galahad never was tempted by a woman. But Lancelot bears the guilt of what happened. It's why he entered a monastery after Arthur's death. This actor has the look of a man who wants to atone for his sin."

Monastery? What a waste of beautiful manhood that would be. Morgan refrained from rolling her eyes. How could anyone have such a wrong impression of Lancelot? "I don't think Lancelot felt guilty at all." She ignored a quick look from Cernunnos. "I think there was this thing called love between him and Gwenhwyfar." Beside her, Cernunnos groaned.

Andy laughed. "Love? Lust, you mean." He pointed to the actress who would be playing Gwenhwyfar and then leaned over to Cernunnos. "Does she not look like someone any red-blooded man would lust over?"

Cernunnos grinned and Morgan was tempted to rake his arm with her nails, but then was surprised when his gaze didn't linger over the beautiful blonde whose well-endowed assets nearly burst from the low neckline of the little halter top she wore to the audition. Had Cern taken ill? She turned her attention back to Andy.

"I really think it was love between them and not lust," she said adamantly.

Andy gave her a curious look. "Tell me why."

Well, she couldn't very well tell him about bannocks. She still wasn't quite sure she understood that little gesture anyway. There was the fact that Lancelot had refused *her* and that Cernunnos hadn't been able to seduce Gwenhwyfar... But how could she explain *that*? She thought back to the time she spent at Camelot perched invisibly on Myrddin's shoulder.

"I have a slightly different idea of what Camelot may have been like."

"Tell me then," Andy said. "As a director, I'm always looking for the best angle to present a story."

"To begin with, Myrddin didn't want Arthur to marry Gwenhwyfar. He was quite opposed to it." She glanced at the elderly actor whom Andy had picked to play the part. Mryddin would be furious if he knew. "He always said Gwenhwyfar was destined for someone else."

"I think that's pretty much accepted," Andy said. "Star-crossed lovers like in Shakespeare. It's still lust though."

Shakespeare. There was that name again. The one Tillie had mentioned with a man named Macbeth. She didn't think Macbeth had sounded like a lover. She shook her head. "Arthur was older than Gwenhwyfar and he was busy trying to keep the Saxons out of Briton." How many times had she yawned and tweaked Mryddin's ear, totally bored with talk about war? "Lancelot was closer to Gwenhwfar's age and he'd been sent to escort her to Camelot. I think they became friends." She stopped suddenly as a thought struck her. Was being friends important for love? She glanced at Cernunnos to find that his amber eyes were fixed on her. Ummm. Friends. "Then when Morgana tried to poison—"

"You mean Morgan le Fey?"

Morgan gaped at him. Beside her, Cernunnos looked suspiciously as though he would burst out laughing. "Certes not! Morgana. Arthur's sister."

Andy looked puzzled. "But Morgan le Fey was Arthur's half-sister."

She sputtered. How could anyone have gotten *that* piece of information wrong? She straightened in her chair. "Morgan le Fey is queen of Faerie. Her consort is Cernunnos—"

"The devil-god? With horns?"

It was Cernunnos' turn to look outraged and Morgan knew that if he'd had his powers, Andy would probably be reduced to a smoldering pile of ash. She laid her hand over Cernunnos' and was surprised that he didn't pull away. It actually seemed to calm him. Another strange behavior from him. She would have to ponder later.

"Cernunnos is the lord of the Wild Hunt," she said. "A very powerful demi-god, who looks very much like my Ken here." She didn't dare look at him for fear she would be the one laughing as he swelled his chest. "And he wears antlers, not horns." She just hoped he wouldn't feel the need to show them at the moment.

Andy frowned slightly as he digested that. Then he nodded. "You were saying about Gwenhwyfar?"

"Things seemed to happen to her. She was nearly poisoned, then there was a near-rape and another time an abduction. Each time, it was Lancelot who came to her rescue, not Arthur." She slanted a look in Cern's direction. Had he ever—would he—rescue *her* if it came to that? As immortals, they had never had that challenge. "Arthur actually appointed Lancelot to watch over her."

Andy grimaced. "How convenient that a cuckolded husband doesn't know who his wife's protector really is. Even more ground for Lancelot to be guilt-ridden, don't you think? And penitent, in the end?"

"But Arthur gave her to Lancelot. After Cam's Landing. When he thought he was dying."

"He *thought* he was dying? That he really waits in Avalon still?" Andy bit his lip. "I know what I named the play, but do you believe that 'once and future' king stuff?"

Morgan worried her lip. She couldn't very well tell him that is was *she* who took Arthur to Avalon to be healed and that he had returned to Briton and assumed life as Armel, a counselor to young King Judwel of Armorica. Nor could she tell this young mortal that Cernunnos had also abducted Gwenhwyfar and held her captive in Faerie.

She shrugged. "He went to Avalon. Lancelot and Gwenhwyfar raised Galahad."

"Gwenhwyfar went to a convent. Lancelot took her there."

Beside her, Cernunnos made a strangled sound. She didn't dare look at him. "The only time Gwenhwyfar spent in a convent was after her son died."

Andy's eyebrow lifted. "She had a son? Your story grows more interesting by the moment. Either you have quite an imagination or you've gotten your hands on research that isn't readily available."

What would he say if she told him that son was Lancelot's?

"Wait," Andy said suddenly. "I do seem to remember something about Arthur having a legitimate son that he took to battle with him, only the child was killed. Is that what you're talking about?"

She decided not to correct him. "Gwenhwyfar didn't want to see Arthur after the boy died. It was Lancelot who convinced her eventually to return to the world. Then, when Cam's Landing happened..."

"You're saying Lancelot and Gwenhwyfar survived and raised Galahad?" Andy tapped his fingers on the table. "Interesting." He got up and walked over to a bookshelf, running his hand over bindings until he finally pulled one down. Flipping it open, he returned to the table. "Does this look like Galahad?"

Morgan looked down. A picture of a young man astride a destrier stared back at her. He was lightly armored and held a white shield with a square red cross. The look on his face was a mixture of rapture and contentment. The man had brown hair, where Galahad's had been dark, but strangely enough, it did look somewhat like him.

"Yes," she said as Cernunnos peered over her shoulder.

"Ah." Andy flipped several pages over. "How about this?"

This time there were a number of knights in the picture riding charging horses. Instead of the shield though, these men wore white gambesons with square red crosses on their chests. She looked up.

"That's Galahad's cross they wear, but I don't recognize them."

"They're Templars." Andy gave her another quizzical look. "The warrior-monks who protected Christians on the First Crusade?"

"Ah." Morgan tried to look as though she knew all about them. There had been that one at Roslyn... In truth, it didn't surprise her that some of the Christos-followers turned out to be soldiers. The new religion lacked the gentleness of Avalon.

"Anyway, there's an interesting story behind the shield," Andy said, "although almost as strange as your theories about Arthur."

Morgan brightened. "Tell us."

"The shield belonged to King Evelake of Jerusalem who was a friend of Joseph of Arimathea. When Joseph left for Briton, he took the shield as a gift to Evelake's brother, an abbot named Nascien. It was a holy relic, much like the Grail. Many warriors tried to take it, but were struck down because they weren't pure of heart." Andy paused. "The legend says the shield rested at White Abbey until Galahad appeared, centuries later."

Morgan was fascinated. She hadn't paid much attention to Galahad. He had been a quiet child, more wont to play his harp than use a sword. She remembered Lancelot's frustration with him. And, if she remembered correctly, the child had wanted to be a priest of all things. "Are the Templars descendants of Galahad's?" She didn't know how that could be. Eventually, Galahad had fallen in love with the sister of his friend, Peredur, but the girl had been killed.

"In a manner of speaking." Andy flipped some more pages, scanning a paragraph here and there. "The Templars weren't founded until nearly six hundred years later, but the Holy Grail legend was strong at the time and the story of Galahad's having found it was still barded in the courts. Galahad, it was said, refused to acknowledge his father's name or wealth, traveling incognito and alone on his quest. Pleasures of the flesh—from liquor to women—didn't interest him. The Templars' original vows were of poverty, chastity and obedience. Who better to model themselves after than a hero so pure of heart that he was nearly a saint at that time?"

Lancelot would either laugh or curse to think of his son as a Christian saint. Even Cernunnos, who usually ignored any talk about the new religion, was looking at Andy incredulously.

Andy noted the expression and shrugged. "Naturally, their order managed to become incredibly wealthy somehow. They built round churches throughout Europe."

"Round?" Morgan asked.

"As a reminder of the round dome built over the Church of the Holy Sepulchre in Jeresalem. There's even one here in London." He thumbed through the book again and then turned it so she could see the page. "Some of the Templars have effigies there." He flipped a page. "See? They lie with their swords ready and their eyes open, as if ready to obey a summons and spring once again to war. Kind of,"—he closed the book—"like the myth about Arthur and his knights waiting to be awakened."

Morgan felt a chill. Could there be some magical connection between these Templars and Avalon? Did she dare hope for a portal to pass through? She glanced at Cernunnos and saw, from his faint nod, he was thinking along the same lines. It was strange how much more in tune with each other's thoughts they were in this century. She turned back to Andy. "How do we get to this round church?"

* * * *

Cernunnos looked around in disgust as they climbed up the stairs at the Temple station and into the light of day. Trains were bad enough when they were on top of the ground where a person could at least look around and spot an enemy advancing. This train went into a tunnel and moved so fast in dim light that a mortal could nigh well be killed before he had a chance to defend himself. They wouldn't be returning by that method. At the moment, Cernunnos wasn't sure just how much of a demi-god he still was.

Beside him, Morgan was fairly bouncing with impatience. They hadn't been able to get to the Temple Church yesterday for Andy had immediately scheduled a meeting of cast members and by the time that finished and they'd found something to eat, the building was closed to tourists.

Tourists. Cernunnos nearly growled. They were everywhere, swarming like flies on horse dung. And buzzing louder than flies.

"I know." Morgan took his hand. "I miss our quiet world, too."

He looked at her in surprise. "Did I speak?"

She blushed a little, something he had never seen her do. "No. We just seem to be...closer, mayhap? I can feel your emotions."

He squeezed her hand. "Mayhap because this world is mad and we are the only two sane ones in it?"

Morgan slanted a mischievous look at him. "Well, you do understand me better than anyone." She suddenly sobered. "Oh, Cern. I hope there is a portal here. I want to go home."

He put his arm around her. "I do too."

The crowd around them started shuffling forward as the doors opened and they moved forward past the tall pillar in the courtyard that held aloft a horse with two mounted riders.

It truly was a remarkable building. Just past the Norman door were free-standing columns, somewhat like the ones they'd seen at Roslyn. Above them, two Gothic arches rose to the drum ceiling. To the east was the long, retangular chancel, but it was the Round that truly captured Cernunnos' attention. The ten stone effigies lay in pairs on the floor. Fully armored, holding swords, they did indeed look as though they merely waited to be called to service again. The hair on Cernunnos' nape bristled. Though he hadn't entered the tomb on Avalon, he could imagine much the same picture. Mayhap there was a portal here.

He looked up and noticed a face protruding out of a wall. A 'grotesque' he heard someone call it. It wasn't unlike the green men's faces found at Roslyn, although somewhat more fierce-looking. Then he saw another and still another. It seemed they were all watching over the knights that lay on the floor. Protectors?

Cernunnos saw Morgan staring at the rose window that was situated beneath a gothic arch and over the doorway. He moved closer. "Have you found something?"

For a moment she didn't answer him, tilting her head slightly. "Passing strange," she finally said.

"What?"

She tilted her head the other way. "Nimue told me about a window such as this once--well, she told Gwenhywfar, but I just happened to be listening—it is a symbol for the goddess, yet this one has a picture of the Christos in the center."

Cernunnos followed her gaze. "I do not see a goddess, unless all those faces in the other pieces are goddesses looking toward the god."

Morgan laughed and again Cernunnos was surprised. Normally, she would have argued that no goddess worships a god. What was this world doing to her? He rather liked some of it. "So tell me what Nimue said."

She pointed. "It's called a rose window. The eight petals track Venus as she moves each year from morning to night star. The stages of a woman's life, Nimue said, from birth through maidenhood, motherhood, and death."

Cernunnos nodded. "Life cycles. Not unlike the Oak and Holly Kings."

"Yes." Morgan smiled mischievously. "And if the 'e' from r-o-s-e is moved to the front, it spells e-r-o-s."

"Eros." Cernunnos ran a finger along Morgan's cheek. "So we have the god and goddess of lust and love here, eh?"

Her face became seductive. "Nimue didn't exactly say that, knowing how sensitive Gwenhwyfar was about the old religion, but I knew."

"You would."

She caught his hand as he was about move it lower. "Who better to guard a portal to Faerie than Venus and Eros?"

"Can you feel anything?"

"Besides what's lurking in your mind?" Morgan sobered. "There are too many people about. If there is power here, I cannot concentrate it, especially with my own powers nearly gone. We must come back tonight."

"We won't be able to get in."

"We have to try. We can slip in just before closing and hide like we did at Roslyn."

"I'm sure someone checks to make sure everyone is gone," Cernunnos said.

Morgan frowned, her lower lip sticking out.

Here was another new endeavor on Morgan's part. Instead of being argumentive, she was quiet. He found the pout quite beguiling. "All right." He put his arm around her. "We'll try tonight."

Instantly, she was all smiles and stood on tiptoe to brush her lips against his cheek. "Thank you, Cern."

It was such a little kiss, hardly a touch at all. Yet, she had *thanked* him. He didn't think she had ever done that before.

He wondered why he felt like he should be thanking her instead.

* * * *

Cernunnos glanced over at Morgan as they walked along the bank of the Thames. She had grown more quiet ever since their return visit to the Round hadn't revealed any portals a fortnight ago. There was an energy there that even Cernunnos could vaguely feel, but Morgan hadn't been able to harness it.

He sighed. It had been the same with him. They had sought out parks—Regent's, St. James, the huge expanse of Hyde—and even gardens like Kensington where he had hoped to be able to communicate with the beasts and establish a link of his own.

But the rabbits, squirrels and such had merely scampered off, refusing his command.

They stopped near the church of St. Magnus and looked up at London Bridge. "It looks a little different than it did in our time," he said in jest.

A suspicious brightness welled-up in Morgan's eyes. "Nothing in Londinium is the same. There were only a few hundred people here then. The Romans had a piked bridge crossing this river and there was open ground between here and the Saxon settlement of Lundenwic." She looked at the churning brackish water as the tide swelled against the natural flow. "Do you remember when this water was clear and longboats tied up alongside coracles?"

Cernunnos took her hand and tucked it inside his arm. "I don't think we'll ever fit into this century."

"I don't want to. Did you hear what was said on that thing that Andy calls a telly this morning? About the group of eight countries coming here to talk about what is going on with the Saracens in Byzantium?"

Cernunnos hid his pleasure. "I think the term now is 'Middle East'"

"I don't care what they call it. Arthur didn't have any problem with Palomides or any of his people."

"True, but Arthur would have been the first person to agree that bringing countries together to talk can only help. Even at that, he was still fighting rebel Saxons when we brought Gwenhwyfar and Lancelot back."

"The Saxons were fighting for land," Morgan said mulishly.

Cernunnos lifted an eyebrow. "I didn't realize you paid any attention to warfare."

"What choice did I have? If I wanted to exist in the mortal world, I had to stay attached to Myrddin. And *he* was attached to Arthur who was attached to *war*."

"Well, look on the bright side,"—they turned and started to walk toward the bus stop—"that man on the telly also said the whole world was going to be playing games here in 2012. Just like one of Arthur's tournaments."

"I hope we're not still here." Morgan shuddered as a motorscooter whined past, spraying up tiny pebbles from the street. "You did promise to take me to the British Museum tomorrow. Andy said we could research past—culture?—I think he called it. Mayhap, we can find some other kind of clue to know where else to search for a portal."

Cernunnos didn't think they'd find anything in a building since they were both creatures of the elements, but he put his arm around her shoulders and gave her a hug. "We'll try," he said.

* * * *

"Did we have to take the underground?" Cernunnos said the next morning when they descended to the train at King's Cross. "Especially the Picidilly? It's even farther underground than the others and you know how I feel about these things anyway."

"Don't worry." They found seats in the second car. "It's not that far to Russell Square. Just close your eyes and I'll nudge you when we're there."

Close his eyes. That's about all he could do. A demi-god meant to ride the open skies should never have to put up with being enclosed like this. He cursed silently as the train lurched forward. The damn tunnel was even tighter than the Circle line. Walls flashed by so close that he could have touched them. Close his eyes. Why not?

Suddenly there was a loud blast, followed by the train jerking to a stop, billows of smoke filling the car. People were ejected from their seats. One man crashed his head against the roof of the train, smashing his skull. Others flew across open space to land with heavy thuds on other passengers. A woman and child careened down the aisle, their mad slide stopping when her shoulder collided with the bent steel of a torn off seat. Cernunnos heard screams, groans, and muffled moans as he choked on the dust and ash-filled air.

With a start, he realized Morgan was no longer beside him. Staggering into the human-littered aisle, he saw her legs and feet sticking out from beneath a mass of twisted metal. He sank down beside her, lifting and tossing aside what had once been a side panel of the train. The metal was still hot, but he didn't feel it as he lifted Morgan in his arms.

Her face was deathly white and she was bleeding from several wounds. He bent down and could detect no breath. He put his fingers to her throat and felt no pulse. She lay limp and lifeless in his arms.

His antlers grew as he lifted his head and bellowed in helpless rage.

Morgan—his beloved Morgan—couldn't be dead!

Chapter Twelve

Sweet Mary! Why hadn't she trusted her instincts? Gwenhwyfar tugged at the ropes that bound her hands behind her even as she scrambled to a sitting position on the makeshift pallet on the ground and then scooted back until she bumped against the wall of the cave. She brought her knees up to her chin and glared at Melehan.

He seemed not to notice as he sat in a large, over-stuffed chair across from her and poured himself some wine from a decanter on the flat rock that served as a table.

"Are you thirsty?" he asked.

He knew she was. Once she'dawakened from the blow he'd struck, he forced dried, salted fish down her throat until she had started to retch. That had been several hours ago and she'd had no water since.

"No," she said.

His eyebrows rose. "Are you hungry then?" His gaze went to the platter of fish that hadn't been finished.

Gwenhwyfar refused to look at it. "I'm quite full, thank you." It galled her to be so polite, but given her trussed-up situation, it was the best course. She'd been abducted before. Keeping a civil tongue was better than suffering unneeded bruises. Or worse. She just didn't know how long she could keep him talking.

"Why are you here?" she asked.

"Why am *I* here?" He looked amused. "Shouldn't the question be, why are *you* here?"

"At the moment, I'm more interested in you."

"Are you? Perhaps you'd like to join me then? The chair is big enough for two." He let his gaze roam to her breasts and linger there.

Gwenhwyfar gritted her teeth. "What I'm interested in is a straight answer from you."

He gave her a charmingly boyish smile. "What is the question?"

She wasn't about to be charmed by his apparent innocence. "Why are you here in Faerie? And where did you send Morgan and Cernunnos?"

"I didn't send them anywhere. That was Mother's doing. I told you she liked to get into mischief."

Gwenhwyfar nearly rolled her eyes in frustration. "Then *where* did your mother send them? And why?"

"That's two questions," he said mildly as if they were having just a normal conversation. He poured some more wine. "Given your present condition and the fact that this cave is shrouded by magic, I suppose I can be honest."

Gwenhwyfar doubted that he knew the meaning of the word. That he wasn't concerned, though, about telling her, didn't bode well for her future. Especially not if the place was be-spelled. Lancelot would never be able to find her.

"Please do be honest," she managed to say.

"They are in the twenty-first century, I believe."

Gwenhwyfar gasped. "Fifteen hundred years in the future? Why?"

"It was as far as she could send them." He shrugged. "I guess that's as far as the future goes right now."

"But why?" Gwenhwyfar asked again. "Aoibhill is a queen— or so she says—of her own land—"

"She is a queen. I can assure you of that."

"Then why is she so desperate for Faerie that she would banish Morgan and Cernunnos?"

"It was only Morgan she wished to banish," Melehan said as he poured another glass of wine.

Gwenhwyfar glanced sideways at the decanter. It was half-gone. Should she encourage Melehan to get drunk? If he passed out, she'd have a chance to find something to loosen her bonds with and escape. If he *didn't* pass out, though, would he become amorous? He already had eyed her. There was little way to reason with a drunken man, hard with lust.

"Why just Morgan?"

He stopped with his cup half-way to his lips. "That should be obvious."

159

Gwenhwyfar furrowed her brows. "I don't think I understand."

Melehan smirked. "She wants the horned god."

"Cernunnos? But she never met him."

"Yes, she did."

Gwenhywfar was stunned. "When?"

He laughed a bit drunkenly. "They go back a long way. It seems my mother was Cernunnos' consort until Morgan came along. Aoibhill wants him back."

Sweet Mary. Two faerie queens fighting over a demi-god. Would such a battle be contained in Faerie or would it spill into the real world? The world where Morgan and Cernunnos were now? "What's your mother going to do? Follow them?" Gwenhwyfar could just imagine the havoc—if not total destruction—that two jealous and powerful immortals could cause, hurling lightening bolts, having forests catch on fire. Summoning the wind that would destroy anything in its way. Causing waves to rise and seas to roil in fury. To say nothing of Cernunnos splitting the earth open with his rage.

"She prefers to fight on familiar ground. The mortal world has such limits."

Gwenhwyfar felt a hysterical bubble of laughter rise in her throat. Thank the heavens for small miracles.

"She's been working on spells to contact Cernunnos," Melehan continued, "but without her horn to call him back, it's been difficult. She's been difficult." He reached for the decanter once more. "In truth, I am trying to avoid her." He winked at Gwenhwyfar. "You're much better company."

"I don't seem to have much choice, do I?"

He straightened and something in his eyes changed as he set the wine back down. Gwenhwyfar thought she saw a red glow and then realized she was mistaken as the flames in the small hearth snapped and crackled. The light had played a trick...

"No, you don't have a choice." He stood and moved toward her.

Keeping an eye on him, Gwenhwyfar tried to scuttle farther backward, but had reached the wall. She yanked at the bindings on her hands, but they held fast. Slowly, she brought her knees closer, ready to kick.

Melehan crouched down on the pallet next to her and reached to touch her face. She kicked out with both feet, but he moved with preternatural swiftness and she found herself on her back with Melehan's body draped over hers, pinning her legs. He traced her cheek with his hand. She turned her face away which only caused him to grip her jaw and jerk her head back.

"What was it you did to my father to make him so besotted?" he asked, his face inches from hers.

"Nothing," she managed to say between clenched teeth. "When Medraut came to court, he was two-and-ten. I did nothing but treat him kindly as a sister would."

Melehan gave amirthless laugh. "A sister? I think not. I heard Medraut tell tales of how you encouraged him to come to you."

"Lies! Your father was mad."

"Mad? Madly in love with you, Gwenhwyfar. He died for you."

She tried to move her head from his tight grasp. "He died because he tried to rape me!"

"Rape you?" Melehan released her chin and ran his hand down her shoulder to her breast. He pinched a nipple and it hardened. He laughed. "Rape you when you respond like this?"

She tried not to squirm under his weight. "I'm not responding to you. It hurts."

He looked mildly surprised and eased the pressure. "Forgive me then."

"I'll forgive you if you let me go,"

"Not just yet." He tilted his head and stared into her eyes. "Why didn't you let me into your dreams?"

"My dreams?" *Sweet Mary.* Had Medraut's lunacy been inherited by Melehan?

"Yes." His hand stroked downward. "I came to you that one time. You woke too soon. I'm sure you remember?"

Ice flooded her veins. Gwenhwyfar closed her eyes, not wanting to let the fear show. That horrible night when that...half-human monster...it couldn't have been! It had been a dream. Melehan was simply trying to... Cautiously, she opened her eyes and stifled a gasp. A tiny red spark had ignited in his eyes.

"So you do remember." He gave a bone-chilling laugh. "I am curious though. How did you block me after that? I hovered above your bed nights in a row."

"Lancelot protected me," she hissed.

Melehan raised an eyebrow. "Interesting. A mere mortal kept me from you?"

Gwenhwyfar suspected Lancelot's fey powers from his mother might have emerged in Faerie, but there was no sense in letting Melehan know that. "He loves me. He kept watch."

Melehan snorted. "This love thing is stupid. Morgan prattled on about it too." He lifted the hem of Gwenhwyfar's gown and put his hand on her bare leg. "There's only one thing between a man and a woman that's important."

"You're going to be a dead man if you go any further," Gwenhwyfar spit out.

"Really? Who's going to stop me? Lancelot's not here."

"It won't matter. Remember how he hunted Medraut down? He'll do the same with you."

"I don't think he'll be able to. My mother has him safely woven into a binding spell that he can't break."

Although she tried to keep her face impassive, Gwenhwyfar felt as though a sword had been run through her. Lancelot couldn't be taken from her. Not now. Even so, a tear managed to leak from one eye.

"Don't cry, my lady." Melehan ripped the silk gown from her. He curled his lips back, extending his fangs. "Once you've been bedded by an incubus, a mortal will never matter again." His eyes glowed red as he bent to take her neck.

The last thing she remembered was letting loose a blood-curdling scream.

And then there was dark silence.

* * * *

Aoibhill hissed a curse as flames from her fingertips did nothing to penetrate the wall of mist that surrounded her. It was *her* mist! A binding-spell of her own making that now held her captive. She had seriously underestimated the mortal, Lancelot.

She sank down and then muttered another curse as her sore backside made contact with the earth. She hadn't even felt him toss her down. Hadn't felt herself be lifted either. Just hard, fast contact with solid ground. She narrowed her eyes. *No one* walked away from one of her spells.

How had Lancelot gotten the power?

Taking a deep breath, she forced herself to recall what she knew about the man. His father had been king of Benoic and his mother, Niniane, was the Lady of the Black Lake of Brocéliande. She, along with her sister, Vivian, the Lady of the Lake at Avallach, had practiced much white magic. How much had Lancelot been taught?

Medraut had always seen him as the enemy, the obstacle that stood between Gwenhwyfar and himself. Not that Aoibhill had cared, but Medraut must have been a complete fool not to see that Lancelot was bound to Gwenhwyfar by far stronger ties than mere lust. Aoebhill had always scoffed at the mortal emotion of *love*. Aphrodite had once tried to convince her that love had power. Had that been the force that allowed Lancelot to break through the mist barrier?

If it was, then she must think of a way to use that against him.

But first, she must escape her own binding. She hurled more fire at the mist, but it just sizzled. Strangely, she could vaguely hear the activity that continued beyond her invisible barrier. Sounds of laughter as the faeries made their way across the yard and disappeared into the forest. The rustle of small creatures burrowing through the brush. Behind her, horses stomped in their stalls, while grooms that were low-born fey moved about the barn. Perhaps there was one that was weak enough to be enchanted by a siren's song? All she needed was for someone to walk through the barrier from the other side and she could slip through the opening that would be created. She closed her eyes and concentrated on bringing the siren spirit close to her. She heard nefarious laughter so subtle she wasn't sure it was real until something landed on her shoulder. Something unseen, but there. The laughter came again, close to her ear.

"Sing," the spirit said.

Aoibhill began to hum and then realized the siren had melded with her for she no longer felt it perched on her shoulder, but heard the nymph in her head. The music was beautiful. Haunting, it rose and fell as soft wails upon the wind.

She was nearly swept away with the sound herself when she sensed that a being had approached. She peered through the mist barely able to make out a form.

It was a gnome. Black as night, thin, lanky, and cadaverous-looking, it swung its huge head from side-to-side as if to locate the source of the mesmerizing sound. The creatures were usually not seen, since most of faerie shunned them due to their appearance, and they preferred to live in shadows. Perhaps this one was lonely.

Perfect. Aoibhill increased the dulcet melody, letting it waft gently as faerie dust toward him. The siren sniggered.

"Come to me," Aoibhill purred.

A perplexed expression crossed the slack-jawed face. The gnome looked around.

"This way," she said softly. "Step through that which you do not see."

Puzzled, the creature took a step forward.

"Ah, that's it," she breathed. "Come to me." Then she gasped as she felt the siren's strength course through her and invisible tendrils snaked out to wind themselves about the gnome's neck.

"He's ours," the spirit whispered.

The mist separated as the black creature was jerked through. Aoibhill barely took note of him although she felt the siren leaving her head to devour the fresh morsel.

She was through! Aoibhill inhaled the freshness around her. The muted sounds from inside the mist were now all clear. She glanced once at what looked like a bit of fog lingering on the ground and laughed.

The thought of Lancelot mocking her brought a quick stop to her laugh. The half-fey prince had actually over-powered her. Aoibhill, Queen of Eire Faerie!!! She narrowed her eyes. For that, he would pay.

The best revenge would be to hurt him, not kill him. The best way to hurt him was to take away the one thing he loved most.

Gwenhwyfar.

Perhaps it would also be ironic justice for Medraut as well, Aoibhill rapidly moved toward the magicked cave. After all, he *had* sired Melehan for her to use. She never had thanked Medraut for that. Now she would.

Gwenhwyfar was about to die.

* * * *

Lancelot had lost the trail. Any traces of broken branches or bent grasses had stopped as the path ended abruptly at craggy boulders. He circled the rocks, looking for any sign of a footprint on the other side, but all he found was shale.

Gwenhwyfar was somewhere in Faerie. With Melehan. All of Lancelot's warrior senses went on alert. Danger lurked. He could feel it. Smell it. Almost taste it. But where was the source?

He made his way across a small glen and entered another grove of trees, not stopping until he reached the small outcropping of granite that was the unicorn's home.

To his relief, Prince nickered his welcome.

"Gwenhwyfar's been taken," he told the unicorn, hoping the animal would understand him. "You've got to try to get to Avalon and bring help." Bel's Fires! Why hadn't he brought pen and vellum to send a message? There wasn't time to go back to the cottage. He had to keep searching. "Make Nimue—or someone—understand. Can you do it?"

Prince's silvery-blue eyes stared at him solemnly. Then the unicorn bowed his head once and trotted out the entrance. Lancelot watched him disappear through the trees. It was a desperate measure. Even if the unicorn managed to break through the roiling, thick vapors, would anyone in Avalon understand the danger?

Lancelot strode rapidly into the heart of the forest to where a massive, partially-hollowed oak tree stood. As impressive as the towering tree was, he knew it was merely a portal to Cernunnos' secret chambers.

Ganus stepped out from the hollow, assumed a warrior's stance and crossed his arms across his bare chest. Lancelot halted.

"The lord is not here," Ganus said.

"I know. I need his sword," Lancelot replied.

Ganus' blue eyes turned metallic. "Not likely, mortal."

"I don't have time to argue with you! Gwenhwyfar has been taken by Melehan."

The faerie's mouth quirked up. "A bit of bed-sport hardly requires a sword threat. You mortals are much too jealous. You should be more like—"

"I don't have time for this!" Lancelot thundered, feeling the battle frenzy rising. "She's in danger!"

Ganus took an involuntary step back. "There is no danger in Faerie, my lord. Not unless Lord Cernunnos or Queen Morgan wills it so."

"Neither one of them is here, you fool!"

A muscle twitched in Ganus' jaw. "I don't think I like being called a—"

"Then stop acting like one." Lancelot took a deep breath and refrained from placing his clenched fist squarely in the faerie's face. "Why do you suppose neither Cernunnos or Morgan have returned?"

"I don't question my lord or my queen. 'Tis not wise."

"By Mithras! *Think*. You've got a faerie queen from Eire and her son here. Do you think Morgan would just let Aoibhill freely roam?"

A look of confusion crossed the other's face. "Queen Aoibhill said she and Morgan were friends."

Lancelot snorted. "They're friends about as much as Medraut and I were—" He stopped when Ganus looked even more perplexed. "Never mind that. Do you think Cernunnos would let Melehan walk his forests and command his creatures?"

Ganus considered. "No, I don't suppose so."

Lancelot began to wonder if this handsome lad that all the faerie maidens swooned over had any wits in the head above his shoulders. "I can tell you that Cernunnos would not tolerate it if he were here. And the reason he is *not* here is because he *cannot* return. Aoibhill has closed the portals. She and Melehan intend to rule here."

Ganus' brows furrowed. "I do not think I would like that. The maidens already plot and lie-in-wait for Melehan."

"Jealous, are you?"

The furrow deepened. "No. Melehan can't compete with me. I'm a—"

"I know what you are," Lancelot said. "But what we don't know, is what Melehan is."

"Certes we do. He's only *half*-faerie," Ganus said smugly.

Lancelot prayed to the goddess that she would grant him patience. "True. But his sire was pure evil. I knew him. I see that evil in Melehan as well. I need the sword. Gwenhwyfar is in danger."

Ganus hesitated. "I've always liked Gwenhwyfar, even though she never—"

"The sword, man!"

"My lord would be most angry with me—"

Lancelot grabbed the faery's tunic and lifted him until his toes were scraping the ground. "It won't matter if Cernunnos is angry with you if something happens to Gwenhwyfar while we stand here talking. You'll be dead."

White rimmed the faery's eyes as comprehension finally penetrated. "I'll get it for you."

Lancelot dropped him. "I'll get it myself." He stepped through the trunk's opening. He emerged a short time later, sword in hand and a dagger in his belt. "I'll return these some day." He left Ganus on the ground, still rubbing his throat.

As he was returning to the deer trail that led through the trees, a black shadow confronted him. Lancelot whirled, sword in one hand, dagger in the other. Then he lowered his weapons. It was only a gnome. Strange, though, since they were rarely seen and never had one approached him.

"What do you want?" he asked.

"The woman is loose," the creature said in a gravelly voice.

"Gwenhwyfar? Where is she?"

The gnome shook its large head. "Not your woman. The other. The one you locked in the fog."

Aoibhill. So now he had two enemies to watch for. Lancelot looked at the gnome's homely face and then blinked. Was that a tear that trickled down its wrinkled face? Lancelot realized he must be looking at the female of the species. "Do you know where Aoibhill is?"

Its lank, gawky frame quivered, as more tears spilled. "No."

"Did she hurt you?" Lancelot asked, even though he was impatient to move on. "Why are you crying?"

The creature looked at him with large eyes so black they were almost invisible in her face except for the sparks that flew from them. "I am Kalere. The woman stole my mate." The gnome's body shook again. "There was this awful music that sounded like a banshee screeching and Malach—that is... *was*...my mate—walked right into that black cloud." Kalere began to sob and then stopped herself. "The woman stepped out and the mist disappeared. Only this—" she held up a bit of dirty cloth—"was left."

Lancelot cursed. Aoibhill had obviously used the gnome as a sacrifice to the dark god she trafficked with. "I'm sorry," he said gently. "I don't know what I can do."

Kalere pointed to the sword he held. "You can kill her."

He doubted that he could, even if Cernunnos' sword was magicked. A centuries-old fey—and who knew who her god was?—would be hard to kill even by another immortal. "I must find Gwenhwyfar first or she might die, too."

Kalere stopped sniffling. "I can take you to her."

He nearly dropped the sword in surprise. "You know where Gwenhwyfar is?"

"I think so," she said. "Come."

They ended up at the set of boulders where Lancelot had lost the trail. "There's nothing here," he said.

"There's a cave," Kalere replied. "I watched the witch make it invisible."

Faerie glamour. Only an illusion. He should have known. How many times had his mother told him that the eye sees what it wants to see and that one must look with the inner eye to see past the illusion? Lancelot walked around the boulders again, looking for any kind of crack. A seam of light mayhap. He thought he detected a small dark line vein in the gray rock. As he stepped closer, he heard a blood-curdling scream from inside the rock. Without hesitation, he charged into it.

The sight that greeted him stunned him momentarily. Gwenhwyfar lay on the floor, her gown ripped open. Part of her face was already a mottle of bruises and a red gash of blood trickled from her throat. Looming above her was a naked creature only half-man. It snapped its head around, snarling at Lancelot's intrusion. Sharp fangs protruded from its elongated wolf-like head and its eyes glowed as red as the gates of the Christians' hell.

With a howl of rage, Lancelot threw the dagger at the beast's head, but it sprang up with lightening speed and the blade struck its shoulder. Lancelot positioned his sword and advanced, only to find his quarry wasn't there.

"Looking for me?" a voice said.

Lancelot whirled. Melehan was standing across the room, smiling angelically. Only there was blood on his teeth.

"Fight me like a man, you bastard," Lancelot said.

Melehan shook his blond curls. "You can't kill an incubus."

"I can try." He lunged, only to find empty space and the hollow sound of fading laughter. He looked around. The cave was empty.

"Come on," he said to Gwenhwyfar as she rose shakily. He stooped to pick up a blanket and wrapped it around her. "We're getting out of here."

As they moved cautiously outside, she said, "I was afraid you wouldn't get here in time." Tears filled her eyes. "How many times have you rescued me, Lance? I was afraid I'd run out of"

"Nice of you to bring her to me, Lancelot," Aoibhill said from the shadow of the trees. "Now I don't have to unwork the spell for the cave."

Gwenhwyfar gasped as Lancelot pushed her behind him and readied his sword. "We're leaving."

Aoibhill looked amused. "I don't think so. At least, not alive." Her eyes narrowed. "You killed Medraut. Such a waste. He could have sired many more like Melehan." She shrugged. "I could forgive that, but you mocked me, Lancelot. For that you will have to pay. The fee that I extract is Gwenhwyfar's life."

"Never."

Aoibhill arched an eyebrow and looked at the sword. "Do you intend to run a lady through with that?"

"You are not a lady," Lancelot answered.

She gave a chilling laugh. "That hardly matters. You wouldn't be able to do it, *Sir* Lancelot. You're far too honorable when it comes to women." She moved slowly toward him. "Shall I show mercy and make her death quick or shall I bring Melehan back to finish what he had started?"

"Give me the sword, Lance." Gwenhwyfar stepped out beside him. "I have no scruples about fighting her."

Aoibhill laughed again. "I've heard about your skills with a sword, Gwenhwyfar. But you are not a match for this." She lifted her hand and fire shot from it, singing Lancelot's tunic. "Mayhap you'd like to watch your lover burn first?"

"No! Leave him alone. If it's me you want—"

"Hush, Gwen." Lancelot pushed her behind him again and turned to Aoibhill. "I'm prepared to die before I let you hurt Gwenhwyfar."

"Isn't that nice?" Aoibhill raised her arm again, ready to hurl more flames. It froze in mid-air. "What—"

A blinding white light descended from the sky, surrounding Lancelot and Gwenhwyfar. Soft music swirled like the gentle chime of tiny bells as the scent of apple blossoms filled the air. An object hovered in the air above their heads. Lancelot squinted and Gwenhwyfar gasped.

"By the Lady," Lancelot whispered and reached out his hand for the Holy Grail.

Chapter Thirteen

Dust swirling around him, Cernunnos coughed as he carried Morgan up the stairs from the Underground into the street. By all the gods! He would never descend into one of those holes again.

Chaos ruled above ground as well. People shoved each other to get clear of the tunnel. Some fell, blood streaming from wounds, while others leaned heavily on each other. Debris was everywhere and men in uniforms were obviously trying to establish order. Sirens blared and big square trucks came to screeching halts as more men, dressed in white, moved into the crowds.

Cernunnos looked down at Morgan, so completely still in his arms. He had detected the faintest of heartbeats just minutes earlier, but she lay limp and pale, barely breathing.

"Here," one of the men in white said as he rolled over what looked like a narrow bed. "Lay her on this."

Cernunnos eyed it suspiciously. "Is that a covered pyre?"

"It's a gurney. Put the lady on it."

Cernunnos held her closer. "No."

"Mister. I can't help her if you won't let me tend to her."

"Where is your healing woman?"

"Our...you want a woman doctor? You'll have to wait until we get back to the hospital."

"What's a ..." Cernunnos paused as a female dressed in white came over. "What's the problem, John?" she asked the other man. "We've got to move along here."

"He won't put the woman on the gurney," the man replied.

The female turned to him, her brown eyes soft and warm. "Your wife's wounds need tending to," she said gently.

"You're the healer?"

A slight crease appeared between her brows. "Yes, but I can only do so much here in the field."

Cernunnos laid Morgan carefully on the narrow bed. "I go with her."

"Civilians aren't allowed—" the man began but the woman cut him off.

"Let him come. Bloody protocol be hanged. We've lives to save, John."

Cernunnos gave him a triumphant look as he climbed into the back of the big beast and held onto Morgan's hand. He watched as the woman hung a bag on a steel hanger and inserted a tube in it. The tube had a sharp needle at the other end. "Wait!" he said when she brought it near Morgan's other hand.

The woman looked up. "Yes?"

"Are you going to shoot her with that?"

Again, the small crease appeared on her forehead. "It's fluids. To replace what she lost." She inserted the needle and Cernunnos felt his stomach churn. It was a good thing his Morgan wasn't feeling any of this or that foolish woman would pay.

The beast lurched, making that awful screeching sound. He held onto a rail with one hand, the other clutching Morgan's. "You will heal her?"

"I'll do what I can. The ER will do more," the woman said.

He was about to ask what the ER was and then closed his mouth. He didn't want to appear daft. He and Morgan had already had too many curious looks when they asked questions. Right now, all that mattered was that Morgan survived. After all these centuries together, what would he do if she weren't with him?

The silent question hit him like an elf-arrow. Now he knew what Lancelot had been talking about. Gwenhwyfar, too. This was *love*. He, Cernunnos, loved Morgan.

That realization kept him mute until the ambulance pulled up to the admitting door. He sprang into action when more people, dressed in wrinkled blue this time, started to wheel Morgan away. "I'm going with her!"

"We have to take her to triage," a man, with something stuck in his ears, said. Cernunnos noticed the man's hand inching down toward Morgan's breast. "Don't dare to touch her there!" He reached out, but the female attendant who'd followed them out put a hand on Cernunnos' arm. "Easy there. It's a stethoscope. The doctor needs to listen to her heart and lungs."

Cernunnos glared at the man. "Let the woman do it."

"Don't be a fool," the man said.

Cernunnos raised himself to his full height, feeling his antlers begin to grow. A fool? This *mortal* called him a fool? He was beginning to get strange looks and forced the tips of the antlers back. A *fool*?

"Look," the woman said, her hand still on his arm. "It's obvious you've never been in a hospital before. I don't know if it's your religion or something else, but if you want us to save your wife's life, you need to let us do what we must. Trust me."

Cernunnos looked into her eyes and for a moment, hers widened. Then he realized he was mesmerizing her. He shook his head slightly. This woman had the feel of a healer. "You will save her?"

"We will do everything we can. Why don't you wait in that room over there?" She pointed to where other people were gathered. "We'll come and get you when your wife is stabilized."

They were going to put his Morgan in a stable? He narrowed his eyes and looked around. He didn't see any horses. He lifted his head and sniffed. There was no scent of animals either. "Where is this stable?"

She gave him another quizzical look and then pointed in the other direction. "Just beyond those doors. She won't be far away."

He sniffed again. Nothing except pungent odors he didn't recognize. This was the cleanest stable he'd ever been near.

"Come." The woman tugged on his arm. He let himself be led over to a chair and then watched carefully as his Morgan was wheeled through the doors. If someone didn't come out in a little while, he would know where to charge through. He just wished he had a weapon.

He turned his attention to the telly mounted on the wall. He still thought it strange that a person could speak from that box, although he'd learned through Andy that the person was really somewhere else and only his image was being cast. Andy had laughed when Cernunnos asked if it was magic, but what else could it be?

The announcer was trying to maintain the dignified, calm tone they all seemed to use, but he was failing. Excitement pitched his voice high and he spoke fast.

"Three explosions in a matter of minutes have caused a Code Amber Alert to be called. The Underground has been shut down. Police are investigating a possible power surge..." He stopped suddenly and glanced sideways as though someone were speaking to him. Then he turned to the camera again and his eyes grew round at what he was obviously reading from something.

"This just in. At 9:47 a.m., another explosion occurred in Tavistock Square, this time aboard a double-decker bus. The bus had apparently been diverted from Marble Arch to Hackney Wick because of road closures near King's Cross..."

People began to cry, scream and shout around Cernunnos. He heard the word 'terrorists' over and over and something about America and 9/11 and it was "happening all over again."

He looked about the confusion. What or who were *terrorists*? It seemed these people were more upset about the news than they were about the injured people they were waiting for.

Mortals. Cernunnos shook his head. All he was concerned with was that Morgan live. She was all that mattered to him because now, he knew he loved her.

Love. Why had he not known that it existed before? He just hoped he'd have a chance to tell Morgan.

* * * *

They were gone. One moment, Aoibhill held fire in her hands that would destroy Lancelot's lover and the next, a damnable, blinding light had frozen her hand. She had never experienced such a power before. The strange thing was, she had felt no malevolence about it. Power that strong had to come from a strong source. How she wished she could harness it. Whatever the case, it disappeared as quickly as it arrived and when it did, Lancelot and Gwenhwyfar were gone.

"Are you sure it wasn't just glamour?" Melehan asked for the fourth or fifth time as they stood in the cottage the mortals had used.

Aoibhill glared at him. "Do you not think I would recognize glamour?"

He turned slightly red. "Certes you would, Mother. But... but Lancelot did manage to break through your barrier." He caught the way her eyebrow arched and quickly added, "The man has some fey power. Mayhap it's different from our own and we just didn't realize it which gave them time to slip away."

"I've not been able to scent either of the mortals. They are not here." She turned back to searching the room.

"What are you looking for?" Melehan asked.

"I'm not sure." She continued to sift through neatly folded clothing. "Something that they may have brought with them from the mortal world. It would still have strong ties to them and I could use that to bring them back."

"Well, if you do, I'd like to finish what I started with Gwenhwyfar before you kill her."

"Certes," Aoibhill patted his cheek. "We'll make Lancelot watch."

Melehan laughed. "Just make sure you secure him first."

She narrowed her eyes. "Would you care to experience a firebolt, son?"

He sobered. "I was jesting."

"Don't." She turned back to tossing garments from drawers in every direction. "There must be something here—" She paused, her fingers touching metal. Slowly she pulled out a silver chain with a small silver horn attached. "My horn! Lancelot had it all this time!"

"The one that will call Cernunnos to your side?" Melahan inched closer.

She didn't answer. Instead, she lifted the horn to her lips and blew.

Nothing happened.

Aoibhill frowned and tried again. And waited. Her frown deepened. "Cernunnos gave me this horn himself, centuries ago. He said the sound of it would always bring him back to me."

"Mayhap he can't hear it."

Aoibhill looked at Melehan and then she kissed him. "How could I have been so stupid? Certes, he cannot hear it. He is not in our Time." She grabbed Melehan's hand. "Come with me."

"Where are we going?" he asked as she led him outside and ran down the path toward the scrying pool.

175

"We're going to the twenty-first century where I sent him."

Melehan tried to pull back. "Are you sure that's wise?"

She didn't answer until they reached the pool. "For the horn to work, we have to be in the same Time. I can't bring him here, so I must go to him."

"But what do we know—"

"Enough. I studied the future before I decided where to send Morgan. It's quite an interesting place. Mortals mate quite easily."

"I won't object to that. I wonder if Morgan is still wearing the pendant I gave her."

"If she is, all the better," Aoibhill said. "Once I summon Cernunnos, I intend to return here with him. You can keep Morgan occupied while I do that."

She raised her hands and the water began to swirl, forming deep troughs and dark walls of high waves. A black vortex formed.

Aoibhill took Melehan's hand. "To the future," she said as they stepped through, "and to Cernunnos."

This time, my horned one, we will not part.

* * * *

"Prince!" Gwenhywfar wrapped her arms around the unicorn's neck as he nickered contentedly and accepted a slice of apple she'd brought.

"He nearly died coming through the mist," Nimue said as she sat down on a hay bale next to Lancelot in the stable. "Aoibhill has warded Faerie with very dark magic."

"She is even more evil than Morgana," Lancelot said.

"Morgana was mortal. Aoibhill is not," Nimue replied. "What surprised me is that even with the nine priestesses of Avalon combining their powers, they were not able to make the darkness surrounding Faerie disappear. It took their total effort to keep Prince alive when he burst through."

"I'm glad they thought he was worth saving," Gwenhwyfar said.

Nimue smiled. "They would not let a magical animal die. He is one of the last of the breed left in existence."

"Did Astrala send the Grail for us?" Lancelot asked as Prince settled down beside Gwenhywfar and laid his head in her lap.

"Astrala is the Grail Guardian. She does not command its power." Nimue looked at him curiously. "It helps those who are pure in heart. The first time you saw it, you had forgiven Arthur and made peace with Galahad. Was there some need you had that it appeared to you this time?"

Lancelot grimaced. "Other than Aoibhill was going to murder Gwenhwyfar to seek revenge upon me for breaking through her magical bonds?"

Nimue lifted an eyebrow. "So your fey blood finally rose, after all. I never did see that while we were in the mortal world."

"The Lady taught me well. I worship the Goddess just as you do," Lancelot replied.

"Even I have learned that Christos worship is not the only religion that is right," Gwenhwyfar added and took Lancelot's hand.

"Then that is why the Grail appeared. You have recognized its power," Nimue answered and then looked up as a panting Brighid appeared in the doorway, her bright red hair in disarray from running.

"Come quickly," she said.

"What is it?" Nimue asked as they all stood.

"Arianrhod's wheel has stopped spinning!!!"

Gwenhwyfar looked at the priestess questioningly. "Do you mean the Wheel of Fate?"

Brighid nodded as they climbed the marble steps that led to the house of glass atop the hill. "Something has happened in the world that should not have happened."

They were all nearly breathless when they reached the summit. Inanna met them and pointed toward the lake below. "The mist has cleared," she said.

Gwenhwyfar turned. Down past the treeline, the shimmering blue of the lake washing upon white sandy shores could be seen once more. Only a faint white mist swirled slowly above its surface. "Does that mean Aoibhill and Melehan are gone?"

"Quite probably. The darkness would follow its mistress."

"That's good, then, isn't it?" Gwenhwyfar asked.

Cynthia Breeding

Inanna's brows furrowed. "It would be if Arianrhod's wheel had not stopped spinning the exact moment the darkness lifted."

"I don't understand. They've gone back home."

The priestess shook her head. "We've already scryed Eire. They are not there."

"Where else would they go?"

"We're afraid they've gone into the future."

"To find Cernunnos?" Gwenhwyfar asked. "Aoibhill thinks he belongs to her."

Inanna sighed. "I always knew that man would be trouble. I think, though, this has far more reaching implications, for the Wheel would not have stopped for that." She paused. "Whatever Aoibhill's intention is, it has stopped the destiny of mankind."

* * * *

Aoibhill breathed in the smoggy air and coughed. Lucifer's Horns! Londinium in the twenty-first century stank as badly as it did in her time. She sniffed. There was no rotting garbage or human waste in the streets, but the smell from the smoke that belched out of those metal things that roared by was bad enough. And the noise! It could deaden a siren's call.

"This is where you want to be?" Melehan asked skeptically as he looked around the narrow, littered alley that hid them from the sidewalk.

"Certes, it is not," she snapped at him. "We are here only until I can lure Cernnunos back to Eire."

"Blow the damn horn then, and let's be gone."

"I wish it were that simple." Aoibhill sighed. "The leap through Time has used much of my power."

"Then let me blow the thing." Melehan held out his hand.

She slapped it away. "Silly boy. I don't want Cernunnos being summoned to *you*. Besides, you don't have your full powers either."

"What?"

"Try disappearing."

Melehan chanted the words and made a sign in the air. Nothing happened. "Damn," he said again. "How do we get our powers back?"

Aoibhill winked. "We steal someone else's."

178

His eyebrow rose. "How do we do that?"

"You keep an eye on the sidewalk. I want no intruders." She stepped farther back into the shadows. "I will call on the elementals to show me where such powers lie."

"Nasty creatures," Melehan said.

"Only if you don't control them." Aoibhill closed her eyes and began chanting. The narrow passageway grew uncomfortably hot suddenly as the fire elemental arrived, clad in flames of yellow and orange. Some crumbled paper ignited dangerously close to Aoibhill. A sudden gush of wind fanning the fire announced the presense of the wind elemental, but she didn't notice. Her chant turned into a hum and the alley grew colder, as the water faerie, dressed in silver icicles, caused droplets of moisture to turn frosty in the air. The brown and green earth elemental tossed a flower pot from a ledge above them, the pottery shattering and the dirt effectively dousing the small fire still burning. Aoibhill took a deep breath and opened her eyes.

"They have shown me a source," she said to Melehan as she dismissed them. "The pendant you gave Morgan is not far from here."

A glint appeared in Melehan's eye. "I never did finish my conquest of her."

"Well, she is all yours when we find her." Aoibhill moved past him into the crowded street. "Come with me. Power surrounds that pendant and I don't think it is Morgan's."

They walked for some time, steadily moving toward the river. Aoibhill finally paused near some warehouses close to a wharf and scented the air. "This way," she said.

Cautiously, they peered through a grimy window. Seven women and one man, all wearing black robes, hoods forming cowls about their necks, milled around what looked like a pentagram drawn on the dusty floor.

"Where is she?" the man asked impatiently as he paced the floor.

"Witches?" Melehan whispered.

"It appears so," Aoibhill whispered back as they both stepped back. "I wonder who they are waiting for." She turned as she heard footsteps. An attractive, auburn-haired woman approached, a black robe folded over one arm.

"It seems there is your answer," Melehan said dryily.

"I need that robe." Aoibhill quickly looked him over. "Even without your powers, you are an exceedingly handsome man..."

"Say no more. That robe will be yours."

She didn't have long to wait. He returned and handed it over to her with a flourish. "The lady in question was most willing to let me put my arms around her. It didn't take much to squeeze the breath out of her."

"I hope you didn't just leave her lying in the street," Aoibhill said as she donned the robe.

"Give me more credit than that, Mother. Medraut trained me well."

"Then he was useful for two things. Now wait here for me."

She took a deep breath before entering the warehouse, willing herself to look as much like the dead woman as possible. No one seemed to notice any difference as they all turned to her.

"It's about time," the man growled.

One of the women, a striking brunette, hushed him. "There's plenty of time for the ritual, Baylor," she said.

Balor? As in the one-eyed god of evil? Aoibhill glanced quickly at his face. Two eyes, golden as a wolf's, glowed from a sharply chiseled face. Black hair that flowed to his broad shoulders gave him a menacing look. She let her gaze stray to the center of the circle. A rather crude altar of packing boxes stood in the middle. She was beginning to get an idea of what kind of a ritual they had in mind. Rutting always created its own power. Pretending to submit to this handsome priest of theirs certainly wasn't going to be any sacrifice on her part.

"I'm sorry to be late," she said in a sultry tone.

"It's all right," the brunette said as the pendant shown from her partially-open robe. "We're still high on the success of the bombings in the Underground."

"Yeah! I can't believe how synchronized everything was. Three trains in under nine minutes...and then the bus, too," another young woman giggled.

"Power to the terrorists!" a third one proclaimed.

"If that's what it's going to take to bring the Royals down, then so be it!" a fourth voice chimed in.

"Givin' themselves airs and all that pomp and circumstance posh," an older woman said with a sneer. "Tis time for the common people to take over this country."

Aoibhill had no idea what a terrorist was, but abolishing a king or queen was something else again. After all, *she* was a queen! She straightened her shoulders. Stealing their powers would be a *good* thing to do.

While they had been talking, the priest had stripped.

"Enough talk," he said. "We are anarchists. Today we celebrate the disrupted meeting of those eight countries who seek to rule the world."

Silently, the seven disrobed and knelt in a circle around the altar as the priest lit black candles and handed one to each of them. Each time, he rolled back his head and muttered strange words that Aoibhill didn't understand, but she felt the power building. A dark cloud now permeated the air over the circle as the priest held out his hand to Aoibhill. "Come, Priestess. It is your time."

She allowed him to undo her robe and slip if off her shoulders where it puddled on the ground. She felt his predatory hunger as his eyes glowed yellow in the pulsating light from the candles. She placed a hand on his heart and wasn't surprised to find no pulse. A demon-man. Great power to be had.

"To perform this ritual correctly, I must have the pendant," Aoibhill said.

He looked surprised even as the brunette snapped her head up and clutched the medallion. "No!" she said. "It is mine. He gave it to me."

He glanced from her back to Aoibhill. "I bought that pendant in a pawn shop. Why is it important?"

She thought swiftly and looked at the other women from beneath her lashes. None was wearing jewelry. "It's silver," she replied. "The female metal." She stroked the gold torque he wore about his neck. "This is male. If you want to increase the power of this ritual—" she looked at the altar—"you'll allow me to borrow it."

He responded to her seductive look and then motioned to the brunette. With a decided pout, she slipped it off and handed it to him. He put it around Aoibhill's throat. "Shall we begin then?" he asked.

"Oh, yes," she purred and then found herself on her hands and knees on the altar. He spread her legs with his knees and, without preamble, rammed into her. Had she been mortal, it would probably have hurt, but she felt the dark need he had to conquer. To take. To use.

What he didn't know was that she was using him. With every thrust, she took his power. "That's it!" she gasped as his seed spilled into her and she sapped the last bit of his strength.

Aoibhill slid forward, letting him collapse against the hard altar. She turned slowly in the circle, allowing each of the witches to see the swirling silver in her lavender eyes. It was an easy, mesmerizing spell. She lifted her hand and laughed as fire shot from her fingertips and ignited the paper storage boxes.

Bending over, she picked up her robe and moved through the thickening smoke to the door. She turned before she left to see the witches standing frozen, flames licking at their feet. The priest lay lifeless on the makeshift altar.

How fitting.

She met Melehan outside. "Here," she said. "I thought you might like your pendant back."

They were less than a block away from the burning building when two men stepped out of an alley not far from them. Both of them were staring at the billowing smoke coming from the windows.

"What the hell happened?" the taller one said.

The shorter one snorted. "That damn priest probably had too many candles lit. I told him not to perform that stupid ritual in a warehouse with combustibles everywhere." He shook his head. "As if a *ritual* would make for a successful overthrow of the government. We're in this for the money. The drug cartels want the European market eradicated. The easiest way to do that is to locate young radicals who *think* they're working for the good of the common people. Ha. No government worries about that anyway."

The other one snickered. "It does make our job easier with all the terrorism that's taking place. People will never believe North Americans might be behind any of it."

Aoibhill had heard enough. "Excuse me, gentlemen."

Both of them looked startled to see her standing there. Certes, they would be. She had cloaked herself and Melehan to hear the conversation. She noticed their eyes drifted to the black robe she still held.

The tall one gestured. "Did you all escape?"

She cast her eyes down and wiped a pretend tear from one. "I'm not sure. I was late in attending and just now got here. I never went inside."

"Do you know who the priest's leader was?" one asked. "Can you take us to him? We've got some...er, a package that needs to be delivered."

She was pretty sure she knew what the package contained. Melehan had been disgusted to find out that drug addicts on the streets of London were all too willing to sell their souls to him without even assuming his incubus form. A plan quickly formed in her head, even as she heard sirens a distance away.

"Yes, I can take you to him. In fact, he has one...um, client that he wants to share part of that package with. A little gift for her."

"What he does with it is his business," the man said. "Where is he?"

She fingered the silver horn around her neck and closed her eyes briefly. Cernunnos' scent was faint—he and Morgan must not have rutted in a while—but still detectable. He was here in the city.

"I'll let you know when I contact him," she said. "Let me have a phone number."

The sirens were coming closer and both men looked nervous. The man scribbled a number on a piece of paper and handed it to her. "Don't take too long. Our boss don't like it."

"You can count on hearing from me," Aoibhill said as the fire engines turned the corner. She almost laughed as the men all but ran from the scene. Linking her arm through Melehan's, she turned and strolled casually away.

This time, when she found Cernunnos, Morgan wouldn't be a problem.

* * * *

Morgan slanted a suspicious glance over at Cernunnos as he opened the door to their room above the theatre and placed one hand at the small of her back to escort her inside. He certainly had been acting strangely since she'd been released from the hospital. She glanced down at the bouquet of roses he'd given her. The last time he'd done that was when she caught him with Queen Boudicca. Apparently, holding the Romans at bay wasn't her only skill.

Morgan glanced around the room. It hardly looked lived-in. Where had Cernunnos been the past three days?

"The doctor said you should rest." He turned down the covers on the bed. "Let me get you settled and then I'll pour you some wine."

She eyed the bed. It didn't look slept-in either. Was that a good sign or bad? She limped toward the bed and instantly, Cernunnos was at her side, lifting her in his arms. He laid her carefully on the mattress and then sat beside her. He had a strange look in his eyes. Morgan took a deep breath. "Is something wrong, Cern?"

"Nothing's wrong." He reached over to push a strand of her hair away from her face. "I'm just glad you're all right. You could have been killed."

She tilted her head sideways and looked at him. "Are we mortal then?"

"I don't know. I don't want to find out. I know that I want you, Morgan. More now than ever before."

She closed her eyes briefly. This was worse than she thought. Cernunnos did *not* make flowery compliments unless he was *extremely* guilty about something. Or someone. Not even with his obvious interest in Gwenhywfar had he been this...*sweet*. All the way home he'd acted like Morgan was made of glass and might break. Whoever her rival was, Morgan knew how to make Cernunnos forget her. Or, at least, she hoped she did.

"Come here," she said seductively. "I've missed you too."

He shed his clothes quickly. He unbuttoned her shirt leisurely, instead of ripping it off, his hands lightly brushing her shoulders as he pushed it back and down. His warm fingers trailed downward, lingering only long enough to pass his thumbs over her nipples before he slid his hands across her stomach and undid her slacks.

He looked up at her, his golden eyes holding a hint of mischief. Morgan lifted her buttocks, trying to press against his hand, but it was already moving a path across her abdomen, reaching up to gently cup a breast, kneading it softly, teasing the nipple with a mere flicker of his finger. She arched her back, her breasts achy, but he'd shifted again to lie alongside her.

Cernunnos rained butterfly kisses across her forehead and over her closed eyelids and down her cheek. He nibbled gently on her earlobe and trailed tiny kisses down her throat. He brushed his lips across hers ever so lightly.

Morgan's body trembled with desire. Never had Cernunnos teased her like this, his easy, slow touch leaving each part of her body tingling and wanting more. She made a slight mewling sound as she grabbed his head and pulled it down for a real kiss.

Obligingly, he slanted his mouth over hers, but still he teased her, keeping the kisses soft and gentle until she thought she would scream with pent-up need. Finally, he slipped his tongue into her mouth, lazily exploring it. Morgan whimpered when his mouth left hers.

That silken tongue worked its way down her throat to her breast. Morgan began to moan in earnest.

Cernunnos shifted again, this time bringing himself over her, his rock-like erection nudging the softness of her core. Morgan groaned as he slipped inside of her. She wanted his thickness filling her completely. She gyrated her hips in a frantic effort to gain relief, but he kept his strokes slow and steady.

"I could go on like this for hours," Cernunnos whispered.

Morgan's eyes flew open and she saw a look of mischief on his face. "No," she panted, barely able to think as he moved inside her and nearly withdrew. "No. I can't stand any more. Please—" She gasped as he suddenly drove in hard and fast. "Yes! Oh, yes..." Her body began to convulse as the mind-fogging pressure built inside her. She clutched the hard, bronze muscles of Cernunnos' arms and screamed as deep muscles contracted and she shattered.

They both lay panting for some time before either of them had breath enough to talk. Finally, Morgan turned on her side. "You've never taken your time like that. We've always let passion just drive us."

Cernunnos rose up on his elbow and looked down at her. "Did you like it?"

"As if you had to ask? You were fantastic." Doubts rolled through her mind again. *Had* Cernunnos been with someone else who had taught him this new technique? Morgan didn't want to be jealous. Not after such a splendid time. She didn't want to ask, but it was as though some other force were driving her. "Why were you so slow and gentle with me today?"

"I told you," Cernunnos said. "I was afraid you were going to die." He took a deep breath. "That scared me. It made me realize that I—" He stopped suddenly, and raised his head, scenting the air, eyes intent, ears pricked up.

"What is it?" Morgan asked as she saw the tips of his antlers begin to protrude. "What's wrong?"

"I'm not sure. I thought I heard the sound of a horn..." Cernunnos shook his head as though to clear it. "It's probably nothing." He reached down to gather his clothes. "Hungry? Let's get something to eat."

Morgan bit her lip as she swung her legs over the side of the bed. There was only one horn that would cause Cernunnos to react like that.

Aoibhill's.

Chapter Fourteen

Morgan looked worriedly over at Cernunnos as the bus turned off A-303 and into the parking lot near Stonehenge. For the past two weeks, he had become increasingly restless and she was pretty sure he'd heard the sound of the horn again.

He glanced down at her. "I don't see how Aoibhill could possibly be here—in this century, I mean."

They'd had this conversation a dozen times since that wonderful day of love-making when he'd first heard the sound. Unfortunately, each time they'd come together in this newly found passion, he'd hear the sound again. Morgan gradually realized that each time they mated, the sound became more clear to Cern and his restlessness increased. Their mating was drawing Aoibhill closer and Morgan finally suggested they not indulge, much to Cernunnos' growling dissatisfaction.

Which was partly why they were here.

Morgan gazed up at the massive stones as they stepped off the bus filled with other tourists. Tears sprang to her eyes. So much had been destroyed. Gone was the beautiful intact circle of sarsens with their flat tops enclosing a second circle of smaller blue stones which in turn protected the five huge trilithons arranged in a horseshoe pattern around a smaller horseshoe of bluestones. Only three trilithons remained fully standing along with a partial outer circle. Tilted and fallen stones lay here and there. The altar stone was still there though.

The Giant's Dance. A Druid place of worship. The Pendragon's burial site. What mortals didn't know was that it had once belonged to Faerie. She had danced inside that circle on many a summer solstice just as the sun rose behind the Heel stone and shown down the avenue. There was no portal here, but she hoped there was enough faerie magic still lingering that she might be able to challenge the power of Aoibhill's horn.

"I just wish I had thought of this a month ago when the sun was aligned with the stones," she said.

Cernunnos took her hand. "I remember the first time you brought me here."

Morgan chuckled. "You said you didn't think Myrddin could build this."

"I admit I was skeptical. But then," he replied as he nuzzled her neck, "I wasn't especially interested in Myrddin or *his* abilities."

They were beginning to get strange looks from the other tourists. A few grinned. "We're drawing attention to ourselves," she whispered.

He arched a brow. "When did that ever bother you?"

"Normally, it wouldn't. But they have strange rules in this world." Just after her coming back from the hospital, she and Cernunnos had been told by some man in a uniform and a tall hat that they couldn't fornicate—what a strange thing to call it— in a public park. Wasn't a woodland the most perfect place to share such wild and free joy? "Let's go in to the circle." She tugged at his hand.

A few steps later, she stopped. A fence surrounded the stones. "I need to go in there," she said to the tour guide.

The woman nodded sympathetically. "We all would, deary, but the place has been closed since the Seventies."

"Why?"

"It became a popular spot with the Hippies and New Age crowd in the Sixties," the guide said. "The land was being eroded by so many people. The stones were in danger of being damaged even more than they are now."

Morgan had no idea what 'hippies' or 'new age' people were, or for that matter, what the Sixties were. "There aren't that many people here now. It won't hurt just to walk inside for a few minutes."

The woman shook her head. "You'd be trespassing, Miss. Wouldn't want to have one of my passengers arrested, you know."

Arrested? That was the word the uniformed man in the park had used, too. What was *wrong* with these people? She narrowed her eyes. It wouldn't take much to vault over the fence and she'd just need a few minutes to feel the power...if it still existed.

Cernunnos' hand clamped down over hers. "No. Don't even think it."

She gave him an annoyed look. He had the most uncanny way of reading her mind sometimes. A trait that definitely was stronger here in the mortal world where she couldn't ward her thoughts.

"You know why I need to do it," she said through clenched teeth.

"And I know I won't be able to get you out of gaol," he muttered back. "I had a hard enough time getting you released from the hospital and you weren't being arrested there."

"Well, everyone, time to get back on the bus!" the guide called out cheerfully. "We still have to see Woodhenge."

Morgan looked back over her shoulder as she stumbled after Cernunnos.

So close... and yet, so far.

* * * *

"Are you sure you know how to use this thing?" Morgan looked at the smaller, older motorcycle that resembled Andy's.

Cernunnos looked pained. "It's not so different from mastering a horse. Hop on. I'll show you."

Still skeptical, she brought her right leg over and settled on the seat behind him. He kicked the start petal. The thing sputtered, shook, and stopped. He tried again with the same results. "Are you sure—"

"Yes!" Cernunnos kicked down hard and then shoutedd victoriously when the engine rumbled to life. "See?"

"Yes, dear." Morgan wrapped her arms around him. At least, that felt good. She missed their lovemaking, but until she figured out a way to combat Aoibhill's strange hold on Cernunnos, it was better not giving the witch power through mating.

Her thoughts were quickly brought to the present as the bike lurched, the engine sputtered again and for a moment, the machine wobbled amid a loud roar. A strong smell of burnt rubber assaulted her nose. Her hair whipped back in the wind and she nearly shrieked as the bike leaned close to the ground when Cernunnos turned a corner.

"We may be mortal, Cern! Let's not risk our lives with this!"

He laughed and revved the throttle as they sped down a straight street. "I've wanted one of these ever since I saw Andy's!"

Morgan rolled her eyes. "Just make sure we get back in one piece!" she shouted above the noise.

"You're safe with me!" Cernunnos dipped into another turn and the bike nearly skidded out from under him.

"Um-hum," Morgan replied.

Sometime later, completely disheveled and having learned to put her own foot out to brace herself and keep them upright, Morgan gratefully crawled off the bike in front of the theatre. She couldn't believe the look of elation on Cernunnos' face. All she felt was relief, at the moment, that she was still in one piece.

She turned on the telly once they got inside their room. Now *that* was an interesting device. She could watch actors actually mating in that box. Andy had explained that they weren't really completing the act, but Morgan wasn't so sure. It *looked* real.

Cernunnos flipped the channel to the local news.

"Today, four more explosions took place in the London Underground and a London bus," the news anchor was saying and trying not to sound excited. "Luckily, only the detonators exploded and the main charges didn't." He paused and then plastered a smile on his face. "No casualties were reported."

Morgan sank down onto the sofa. "Terrorists, again. What is wrong with these people that they want to kill with no purpose and for no reason?"

Cernunnos sat down beside her. "It makes no sense to me either. It does not seem that this enemy wants the land. The attacks are not aimed at soldiers...at least, that fight would be fair."

"These...terrorists...seem to enjoy destruction. It reminds me of Morgana and her plot to bring the plague to Briton," Morgan said.

"Aye. But Morgana had no wish to die. She wanted to survive and have the power to rule. These people kill themselves."

Morgan picked up Cernnunnos' hand. "I don't want to live here anymore."

He brought her hand to his lips and kissed it. "I know. I want to get back to Faerie as badly as you do."

"We don't even know if that's possible anymore," Morgan replied as she closed her eyes and savored his light kiss. "But, I definitely don't want to live in Londinium. Don't we have enough money saved from the performances to move into the country? We could find other work, now that we have an idea of how this world operates."

"Certes. I would be happier in the woodlands, too. We'd have to tell Andy though, so he could replace us."

"Then let's do so tonight," Morgan responded and then sighed with pleasure as Cernunnos kissed the soft, sensitive area inside her wrist while one hand stroked up her arm to lightly cup her breast.

She moaned. "Cern, we really shouldn't. You'll hear the horn again. You know how it makes you feel afterwards. Like—"

He slanted his mouth over hers, silencing her protests. "I know how it makes me feel *now*. And wherever that power pull is coming from, I can resist it. I want you."

Morgan found herself melting and she reached up for him. It had been so long...only this once...now...

It couldn't hurt. Could it?

* * * *

Andy looked from one of them to the other as Cernunnos and Morgan sat across from his desk in the small, littered office. "Well, I hate to lose you as cast members, but I understand. The terrorism thing has frayed a lot of nerves."

"I just don't understand it," Morgan said. "King Arthur fought twelve major battles against the Saxons before Briton established peace between them. It was years later that Ida and Wehha invaded and led to a second rebellion. And Childebert in Gaul advanced westward—"

"I'm not sure Andy wants a history lesson," Cernunnos said.

"Actually, I find it quite fascinating that you two know so much," Andy replied. "I know you're historians, but Morgan makes it sound as though you were actually *there*. I can almost hear the clash of swords and the battle cries when she describes it."

"Thank you." Morgan ignored the look Cernunnos sent her. Really. If it hadn't been for her, this medieval play they acted out each night would have *Morgan le Fey—her!—*being bad, not to mention Lancelot and Gwenhwyfar had been cast as traitors. Not that Morgan was *fond* of Gwenhwyfar, but the facts needed to be set straight. Arthur had, after all, sired a daughter with Nimue. *That* wasn't in any of the history books. It had taken a great deal of persuasion on her part—and mayhap a bit of glamour—to convince Andy to change the storyline.

"What I was trying to say was that those wars may have been vicious and bloody, but the invaders were after land. They wanted to settle it, even if it didn't belong to them. I don't see what the goal is for these explosions on innocent people."

"No one does," Andy admitted, "but religious wars over the centuries have never made sense. The Holy Land—Jerusalem in particular—has been in bloody conflict for centuries. It fell out of Christian hands in 1099. Twenty years later, the Knights of the Black and White—Templars—began guarding the roads for Christians who made pilgrimages to Jerusalem. Or so they say. They got rich doing it. Then look at the Crusades. Richard I decided to defend Jerusalem from Saladin's advance by taking the Cross himself. The fall of Acre ultimately resulted in a three year truce with Saladin. A victory in itself, considering both sides considered each other Infidels that needed to be banished." Andy shrugged. "I doubt the issue will ever be resolved."

"I'll bet King Arthur could solve it," Morgan blurted out before she thought.

Andy gave her a strange look. "I almost wish the legend were true. That King Arthur could return some day to restore peace to the world. But, as much as I love the idea, it is only a myth."

Morgan bowed her head. King Arthur had lived, but she also knew that when Nimue brought him through Faerie the second time, he had been quite dead. Although she hadn't traveled into Avalon with the byre, she'd heard the priestesses' ritual sounds of passing through the mists.

"Well," Cernunnos said as he gave her thigh a pat, "we have a show to do."

Andy glanced at this watch. "Not too much time to get the make-up on either."

Morgan almost giggled. They never wore make-up. They didn't have to. They were playing themselves.

She felt a strange current of excitement, sometime later, as the curtain opened on the first scene. Mayhap because they would soon be leaving this crowded city, but she wanted to give the best performance she could. Her lines seemed to flow naturally as she and Cernunnos threw heated barbs at each other and then indulged in even more heated scenes in which they made up for their behavior. It was the one time she felt safe about kissing him anymore. The curse of the horn didn't seem to faze him when they were on stage. She opened her mouth to let him indulge himself and felt his surprised tension, just before his tongue swept inside. She lingered with the kiss as the audience clapped enthusiastically and the prompter behind the curtain hissed to move on.

Reluctantly, she let her hands slide down from Cernunnos' neck and over his hard biceps. She let her body slither against his—it was in the script!—before she turned toward the audience and winked.

Red eyes glowed back at her from near the back of the theatre. She blinked. Melehan winked back at her. And then her blood chilled.

Sitting next to him was Aoibhill.

* * * *

Aoibhill fingered the small silver horn and watched carefully as Morgan froze. So the little mouse did recognize her. She frowned. She didn't remember Morgan being so animated before. Did she always have reddish glints in her hair? And were her eyes always the deep color of the forest? That she lusted for Cernunnos was obvious in every move she made on the stage. Aoibhill's brows knitted together. Cernunnos had played his role very well. Mayhap, too well.

"Go ahead and blow the damn horn," Melehan said at her side. "I want to get Morgan alone."

"Oh, you will." She toyed with the little horn again. She had blown it twice before and gotten only a faint trace of a trail. Apparently, in this century, she needed to be closer to Cernunnos for the enchantment to work. Or mayhap, the magic had worn thin. At any rate, she picked up a scent—one of earth and woodland that was Cernunnos—that had led to the King's Cross area. She'd almost lost it with the crush of people milling about after the explosions, but the unbridled muskiness of the demi-god had come to her again this afternoon.

Now that she had Cernunnos in her sights, she could afford to toy with him a bit.

Or with Morgan. Let the bitch stew. At this close distance, the horn wouldn't fail. Cernunnos would come to her. Just as he had so many centuries before.

"Patience," she said to Melehan.

He snorted. "Women."

"Careful, son. Your fangs are showing. *Women* much prefer the glamour of your adorable grin and halo of golden curls."

He turned that grin on her. "Like this?"

"Better," she said, "but keep your eyes blue. Red scares the mortals."

The curtain closed on the line of actors taking their bows and Aoibhill stood. "I think I'll wander backstage," she said.

"About time," Melehan muttered as he followed her down the aisle.

A rather skinny-looking young man dressed in black that matched his hair and goatee stopped them. "Sorry. I'm the director. No one's allowed back stage."

Aoibhill fixed her lavender gaze on him. "I'm a friend of the actor who played Cernunnos," she said. "An old friend."

For a moment he looked dazed, but then his eyes cleared behind his glasses.

"Sorry. If you like, I'll give him a message."

Aoibhill kept a smile on her face. The little twit should have been mesmerized with her look. Why wasn't he? And what nonsense was this about trying to stop her? She could, certes, conjure a spell to place on him, but she didn't have the time. Simple, feminine wiles would have to work. She lowered her lashes and then tilted a look upward at him. "Please. I've come a long way. I'd just like to say hello."

"I'm quite taken with the actress who played the faerie queen," Melehan added. "Wouldn't she be flattered to meet a fan?"

Andy shrugged. "Neither of them seem to care for fans. Only the acting." He brightened a bit. "In fact, they've helped change the plot to make the show even better."

Aoibhill sighed inwardly. Mayhap if Melehan could keep the fool talking, she could slip by...she shot her son a glance.

"How so?" he asked promptly and moved a little closer to the other man, leaving space behind him for Aoibhill to slip through.

"Well, I originally had Morgan le Fey cast as an evil, conniving witch," he began, "and then—"

Aoibhill wanted to shout, "She is even more than that!" but Melehan maneuvered himself into position where the other man had to turn away to keep talking to him and she decided it was more important to move.

She walked down a dark, narrow hall. To her right, she heard a babble of excited voices. Peering inside the open doorway, she saw the young actresses removing make-up. Morgan wasn't there. The next doorway opened to the men's area where several actors were in various stages of undress. She stopped. Young men...lean, well-muscled torsos...

"Like what you see, lady?" a blond Adonis-type asked as he put his hands on the towel that wrapped around slender hips.

"Very much," Aoibhill said, "but I'm looking for Cernunnos."

He grunted. "That figures."

A tall, dark-haired man who'd played Lancelot and looked uncannily like him, came over. "I think I heard him say he's leaving."

She tried not to panic. "Well, I can see he's not here."

He inclined his head as a loud noise rumbled through the hallway. "That sounds like him now."

Aoibhill turned and ran toward the open door that led into an alley. The noisy machine—they were called motorcycles, she remembered—was leaning into a sharp turn toward the street. Cernunnos was driving it, with Morgan holding on to him.

Aoibhill cursed roundly, causing the building behind her to shake. The little bitch must have given him some line to make him drive away like that. She lifted her horn and then lowered it again.

Now that she had his scent, she could follow him. Melehan would do away with Morgan, once and for all. When she finally blew the horn, Cernunnos would be all hers for all eternity.

Soon. Very, very soon.

Chapter Fifteen

Morgan pressed her face against Cernunnos' back when the bike leaned into another turn as they sped away from Upper Street and made a sharp left turn on Pentonville Road. Cernununnos didn't say anything until they raced past Regent's Park and were on the A-40.

"You're *sure* it was Aoibhill?" he asked through the headset attached to his ear.

"I don't think I'd forget her," Morgan spoke into the tiny metal thing near her mouth. For once, Cernunnos' fascination with this new technology paid off. She didn't think she'd be able to shout over the wind that tore at them.

"How did she get here?" he asked. "The laws of Faerie forbid her entrance on Briton soil unless you permit it."

If she hadn't been afraid of getting a bug in her mouth, Morgan would have laughed out loud. Or cried. "This is the twenty-first century, Cern! Faerie may not even exist. Anyway, when I stepped through the pool, I left Faerie open."

Cernunnos' hand on the throttle, revving the bike up, was a good indication of his anger, yet his voice was calm. "She must have sent that damn Melehan to lure you away. I wish I had been there."

Morgan was glad Cernunnos couldn't see her embarrassment. Her face must be as red as a rowan berry with shame. How could she have been so gullible as to believe Melehan's story about Custennin? Once again, she'd let her interest in mortals—and especially handsome males with strong, muscular bodies—override her logic. She *did* have thinking skills, despite the free-spirit faerie instinct for impulsiveness and instant pleasure. Melehan's golden curls and boyish visage had captivated her. How foolish she had been.

"Don't blame yourself," Cernunnos said through the headset. "He had the pendant, remember?"

Morgan almost smiled. "Are you able to read my mind these days?"

Cernunnos laughed. "No. You're kneading your nails into my ribs like a cat. You only do that when you're upset."

With a jolt, she realized he was right. No doubt she had claw marks in his skin in spite of the shirt he wore. She relaxed her fingers. "I didn't know you ever noticed that."

He took his left hand off the handlebar for a moment to pull her arms around him again. "There's lot of things I've noticed about you lately, Morgan. Little things like how you're eyes lit up when I made that pizza food you like so much." He glanced in the rear view mirror. "And how you managed to choke it down without making too much of a face."

Morgan grinned back. "Well, it did have a bit of extra garlic on it."

"A little? The whole room smelled for hours after."

"Well, you were equally brave at swallowing my attempt at American fried chicken. I just didn't know it would be raw in the middle."

Cernunnos chuckled. "I don't think either of us is a cook." He glanced in the mirror again. "But we *are* really good at something else. When we stop tonight—"

"Hush! Pay attention to your driving," Morgan chided him even as her hand slid down toward his belt.

He swerved, barely missing a huge truck. "Do I need to make a stop sooner?"

She let her fingertips graze the hardening length of him that strained against his jeans and sighed as she withdrew her hand. "I would love to, but we need to put distance between us and Aoibhill."

For an answer, he throttled the bike again, the tires nearly smoking as their speed increased. Morgan rested her head against his shoulders.

How much distance did they need to put between themselves and Aoibhill to be safe? Would she be able to find them? What powers did the Eire queen retain?

That she wanted Cernunnos back was obvious. After all these centuries when Morgan thought Aoibhill had been satisfied with other conquests. By Avalon's Goddess, there had been a number of them: Achilles, Hercules, Dionysus, Loki—

who should have been a perfect match—Taliesin, Julius Caesar...Aoibhill had even given Cleopatra a scare when she tried to lure Marc Antony away. Morgan smiled, remembering. Like Lancelot, he stayed true to his mortal queen. Yet, Aoibhill still wanted Cernunnos.

She shuddered and clenched Cernunnos. Would they ever be safe from the Eire queen?

Morgan felt Cernunnos gently pry her digging nails loose. His warm, strong hand covered hers.

"We'll be safe, Morgan. We'll be safe."

She closed her eyes, inhaling his clean, earthy, male scent. He may not be reading her mind, but he had gotten to know her, in the past few weeks, in a way that their relationship over the centuries never had. Resting her head against him, she sighed contentedly.

* * * *

Morgan held Cernunnos' hand as they gazed up at the ancient hill fort the next morning. They hadn't dared to make love the night before because even Cernunnos had grudgingly agreed that the power that was created in the act might allow Aoibhill to find them. Strangely enough, cuddling and being held had been very satisfying. Morgan looked over at Cernunnos, loving the strong set of his jaw, the tawny mane of hair that blended with his bronze skin and amber eyes that glowed with warmth as he looked down at her.

He gave her fingers a squeeze and looked back at the fort. "Do you think this was Camelot?"

"I'm not sure." Morgan looked back at the village of South Cadbury and the church they had just passed. "The village is different and this—" she gestured toward the notice board and the earthen path that led up the hill—"is not where the gateway was."

"No," Cernunnos answered as he started walking, "but let's see what's at the top."

Morgan followed him, Trees lined the uneven walkway, gnarly roots sticking out as if to defend the hill once more from unwelcome invaders. They went through a gate in wall and then the path became steep as it wound through trees before finally opening onto a grassy enclosure at the flat top of the hill.

"There should be four lines of banks and ditches," she said, "but everything is covered with trees."

"Over here," Cernunnos answered from a spot to her left. "You can still see them from here."

She joined him and looked down at the grassy banks, the ditch lines now clearly seen. "This looks familiar." Glancing around, she pointed toward barely visible stone foundations. "The castle walls, I think." Moving farther along to her right, she stopped and gazed down at another village. "There! That's the village spot I remember! The original cobblestone road led up the hill from there."

Cernunnos walked over and put an arm around her shoulders. "There was a gatehouse here. Double doors into a square tower with another set of doors into the bailey. Good trap for anyone who managed to breach four lines of defense."

"And the Great Hall was here," Morgan said as she tugged Cernunnos along with her over the hollows and dips in the pastureland. "The kitchens were over there." She peered more closely at the ground. "I don't see where Nimue's small stone cottage was."

"Why is that important?" Cernunnos asked.

"That's where Lancelot *thought* he was meeting Gwenhwyfar the night Elaine lured him to his fate. I really wanted to put a snake in the twit's bed, but Myrddin wouldn't let me."

Cernunnos arched his brow. "*You* wanted to help Gwenhwyfar keep Lancelot? I would have thought you'd welcome Elaine's...intervention."

Morgan shrugged. "Elaine was a nasty little piece of work. Acting so piously a follower of the Christos, yet secretly working with Morgana."

Cernunnos frowned. "That woman called on me more than once for help."

It was Morgan's turn to arch a brow. "Did you?"

"No. Her kind of magic only spelled trouble. For everyone."

"Well," Morgan said, "at least *she's* not here. Medraut either." She shivered suddenly even though the day was warm.

"What is it?" Cernunnos asked. "You have a strange expression on your face."

She shook her head. "I don't know. Just now, I had the strangest feeling that mayhap they were here...some part of them, anyway. It's probably nothing."

He moved closer and drew her to him. "It's too bad neither of us has Nimue's gift of sensing spirits. I can't even sense if anything lingers here, even though I'm sure this was Camelot. That person at the church said there was supposed to be a cave in this hill that serves as Arthur's grave, but no one has been able to find it."

"That's because we know Arthur isn't here." Morgan stiffened suddenly, then began to tremble.

"What is it?" Cernunnos asked.

For a moment, she didn't answer him as his gaze shifted over the fields and to the surrounding hills. Then she reached up and gave him a quick kiss.

"We've been so stupid, Cern! Arthur may not be here, but someone else is. Someone that might be able to help us get back. I don't know why I didn't think of this before."

"What? Who?"

"Myrddin. Nimue said she placed him in a crystal cave."

Cernunnos furrowed his brows. "But the man at the church said no one has been able to find the cave."

"That's because it's not *here*."

"You're not making sense, love."

"Yes, I am." She suddenly pointed. "Look over there. What do you see?"

He followed her direction. "Another large hill with a tower of some sort."

"Look more closely."

"I see smaller hills. What am I missing?"

Morgan let her eyes glaze. "Um. It could be a woman lying on her side. The large hill with that tower is a breast. The long sweep of lower hills could be a leg...the other mounds could be a second leg." She turned to Cernunnos. "Nimue once had this long conversation with Myrddin—while I perched on his shoulder and tried to tweak his ear so he would leave—about those hills being a symbol of the Great Mother, lying in the birthing position. The water around her was the fluid that spills once the babe is born."

Cernunnos shook his head. "There's no water."

"There *was*. Look at the valley, Cern. Picture it as a lake. In the middle, the tall hill stands as an island, shrouded in mist. Picture it." She watched him as his eyes suddenly widened.

"Do you mean—"

"Yes. That was the Lake. Nimue was the Lady. That is Avallach." She turned back to it. "And somewhere on that hill is a crystal cave where Myrddin sleeps. All we have to do is find it and awaken him."

"That sounds easy," Cernunnos said dryly. "Some people die and remain dead."

She stuck out her tongue at him. "You forget that Myrddin and I had a pact. He needed my help in transforming Uther into Gorlois' likeness for Ygraine so Arthur could be born. In return, through being attached to him, I could remain in the mortal world and experience its pleasures."

"Pleasures that I assume you're willing to give up now?" Cernunos asked.

"If we can get back to Faerie, I wish to stay there forever," she said fervently.

"So how can a long-dead Myrddin help? It's been...what? Over fifteen hundred years?"

"For him. But I still carry a bit of his essence in me from our time together. If I can give that back to him—"

Cernunnos didn't wait to hear more. "Let's go," he said.

They ran down the hill to the small parking space where they'd left the Harley. Gravel spurted up from the tires as Cernunnos gave full throttle and Morgan prayed to the Goddess of Avalon that she was right.

That they would finally be going home.

* * * *

Cernunnos parked the bike and they joined the throng of visitors milling about the ruins of Glastonbury Abbey. It seemed a strange assortment of people, from neatly dressed, middle-aged couples to young people in wildly colorful shirts and torn jeans. A bearded man in a long, white, hooded robe strolled slowly by.

"Who's he supposed to be?" Cernunnos asked Morgan.

She shrugged. "Probably a New-Age druid like we saw at Stonehenge."

Cernunnos snorted. "Myrddin would have a good laugh at that."

Morgan managed a smile. "I hope he has a chance to. The land looks so unfamiliar, I'm not even sure we're in the right place."

"It's hard to miss that hill," Cernunnos pointed to the mound with the tower on it.

"That's what you saw from Camelot, wasn't it?"

"I think so," she said, "but there's no water. In our time, Ynys Gutrin—Glastonbury—was near the edge the Lake. And the hill was always shrouded and never clearly seen." She looked at the stone walls of what was left of the abbey. "There was a Christian church, but nothing like this."

"Well, don't worry about the church." Cernunnos guided her past the Lady Chapel toward a small plot with a marker on it. "Here's part of what we came to see. You've learned to read. What does it say?"

Morgan looked down at the sign. "Site of King Arthur's tomb. He and Gwenhwyfar were found here in 1191. In April, 1278, King Edward had them removed to a black marble tomb that survived until 1539." She looked up at Cernunnos. "Nimue said it was Lancelot's former body she buried with Gwenhwyfar's after we took them back to Faerie."

"No one was supposed to know that Arthur survived, remember? He even changed his name to Armel."

"Um," she said as they continued to walk about the grounds, "it's surprising how much legend has sprung up about Arthur and the Grail as well. People want to believe it's here, buried under the Chalice Well we saw earlier. But people also think it's buried somewhere in Roslyn Chapel, way up north. If they're so willing to believe these stories, I wonder why the Grail Maiden is not spoken of."

"Astrala, like the Grail itself, only appears when she is needed," Cernunnos replied. "Even I have never met her...or seen the Grail."

Morgan rolled her eyes. "I think you're supposed to be 'pure of heart,' Cern. That hardly describes you."

"And you should be glad it doesn't," he answered, his face lighting up. "Once we get back to Faerie, where Aoibhill can't hunt us down, I'm going to show you *exactly* how impure my thoughts are. I hope you'll be ready."

Morgan batted her eyelashes at him. "Have you ever known me *not* to be?"

His grin widened. "I can't say I have. Do you want to give me a little taste right now?"

Her eyes dilated to almost black and Cernunnos drew a deep breath. When Morgan looked at him that way, it was all he could do to keep from taking her wherever they were. Once, not too long ago, he would have done so, and forget whatever public embarrassment it might cause. Lately, though, he'd become very protective of Morgan. He shook his head. He must be picking up human traits.

"I'll give you more that a little taste once we find Myrddin." She inhaled deeply. "I think it's time we go to Avallach—or the Tor—whatever it's called now."

With the bike, it only took them a few minutes to arrive at the foot of the hill. "This seems so strange," Morgan said as they began climbing. "First no water surrounding it, only grassy fields. No mists. Even the labyrinthine maze is gone. There's only this path."

Cernunnos took her hand and they walked in silence the rest of the way up. His antlers began to grow as he surveyed the vast open lands from the summit.

"Cern." Morgan pointed to his head.

"Oh. Sorry." He glanced around at the few people who were also enjoying the view. "The land calls to me here more strongly than anywhere we've been."

"I know." Morgan paced slowly. "The stones that used to stand here left some power. I can feel it."

"Can you capture it?"

She closed her eyes and concentrated. Cernunnos watched as she swayed to some unknown rhythm. He, too, could feel a sort of different energy. He looked up at the tower. It was dedicated to some Christian saint named Michael. From what he knew, the followers of the Christos didn't believe in this kind of magic. The source of the power must be older than that.

Morgan opened her eyes and he could see disappointment in them. "It's here," she almost whispered, "but I can't touch it. I feel traces... Myrddin was here. I'm sure of that."

"Which means we have to find him," Cernunnos said. "Didn't Nimue say she placed him in a cave?"

Morgan nodded. "It has to on this hill somewhere." She glanced down the path they'd come up on. "The place is so big. An entrance could be behind any bush or large rock. We'd be better off separating to look."

"I really don't want to leave you alone."

"I think I'll be safe, Cern. It's the middle of the day and there are tourists around. We haven't seen Aoibhill or Melehan since London."

"I don't trust that bitch. Or the bastard with her."

"I don't either, Cern, but think. What drew her to us was the scent—or the power—of our mating. We purposely have not been indulging ourselves. We barely even touch."

Cernunnos growled. "Don't remind me."

"The sooner we can find Myrddin's cave, the sooner we can...you know." Morgan smiled seductively. "It'd save time if we each searched part of this place.

"I don't know—"

"I'll stay near the path," Morgan said. "There are people around. I'll be safe."

What she said made sense. They could cover more ground. He looked around, trying to pick up any non-human scents. Apart from some small animals, he sensed nothing. "I suppose it might be all right," he said reluctantly. "Just stay where people can hear you if you have to scream."

"Certes." Morgan skipped away. "Don't worry about me. We'll meet at the foot of the path in two hours."

He watched her move away and then turned in the other direction. He remembered hearing Nimue calling to Gwenhwyfar that long ago Samhain night when he had ridden the Wild Hunt. Gwenhwyfar had been left on Avalon when Myrddin took Arthur back to Briton. Cernunnos had been so focused on capturing her that he hadn't paid much attention to the spot Myrddin had actually returned to. But Nimue had said something once about a cave of crystal lights on Avallach. It had to be here somewhere.

He searched, looking behind rocks barely large enough to hide any kind of hole and pulled bushes away from the ground. Nothing.

Mayhap, Morgan had found something. Slowly, he started back toward their meeting point. He was passing a small clump of gorse when he felt the hair rise on his nape. He looked up.

Standing not far away was a white stag.

Cernunnos let his antlers show, hoping this one wouldn't charge him. "Brother," he said.

The hart dipped his own head in acknowledgement and then he turned and trotted off. Cernunnos quickly followed. Rounding a small, moss-covered boulder, he stopped. The stag had disappeared. Cernunnos looked around, his tawny mane bristling. The air fairly sparked with something here.

Then he saw it. Nestled beneath the ledge of the stone was a semi-circle of primroses. In bloom, in the shade and not in season.

The entrance to the cave. It had to be.

He spun, wanting to sprint back to Morgan, but knowing the last thing they needed was to attract attention. It seemed like an eternity before he saw the beginning of the path that led up the hill. Morgan was there, her back to him.

He stopped abruptly. Standing beside her was Melehan, holding the pendant. "Morgan!" Cernunnos shouted and started to run. She paid no attention. Did Melehan already have her mesmerized? And how had he gotten hold of that damn pendant anyway? Morgan had thrown it away. Cernunnos cursed. He should never have let that happen. He should have kept it. "Morgan!" he shouted again.

She turned, her green eyes glassy as she stared at him.

"It's me! Cernunnos! I've found the gate! Wait—" The words died in his throat as the soft, silver-tinkling sound of the horn lulled him. Like a magnet, he felt himself pulled back by an invisible force. He met Morgan's startled eyes for one instant before he was compelled to turn around. He didn't have to look to know who held the horn.

Aoibhill smirked. "Come to me, Cernunnos. You are mine."

Chapter Sixteen

Numbly, Morgan let herself be led toward a small car. Aoibhill had won. Cernunnos had turned away from Morgan when he heard the silver horn. After centuries of being with her, he still heeded Aoibhill's call.

"It's better this way," Melehan spoke soothingly in her ear even as his firm hand moved her along. "You have no idea of the pleasures I am going to introduce you to."

How could anything ever be pleasurable again? Morgan fingered the pendant around her neck. The metal felt strangely cold, yet her hand tingled as though burnt. She started to remove it, but Melehan placed his other hand on hers.

"It stays there."

Morgan frowned. She didn't want the pendant, yet his command was compelling. Her hand suddenly felt heavy as iron beneath his and she dropped it to her side.

"Good girl," he said.

She tried to turn around, but Melehan kept moving. She didn't resist. She'd managed to look over her shoulder. Aoibhill and Cernunnos were not there.

They'd reached the car and Melehan opened the door for her. She looked longingly at where Cernunnos' motorcycle still stood. So he'd left that too. She got into the car. It didn't matter much where Melehan was taking her. Cernunnos was gone.

They didn't go far. Melehan stopped the car in front of a small, wooden frame house that had seen better days. Morgan merely glanced at two men, dressed in suits that didn't fit with their burly frames, who greeted them once they were inside.

"Did you get the stuff?" Melehan asked one of them.

The taller one nodded and reached into his coat pocket and brought out a syringe with a long needle. He handed it to Melehan and then tossed a small, plastic bag containing a white powder on the table by the entrance.

"That should keep her quiet," he said.

Morgan fingered the pendant again. "What is that?"

Melehan moved closer. "Remember when I told you I was going to introduce you to pleasure? This is just the beginning." Quickly, he caught her arm and jabbed the needle in.

It stung and Morgan slapped at his hand. Something was wrong. She needed to leave. But her head... She felt dizzy and then another feeling flashed through her body. Suddenly she was flying. Floating like she did in Faerie. Blurry-eyed and confused, Morgan looked up at Melehan.

"Just relax. You'll get the real rush in a minute."

His eyes were grey. Where had she seen those eyes before? On someone else... Arthur? *Arthur had grey eyes. Arthur had been king when I still lived in Faerie. I remember floating by Arthur's boat on the way to Avalon. Arthur had been kind...* Morgan stumbled and Melehan jerked her arm roughly. *Arm hurts. Arthur wouldn't hurt...* She blinked, trying to clear her head and her eyesight. *Medraut's eyes. But why did Medraut have golden curls? His hair was black.*

"She sure isn't used to the stuff," the shorter man said. "Some high. Her eyes are completely black."

"Yes," Melehan replied. "She'll be addicted in no time."

Morgan danced to the corner of the room and tilted her head. "Is Cernunnos coming soon?"

Melehan smirked. "I imagine he's already come. At least once."

She looked around. "Where is he?"

"He's around. Have patience."

She shrugged and turned her attention to an abstract painting on the wall.

Morgan lifted her arms and twirled across the room. She was happy. She hadn't been able to float since she'd stepped through the pool.

* * * *

Cernunnos swore under his breath. In the momentary reaction he'd had to the sound of that damn horn, Aoibhill had managed to transport them to a room in some house. She obviously hadn't lost her powers as he and Morgan had.

Morgan. The look on her face as she'd turned had been devastating. Her gaze had gone from glassy enchantment to startled recognition of Aoibhill. Did Morgan think he'd gone willingly with the bitch?

Worse, Melehan had Morgan. Jealousy surged through Cernunnos at the thought of Melehan even touching Morgan's flesh. Rage followed the thought that Melehan might rape her. Without her powers, she only had the strength of a mortal woman. Cernunnos needed to get to her.

But there was that damn horn. He'd used every bit of his considerable strength to resist its spell. He cursed again, ruing the day he'd accepted the 'gift' from Aphrodite and given it to Aoibhill. His own brain must have been addled to do so, but that had been before he'd met Morgan.

Aoibhill walked over to the sofa he was sitting on and sank down gracefully beside him, the side of her breast brushing his arm. Centuries ago, that would have been all that was needed for him to take her. Now, he only wanted Morgan. Still, best to let Aoibhill think he was under her spell until he could escape.

"It's been awhile," he said.

She traced her fingers lightly across his chest. "*That's* all you can say, lover?"

Cernunnos forced a snarl from his face. "How did you get here?"

She nibbled his ear. "Do we need to talk?"

He turned his head slightly away. "What kind of a lover would I be to not want to know what's happened to you since we last saw each other?"

Aoibhill narrowed her eyes. "The last time we saw each other, you were with *her*."

"I tried to explain that to you before I left. You didn't want to listen."

"And I don't now. Anyway, I don't have to worry about her anymore."

The hair at his nape bristled, but he managed to keep his voice calm. "What do you mean by that?"

She shrugged. "Melehan will take care of her."

Anger surged through Cernunnos once again at the thought of Melehan having Morgan mesmerized with the pendant. By all the gods! She might even willingly let him have her! "Morgan told me Melehan had fought with the rebel Saxons and was being hunted by Custennin. How do you know him?"

Aoibhill laughed. "He's my son...and the rightful king of Briton."

"What are you talking about? Arthur left no heir."

She arched a look at him. "Arthur left no heir he *knew* of."

"I think you'd better explain."

With a sigh, she sat back. "I don't know why you're being so difficult. I did all of this for you."

His hair bristled again. "All of what?"

"I had to get you back, Cernunnos." She lowered her lashes and then swept a glance upward at him as she undid the buttons of her blouse. "No other lover has ever been as good as you."

At another time, the vixen would have done him in. At another time, he would have let himself believe her words. Now, he was just irritated at being fawned at. "I find that hard to believe."

"But it's true." Tears welled up in her lavender eyes. "You're the only one I'll ever love."

Love. She didn't know the meaning of the word. He glanced at the exposed breasts that didn't even create a stir in his jeans. *Love is more than just wanting to rut.* The thought would have shocked him once. Morgan had been trying to get him to see that.

"You only think that because I left."

Her eyes suddenly glittered like ice. "You really shouldn't have done that, Cernunnos. I'll have to punish you for it."

"I don't think I care to play that game, Aoibhill."

"It's not a game, I assure you. When you went off with that little mouse, I used the horn to call you, but Myrddin, damn him, deflected the sound. I couldn't enter Briton's Faerie without permission and Morgan le Fey was not about to grant that. So I did the next best thing. I let Arthur's son have me."

Cernunnos frowned. "Medraut?"

"Yes. He'd come to Eire to hire mercenaries. It seemed a golden opportunity."

"For what?"

She looked at him as though he were dim-witted. Mayhap he was.

"If Melehan became king, I could, by royal command, enter Briton," she said patiently. "Then it would only be a matter of time before he'd get rid of Morgan and you would be mine again."

The woman was mad. She had to be. Still, it was wise to placate her to find out where Melehan might have taken Morgan. "You're a Faerie queen, Aoibhill. You reign supreme in your land. What makes you think Morgan would allow the king—whomever he might be—into her queendom?"

She laughed again. "Melehan is not just a man. The other reason I chose Medraut as his sire is because of the intense evil darkness in him. All I had to do was add a few spells to create what I wanted."

His hair practically stood on end. "Which was?"

She looked him squarely in the face. "An incubus."

Cernunnos' blood ran cold. Not only was Morgan held mesmerized by an enchanted pendant, the man who was her captor wasn't human.

* * * *

Cernunnos paced the small bedroom later that afternoon. He glanced at the door with no lock. Evidently, Aoibhill felt the wards she had set around this room would keep him effectively a prisoner. Mayhap she was right. He had tested the invisible barriers earlier, only to find himself shocked and flung backwards each time he tried to open the door or the window. And she had the silver horn. Would he be strong enough to resist it twice?

She had lured him to this room, using every seduction trick he remembered. He'd played along, pretending to be unable to resist.

He heard the front door open and close and then a male voice. Turning down the volume of the actors on the telly, he thought he heard Melehan's voice. Cernunnos inched closer to the door, careful not to touch it.

"Everything is going just how you planned it, Mother. Morgan reacted to the heroin even better than I thought."

"It was a brilliant plan of mine to employ those two Americans we found in London, wasn't it?" Aoibhill purred.

"They have strong stuff. It shouldn't take more that two or three days for her to be completely addicted. She was already scratching and itching when I left."

"Good. I want you to make her beg for it. Wait until she screams and thinks she's going insane, then give her just enough to—"

"I know what I'm doing, Mother. You taught me torture well."

"See that you do it well then. I want that little bitch degraded and humiliated. I want only the most ruthless of men using her. I want her begging them to use her. I want her to have no pride left. Nothing to cling to except the drug."

"Don't worry. Cernunnos won't even recognize her by the time I'm finished," Melehan said with an evil chuckle.

Inside the bedroom, Cernunnos fisted his hands and cursed. The situation was even worse than he thought. Andy had talked about crack addicts on London's streets and that heroin was even worse.

The front door closed and he went to the window. Melehan was getting in a small, black car. Cernunnos only hope of finding Morgan before it was too late was to follow that car.

Summoning every bit of energy he had, he closed his eyes and concentrated. He felt his antlers grow. His tawny mane sleeked down, covering his skin. Hearing and eyesight became more acute while his muscles elongated and stretched into the powerful legs of an enormous stag.

With a roar or rage, he lowered his head and charged the window. He felt the pain of piercing the ward shoot through him like a dozen arrows, but he ignored it. Morgan needed him.

Landing on the soft dirt outside the house, he spotted the car in the distance and broke into a bounding run to follow it.

* * * *

"Why am I so cold?" Morgan rubbed her arms with trembling hands.

Just wait. It gets worse. Melehan watched as Morgan paced the living room in agitation. The drug was wearing off. Soon, she would want to feel its high again. Then he would have her where he wanted her.

"Maybe you should lie down, Morgan. You're looking somewhat ill."

"It's so strange," she said. "I was feeling so good. Now I'm cold. And weak. My legs feel like I've run for kilometers."

"You'll feel so much better after a nap." Melehan soothingly took her arm. "Come with me."

She let herself be led into the bedroom. Melehan set her down on the edge of the bed and knelt to remove her shoes. He reached under the covers for the leg shackle and with a practiced hand, slipped in on her ankle.

Morgan stared down at him. "What are you doing?"

His fangs began to extend as he deftly caught her wrist and cuffed it to the post as well. "We're going to have some fun, Morgan. Trust me."

"But I don't want—"

Her words were cut off by a loud crash and a muffled, "What the hell?" from the one of the bodyguards in the living room followed by another heavy crash. Melehan turned to see a massive stag hurdle through the doorway. It swung its magnificent rack of antlers in his direction and pawed the ground once, before bellowing a challenge.

Melehan hissed as he shifted into his true incubus form. Where the giant creature had come from he had no idea. Deer—especially ones who stood well over five meters at the shoulder—didn't just appear on the streets of Glastonbury.

A shifter then. Wary, Melehan pulled a knife from his boot and began to circle the animal. The stag pivoted slowly, its hot, molten-gold eyes never leaving his face. Why didn't it attack? Melehan had the distinct impression the stag was waiting for him to make a mistake.

With his free hand, he sketched a sign to make him invisible, invoking the words he'd been taught. The stag wouldn't see him coming. One quick jab to the heart and it would be over. He moved in to strike.

And found himself speared and lifted by the wide rack. He landed with a hard thud in a corner and looked up. Lucifer's horns! The animal looked like it was grinning at him. How could it see him? The enchantment always worked.

Blood spurted from the wound in his side. Melehan cursed and put his hand against it to staunch the flow. He muttered another incantation and a firebolt fashioned itself from his blood and flew to the bed, igniting the end of the coverlet.

Morgan screamed.

In one bound, the stag was beside her. He bent his head, one honed prong ripping the links of the cuff from the post. A sharp hoof slashed the leg shackle and Morgan fell from the bed as the flame engulfed her pillow.

Melehan rose to his knees and threw the knife. The stag grunted as it imbedded itself deep in his shoulder and swung his antlered head toward Melehan.

"No, Cern! There's not time!" Morgan coughed with the rapidly rising smoke. The deer hesitated and then turned back to her, nudging her arm and bending down quickly on one leg. She scrambled onto his back and in one tremendous leap, he cleared the door.

Melehan heard sirens in the background, becoming louder. He staggered to the door, leaving a trail of blood in his wake. He barely glanced at the two bodyguards lying on the floor. A lot of help they were.

As he slid into the driver's seat and headed for Aoibhill's place, a thought struck him. Morgan had known the deer. Had called him Cern.

Cernunnos? How in the hell had he escaped Aoibhill?

* * * *

Ignoring the pain from the shoulder wound, Cernunnos carried Morgan into the rented motel room, kicked the door shut, and laid her gently on the bed. She was shaking, her skin cold and clammy, her breathing shallow. He brushed her hair away from her forehead.

"What's happening to me?" she asked in a weak whisper.

"Melehan told Aoibhill he gave you heroin, that you would have a terrible reaction to it soon and want more."

Morgan closed her eyes. "It felt so good, Cern. Now it feels so bad."

He cursed under his breath. "I'm sorry I didn't get to you sooner." He went to the bathroom and returned with a damp cloth and began wiping the sweat from her face and throat. "When I think of what they planned to do to you—"

Her eyes popped back open and she tried to sit up, but Cernunnos stopped her.

"I have to tell you what else they planned."

"Tell me later. Just rest now."

"No." Her voice was weak, but she stuggled on. "Those Americans that were with Melehan...they weren't just body guards that supplied that horrible drug. They're terrorists. I heard them talking about another set of explosions in the London underground."

Cernunnos stared at her. "Are you sure the drug wasn't making you hear things? From what we've read, it isn't Americans that are doing these things."

"That's just it," Morgan said. "They laughed and said they'd never be suspected. They said they were anarc...anarchists. That there was a movement of some sort to overthrow governments. Then Melehan laughed and said with his help, and his mother's, they wouldn't have to worry."

"Aoibhill," Cernunnos said bitterly. "She's got to be stopped."

"But not by us, Cern. You said you found the entrance to Merlin's cave. We must get back home."

He knew she was right. He couldn't risk Aoibhill sounding that horn anywhere close to him. He was weakened through loss of blood and the effort to force the wound to heal. He didn't know if he'd be able to resist. "As soon as you're feeling better, we'll write a letter about their plans and leave it with the clerk to take to the police."

Reaching out to grasp his hand, she gazed up at him. "I thought you had gone with her."

"Never. I made the choice to leave Eire and her long ago." What had he ever seen in Aoibhill? He traced the curve of Morgan's jaw lightly with his thumb. "I've never regretted choosing you."

She managed a wavering smile. "We've always lit the spark for each other, even if there have been other lovers at times."

"Not one lover has been as satisfying as you, Morgan. Ever."

"Not even Gwenhwyfar?"

Cernunnos shook his head. "I think when I first captured her, I wanted to make you jealous because you flirted with Lancelot. Then I wanted to prove to Lancelot that I could get her."

"I flirted with him because you flirted with—"

"Hush." Cernunnos put a finger to her lips. "There'll be no more flirting for either of us."

Tears filled her eyes. "Am I dying then?"

Startled, it took him a moment to understand her, then he gathered her quickly in his arms. "No. I'm saying this is all wrong. These weeks we've been in this century—without our full powers—we've learned to depend on each other. We've had to cope. I never realized how strong you are, Morgan. You had more courage than I did when it came to having to adjust to all this. I don't think I could have... Bel's Fires! What if I had lost you today? To the drug or the fire? Or to that damn incubus? I nearly failed to protect you!"

Morgan leaned back in his arms and looked up at him wonderingly. "You risked your life for me just like Lancelot did for Gwenhwyfar."

Cernunnos cupped her face in his hands. "I think I understand now what they were trying to tell us. I couldn't—wouldn't want to—continue to exist without you."

He took a deep, shuddering breath. "I love you, Morgan."

Tears gathered and overflowed in her eyes, but these were tears of happiness. "I love you, too, Cern."

* * * *

Aoibhill paced the room furiously before turning on Melehan. "Those men are dead and Morgan escaped? How could you have let this happen?"

Melehan was in no mood for a lecture. His body was sore from having been thrown and his wound, though closed, still ached. "How did Cernunnos escape from you, Mother?" he asked sarcastically. "I wouldn't have had a problem if he hadn't showed up."

White-lipped, she resumed her pacing. "I don't know. The wards were holding. He'd tested them earlier. Maybe his animal form was able to withstand more pain."

"Or maybe he had stronger magic," Melehan goaded.

She whirled on him, points of fire flashing in her eyes. "There is nothing stronger than black magic."

Melehan shrugged. "It took several times for your horn to work."

Aoibhill fingered it as it dangled from a chain around her neck. "It works when I'm close enough to him." She got a faraway look in her eyes. "I always did like him in his stag form. So powerful and virile..."

"Save your lust, Mother. They're gone."

She focused on him. "I think I know where they might be. Cernunnos said something about finding a gate just before I summoned him to me. If they found some kind of entrance into the Tor, they'll come back."

Melehan narrowed his eyes. "When I was with the Saxons, there was a legend already building that Myrddin lay buried in a cave in that hill, but no one could find it."

"Well, Cernunnos just did." Aoibhill's eyes narrowed. "And when he returns to it, we'll be waiting." She played with the little silver horn. "And, this time, he won't escape."

Chapter Seventeen

Cernunnos parked the bike some distance away from the Tor. He gave it a loving pat. Morgan watched him. "I wish you could take it with us."

A corner of his mouth quirked up. "I'm sure Lancelot would insist on learning how to ride it."

Morgan returned the smile. "Gwenhwyfar, too,"

They moved in silence toward the hill. Twilight hung low, turning the skies a soft shade of lavender, and for a moment, Morgan could almost envision the mists that used to surround this place.

"This way," Cern said as they moved away from the path and came to the place where the white stag had disappeared. "Look down."

Morgan knelt and touched the still-blooming primroses beneath the ledge. "A Faerie circle."

"Yes." Cernunnos put his hand on the moss-covered boulder and pushed. "This cap ledge looks like it should move." He tried another angle, grunting, and then another. Sweat glistened on his arms as the massive muscles strained. "I can't lift it or roll it," he finally said.

Morgan batted her lashes at him. "Well, if you're through being all manly, let me try." She knelt again and picked a flower, murmuring softly.

The air began to sparkle as misty female forms materialized and flitted about in pastel shades of pink, blue and green, taking time to pose gracefully in mid-air as they tilted their heads and eyed Cernunnos.

"It is I who summoned you." Morgan tried to keep the irritation out of her voice. Her faeries had always been attracted to Cern; apparently, it was no different in this century.

One, dressed in a gossamer gown of pale gold, turned her attention to Morgan. "I am Morwen, the queen here," she said in a regal voice. "Who might you be?"

Morgan stared at her. "I am Morgan le Fey!"

The faerie's lovely forehead creased. "My great-great-grandmother was Morgan le Fey."

Morgan felt her mouth gape and quickly closed it. She wasn't anyone's grandmother! Beside her, Cernunnos was looking highly amused. "She does look like you," he said helpfully.

She started to open her mouth again and then didn't, not sure what she could say to that. Morwen was beautiful. Morgan gave Cernunnos a slanted look, but he had an innocent expression on his face. Ummm. "Morwen, we need to get inside the hill. Cernunnos thinks this is the opening."

Morwen's slanted green eyes widened slightly as she turned to him. "The god of the Wild Hunt? You are my great, great grandfather!"

It was Morgan's turn to chucklewhen Cernunnos squirmed.

"Your legend still lives, you know," Morwen said.

Cernunnos' chest expanded. "Does it now?"

She nodded. "Along with King Arthur's, certes." Cern looked like a small boy who had just had his prize trophy taken away and awarded to someone else. "What do they say about Arthur?"

"Well, this *is* Glastonbury. The myth is that King Arthur and his knights are released from the hill at Cadbury and ride ghostly horses across the sky on Samhain and that Cernunnos rides after them from the Tor."

He lifted a brow. "*After* them? I think not—"

Morgan did grin this time. Parts of his personality hadn't changed. "What's important," she said to Morwen, "is that we get inside this hill. We think there is a portal that will take us back to our own time."

Morwen studied them a moment and then she nodded. "The words Nimue used to seal it have been handed down, should the need ever come. But it can only be opened once and it will close behind you."

Cernunnos took Morgan's hand. "We might be entombed in there. Do you want to look for another portal?"

Morgan shook her head as she looked down at his strong, bronze-colored hand holding hers. "We'll be together." Cernunnos tensed suddenly, his head high, nostrils flared and then she heard the silvery tinkle of a small horn.

"Oh, no," she whispered and clung to him.

"Oh, yes," Aoibhill said as she stepped from the increasing shadows of dusk. "He is mine, mouse. Did you really think you'd get to keep him?" She lifted the horn to her lips and blew again. "Come here, Cernunnos."

He stood his ground. "Not this time, Aoibhill. It's over."

She hissed. "Come here."

Melehan stepped up beside her, dangling the pendant. "You, too, Morgan. Come to me."

She felt herself sway and then felt Cernunnos' arm slip around her waist. "No," she said. "You have no power over me."

Aoibhill blew the horn again and then frowned when Cernunnos didn't move. "Dark magic is the strongest there is. Those faeries cannot be protecting you."

"They aren't," Cernunnos answered and then raised Morgan's hand, still clasped in his. "Love is protecting us. It's the strongest magic there is."

Behind them, the ledge of the boulder moved away. Cernunnos stepped backward, pulling Morgan through the entrance with him. "Go home, Aoibhill," he said.

"No!" Screaming with rage, she threw a firebolt but the gap had already closed. For a moment the rock turned red like molten lava and then the heat faded, leaving Morgan and Cernunnos inside a very dark cave.

* * * *

On Avalon, Nimue straightened suddenly from digging in the herb garden. She hurried through the healing house of glass to the top of the small hill behind it. The priestesses would be there to do perform the moon ritual as it rose over the water far below.

Astrala turned as Nimue approached. "What is it?"

"The seal of the cave has been broken," she said.

Rhiannon arched a brow. "Myrddin's ready to go to the Other World finally?"

Arianrhod frowned. "My Wheel did not spin this Fate."

Camelot's Enchantment

Nimue shook her head. "When Arthur and I entombed Myrddin's body, I enchanted the entrance so that no one would ever find it. I also placed a special spell on the seal that it could be opened only once if ever the need arose. Myrddin wanted to be left in peace."

"I imagine he did," Hetaira said with a laugh. "Morgan riding on his shoulder for forty earth years and tweaking his ear every time she wanted something probably was a bit irritating."

Nimue smiled at that. "I was the only one who could see her. Poor Myrddin. Arthur always thought he was talking to himself." She closed her eyes, drawing her energy in. "It's not Myrddin who opened the cave, though." The priestesses were silent while she concentrated. Then, with a gasp, her eyes sprang open. "It's Morgan! She's in the hollow hill!"

Astrala glided over. "Are you sure?"

"I saw her. Cernunnos is with her."

"Well, then," Brighid said as she set down her harp, "you can just go back and bring them home."

Nimue shook her head. "The seal can only be opened once. The portal home is at the top in the circle of stones. Outside the hill. As immortals, they're trapped for eternity."

"My Wheel did not spin that Fate either," Arianrhod said. "We have a full moon. We have the power-of-nine here. Mayhap we can help them."

Inanna looked thoughtful. "It might work." She reached out her hands. "Come sisters. Form the circle. It is time to bring Morgan and Cernunnos back to Faerie."

* * * *

Morgan was glad to feel Cernunnos' strong, warm hand wrapped around her own in the darkness of the cave. As they stood there, the inky darkness faded a little as though some small glow of light emanated from somewhere. Morgan felt her ear points grow.

"Myrddin is here," she said softly. "I feel his essence." She tugged at Cernunnos' hand. "This way, I think."

"Let me go first so you don't run into something." Cernunnos slipped one arm around her waist and held the other one out to feel the wall. The pale wash of light faded the darkness even more as they shuffled along. Cernunnos stopped suddenly.

221

"What is it?" Morgan asked.

"There's a ledge...no, a rock, I think. It seems to be round."

"Myrddin's tomb?"

"Mayhap. Let me see if I can roll it." He let go of Morgan and she heard him grunt with effort and then the sound of earth being scraped. In another moment, the rock moved and she gasped.

Candles flickered in small sconces, illuminating thousands of sparkling crystals embedded in the walls. Their blues, greens, yellows and red twinkled with the draft from the removed stone. A hollow log lay along one wall and across the small enclosure sat a man in long, cobalt robes reading a scroll. He looked up, his piercing golden eyes, so much like an eagle's, appraised them.

"I never thought I'd be glad to see you again, Morgan," he said.

"Myrddin!" She squealed in delight and danced over to him.

He covered his ears before she could get to them. "Still impulsive, I see."

She ignored the barb. "You're alive! How can that be?"

He rolled up the scroll and set it aside. "When I brought Arthur back, I lost my prana—my life force—and Nimue thought I was dead. She entombed me here. When I woke up, I realized she had cast a spell upon this place." He pointed to the scroll. "I've been trying to figure out what it is since then." He peered up at her. "So what year is this?"

"2005," Morgan replied and reached to push a lock of his now-silver hair off his forehead.

He ducked. "No ears!" Then he took a deep breath. "Fifteen hundred years have gone by? What happened to Arthur?"

She told him what had taken place. "Arthur sleeps now in Avalon," she finished.

Myrddin looked from her to Cernunnos. "So what are you two doing here?"

Quickly, Cernunnos explained about Aoibhill and Melehan.

Myrddin stood. "We have to find them before they wreak havoc on the world."

Cernunnos shook his head. "The entrance is sealed. We were hoping to find a portal to Faerie in here."

"Not in the hill," Myrddin replied. "There is one at the top inside the circle of stones. It was where I came through."

Morgan looked at Cernunnos and then at Myrddin. "The stones are gone. Now there is a remains of a church dedicated to St. Michael."

Myrddin snorted. "So the Christos people won?"

"Not entirely," Cernunnos said. "Faeries still exist. Arthur's legend still exists."

"There are those New-Age druids who think they know the Old Ways," Morgan added.

Myrddin closed his eyes in thought. "When you were on the hilltop, did you feel any energy?"

Morgan nodded. "I did, but I couldn't harness it."

"Then the portal still remains," Myrddin said and opened his eyes.

"But how do we get to the top of the hill?" Morgan asked.

He picked up his staff and held it high. Crystals began to break and fall away as a crack opened in the wall, revealing a stone stairway. "This leads to the circle," he said, "and opened at one time through a standing stone. If that's gone, I'm not sure what we'll find."

Silently, they made their way up the rough-hewn stairs. When they reached the top of the hill, a hard layer of rock and dirt formed a ceiling. Cernunnos studied it. "My antlers are sharper than anything we have," he said. "Stand back and let me shift."

Morgan watched as he used them to pick at the rock while Myrddin pounded the hard-packed dirt with his staff. She remembered an incantation Sadi liked to use when Ganus was with her and there was no bed nearby. It softened the earth. Morgan began murmuring it softly in time to the rhythm of the steady beating of Cernunnos' pronged horns.

It fell in suddenly, showering them in grimy dust, but none of them minded as they scrambled out in the cool night air. The full moon hung suspended just over the horizon, its silver ball throwing a misty cast over the fields below. She moved toward the tower of St. Michael's.

"It was here that I felt the pull," she said as Cernunnos and Myrddin joined her.

Myrddin nodded as he tossed his head back and raised his staff. "Goddess of Avalon! Open the portal to your servants that we may come home!"

And, in a blinding flash of light, they were gone.

* * * *

Morgan looked around the living room of her stone cottage deep in the heart of Faerie. They were back! She moved about, touching objects, assuring herself that this was real. Even though the other faeries and the forest creatures as well had gathered to welcome them back, none of it seemed real until now. They were home.

Cernunnos watched her with a strange look on his face. She turned her attention to him. "What is it?"

He shook his head. "It's as though I'm seeing you for the first time. Beneath your impulsiveness and curiosity about everything is a little girl looking for something real and solid."

Morgan walked over to him and laid a hand on his broad chest as she arched an eyebrow. "*You're* real and solid."

His eyes sparked and turned whiskey-colored. "If you move your hand lower you'll find something else that's hard and solid."

She laughed as she complied. "Oh, Cern, if feels so good to be able to do this again without fear of Aoib—"

Cernunnos silenced her with a kiss. "I don't want to hear her name." He nuzzled Morgan's neck softly. "I think it's time we take advantage of being home." Keeping his mouth pressed to hers, he backwalked her into the bedroom. By the time they reached the bed, they were both naked.

"Just like old times," Morgan giggled as she bounced on the bed.

"Only better," Cernunnos replied as he joined her, "because now I know I want to make *love* to you, not just plunder you."

"Oh, Cern," Morgan sighed as she put her arms around his neck and pulled him down to her, "I've been waiting for centuries to hear that and I didn't even know it."

He slanted his mouth over hers again, nibbling gently on her lower lip, sucking it into his mouth. He let his tongue glide slowly over her parted lips, teasing her, loving the feel of her arching against him. He moved one hand slowly along her ribs, his fingertips just grazing the side swell of her breast.

Morgan made a soft, little mewling noise in her throat. When had the man become such an expert as such exquisite torture? Her nipples tightened into tingling buds needing to be touched, yet he lazily drew circles around them with a finger. His tongue only flicked hers as she parted her lips even more. With a whimper, she cradled his head in her palms and attacked his mouth, sliding her tongue in to do battle with his and was rewarded with a low growl. His tongue filled her then, exploring her fully.

"Have mercy, Cern. I can't wait any more."

"I've just begun, my love."

"No! I mean...yes. But... Cern, I mean it. I want you inside of me. *Now.*"

The tip of him brushed against her opening. "You're *sure?*"

"Yes!"

With a smooth thrust, he filled her, relishing the heat of her tight sheath. He could feel the inner walls begin to grasp him and he thrust hard and deep, feeling the smooth dome of her womb just as her body convulsed and she spasmed, screaming his name.

Cernunnos felt his erection swell even further and then, in a burst, he flooded her.

She cried out again with pleasure and he slumped over her, burying his face against her neck. "I love you, Morgan," he said when he could catch his breath again. She murmured her assent sleepily, but when he tried to roll off of her, her legs wrapped around his thighs and she held him captive still inside of her. He gave her an inquiring look.

"*Now* you can make love to me," Morgan said.

Incredibly, he found himself hard again. Making love to Morgan when *real* love was involved gave him a deeper connection than he'd ever experienced in all his long life. Finally, their souls were mated, as well as their bodies.

"If you insist, my lady."

Epilogue

Lancelot and Gwenhwyfar, along with Myrddin, awaited them in the mists of the scrying pool the next morning when Morgan and Cernunnos finally emerged from the stone cottage. Morgan was surprised to see the priestesses of Avalon standing on the other side of the Faerie ward.

"Welcome back," Inanna said quietly. "We had feared you lost to us."

Morgan sketched a sign that made the ward dissolve, although the mist continued to swirl. "There will be no more barriers between us. You will be free to enter Faerie as you wish." She looked at Cernunnos and he nodded slightly. "We have no desire to ever leave here again."

Myrddin raised both brows. "You clung to my shoulder and tweaked my ears for forty years because you wanted to experience mortal life," he said. "What changed your mind?"

Morgan shook her head. "It's a cruel world. I know there have always been wars—I had to sit and listen to the tedious battle plans you made with Arthur—but *those* were for a reason. Defending our lands, defending our way of life. In the twenty-first century, people—they call themselves terrorists—destroy *themselves* even as they kill others. They don't want to conquer the land like the Romans did. They aren't looking for a new place to live, like the Saxons, either. They have some belief that if they kill, they will be blessed by their gods.

"Is there no one who wants peace?" Lancelot asked as he paced.

"There are," Cernunnos answered. "There was a meeting of eight of the strongest countries while we were there. And these terrorists managed to cause explosions on the big metal horses that hundreds of people ride in tunnels while they were meeting."

"Trains, Cern," Morgan said.

"Tunnels?" asked Gwenhwyfar.

"It's a strange world," Morgan replied, "but Cern is right. There are many people who want peace." She paused. "I'm afraid for them though. While I was captive, I heard plans that people from the nation that was heading the peace talks were actually going to do more horrid things than what has already happened...and that the current terrorists would be blamed for it. Melehan laughed and said he and Aoibhill were going to help them wreck havoc in the world."

Lancelot's head snapped up. "*Melehan* is still there?"

Gwenhwyfar gave him a wary look. "Lance—"

He looked down at her. "I can't let Medraut's son follow in his footsteps."

"It's not our world, Lancelot. Destiny and Fate are not ours to play with."

"You know what evil Morgana and Medraut caused, Gwen. Arthur should have let me kill them before Cam's Landing ever began."

"He wouldn't have the blood of murder on your hands, Lance."

"I know." He looked grim. "Yet, because they lived, you were nearly raped and left to die...and Morgana brought the plague to Briton. How many lives did that take?" He shook his head. "Medraut was evil, but he was human. Melehan is an incubus, capable of much more damage. And Aoibhill is much more powerful than Morgana ever was. I must do this, Gwen. I must stop them."

Morgan crinkled her forehead. "How are you going to do that?"

Lancelot straightened and looked at the priestesses. "I want to go to the twenty-first century. Will you send me?"

"Lancelot, no!" Gwenhwyfar cried. "We've made peace with Morgan and Cernunnos. We can be happy here in Faerie."

He took her hand. "Remember when you said that all the days were alike here? That whatever we wanted, we could have? That there were no real problems? It's a nice existence, I grant that, but humans are struggling. Humans will die before their time if we allow Melehan and Aoibhill to roam the earth. I am half-fey. I can track them and destroy them."

"It is a noble thing, this quest of yours," Astrala said gently before Gwenhwyfar could answer him.

Lancelot looked over at her. "Galahad had a quest. He sought—and found—the Holy Grail. I was not pure-in-heart like he was, but the Grail granted me a glimpse of it. Enough for me to come through the portal and find Gwenhwyfar again. Enough to bring us to Avalon a second time." He turned back to Gwenhwyfar. "Please understand. This is my way to repay my debt. You'll be safe here until I can return."

Her eyes sparked green flames. "You aren't going without me, Lancelot du Lac."

"I don't—" He stopped as Astrala cupped her hands and a light began to glow between them.

"Do not argue, my children. Watch."

From within that globe of luminous white, a form took shape. Lancelot and Gwenhwyfar shaded their eyes as the brilliant luminescence nearly blinded them. A silver chalice, etched in runes, a ribbon of gold along the lip shimmered in the air.

The Grail.

"Yes," Astrala said as she opened her hands and the Grail grew, expanding upward and outward, hovering over the scrying pool. "Its power will take you there."

The earth began to shake. Gwenhwyfar clung to Lancelot's arm and then, slowly her eyes widened as shadows began to shift in the tendrils of drifting mist. The forms grew larger and horses emerged, war-hooves pounding the ground. She looked up and gasped.

Arthur and his knights of the Round Table lined up in battle formation.

Lancelot stared too. "Arthur? Gawain. Gaheris. Gareth... Bedwyr—"

"I thought you might want some help," Astrala said to Lancelot before turning to Arthur. "It is time for you to ride once more."

He nodded gravely. "We are ready."

Galahad moved forward, leading Lancelot's favorite mount.

"Pryderi!" Lancelot ran his hand over the stallion's black satin coat. "And Galahad. Son. There's so much I want to say—"

Galahad shook his head. "This time we ride together, Father." He motioned for Peredur to bring Gwenhwyfar's horse,

Safere, forward. "And knowing my step-mother, she's not going to stay behind."

Gwenhwyfar vaulted onto the sorrel's back. "Just give me a sword."

"I suspect you'll be using other kinds of weapons." Astrala raised her hands in supplication. The cup grew larger still, a transparent arch appearing in its bowl. "That is the entrance and the way, May the Goddess go with you."

Arthur's eyes swept over the small group of priestesses and then his countenance beamed. "Nimue."

"I'm not staying behind either," she said as she rode forward on the white stag she favored. Cernunnos looked sharply at the animal and then at her.

"Or I," Mryddin said as he gestured his mule forward. "I might as well find out what I missed sitting in that cave for fifteen hundred years." He gave Morgan a sharp glance. "You're not coming, are you?"

She shook her head and leaned against Cernunnos as he wrapped an arm around her waist. "I've found what I want right here in Faerie."

"Good luck to you," Cernunnos added. "I may ride the Hunt—"

"I don't think so," Morgan murmured. "I have other plans for you."

Arthur laughed and then he pulled Excalibur and raised it high. "For freedom!" he called and spurred Valiant forward through the shimmering arch.

One by one his knights leapt after him, swords drawn. When the last of them was through, Astrala lifted her hands once more and the Grail drifted toward her, shrouding her in its light.

When the brightness diminished, only the battle cry of freedom lingered in the air.

About the Author

An avid reader of anything medieval, Cynthia Breeding has taught the traditional Arthurian legends to high school sophomores for fifteen years. She owns more than three hundred books, fictional and non-fictional, on the subject. More information on Arthur, Gwenhwyfar and Lancelot is available on her website, listed below.

She lives on the bay in Corpus Christi, Texas, with her Bichon Frise, Nicki, and enjoys sailing and horseback riding on the beach.

Readers can reach her on her website: www.cynthiabreeding.com.

Camelot's Enchantment

Praise for
Highland Press Books!

Camelot's Enchantment is a highly original and captivating tale!
~ *Joy Nash, USA Today Best Seller*
* * * *

An anthology by amazing women with character and grace—
incredible writers, wonderful stories! **For Your Heart Only** is
not to be missed!
~ *Heather Graham, NYT Best Seller*
* * * *

Brynn Chapman makes you question how far science should take humanity.
Project Mendel blurs the distinction between genetics and horror and
merges them in a reality all too plausible. A gripping read.
~*Jennifer Linforth, Author, Historical Fiction and Romance*
* * * *

Kemberlee Shortland's **A Piece of My Heart** is terrific romantic/suspense
fiction to savor and share with family and friends.
~*Viviane Crystal, Crystal Reviews*
* * * *

From betrayal, to broken hearts, to finding love again, **Second Time
Around** has a story for just about anyone. these fine ladies created stories
that will always stay fresh in my heart; ones I will treasure forever.
~ *Cherokee , Coffee Time Romance & More*
* * * *

The Mosquito Tapes - Nobody tells a bio-terror story better than Chris
Holmes. Just nobody. And like all of Chris Holmes' books, this one begins
well—when San Diego County Chief Medical Examiner Jack Youngblood
discovers a strange mosquito in the pocket of a murder victim. Taut, tingly,
and downright scary, The Mosquito Tapes will keep you reading well into the
night. But best be wary: Spray yourself with Deet and have a
fly swatter nearby.
~ *Ben F. Small, author of Alibi On Ice and The Olive
Horseshoe, a Preditors & Editors Top Ten Pick*
* * * *

Cynthia Breeding's **Prelude to Camelot** is a lovely and fascinating read, a
book worthy of being shelved with my Arthurania fiction and non-fiction.
~ *Brenda Thatcher, Mystique Books*
* * * *

Romance on Route 66 by Judith Leigh and Cheryl Norman –
Norman and Leigh break the romance speed limit on America's
historic roadway.
~ *Anne Krist, Ecataromance, Reviewers' Choice Award Winner*

Camelot's Enchantment

* * * *

Ah, the memories that **Operation: L.O.V.E.** brings to mind. As an Air Force nurse who married an Air Force fighter pilot, I relived the days of glory through each and every story. While covering all the military branches, each story holds a special spark of its own that readers will love!

~ Lori Avocato, Best Selling Author

* * * *

In **Fate of Camelot**, Cynthia Breeding develops the Arthur-Lancelot-Gwenhwyfar relationship. In many Arthurian tales, Guinevere is a rather flat character. Cynthia Breeding gives her a depth of character as the reader sees her love for Lancelot and her devotion to the realm as its queen. The reader feels the pull she experiences between both men. In addition, the reader feels more of the deep friendship between Arthur and Lancelot seen in Malory's Arthurian tales. In this area, Cynthia Breeding is more faithful to the medieval Arthurian tradition than a glamorized Hollywood version. She does not gloss over the difficulties of Gwenhwyfar's role as queen and as woman, but rather develops them to give the reader a vision of a woman who lives her role as queen and lover with all that she is.

~ Merri, Merrimon Books

* * * *

Rape of the Soul - Ms. Thompson's characters are unforgettable. Deep, promising and suspenseful this story was. I couldn't put it down. Around every corner was something that you didn't know was going to happen. If you love a sense of history in a book, then I suggest reading this book!

~ Ruth Schaller, Paranormal Romance Reviews

* * * *

Static Resistance and Rose – An enticing, fresh voice. Lee Roland knows how to capture your heart.

~ Kelley St. John, National Readers Choice Award Winner

* * * *

Southern Fried Trouble - Katherine Deauxville is at the top of her form with mayhem, sizzle and murder.

~ Nan Ryan, NY Times Best-Selling Author

* * * *

Madrigal: A Novel of Gaston Leroux's Phantom of the Opera takes place four years after the events of the original novel. The classic novel aside, this book is a wonderful historical tale of life, love, and choices. However, the most impressive aspect that stands out to me is the writing. Ms. Linforth's prose is phenomenally beautiful and hauntingly breathtaking.

~ Bonnie-Lass, Coffee Time Romance

* * * *

Cave of Terror by Amber Dawn Bell - Highly entertaining and fun, **Cave of Terror** was impossible to put down. Though at times dark and evil, Ms. Bell never failed to inject some light-hearted humor into the story. Delightfully funny with a true sense of teenagers, Cheyenne is believable and her emotional struggles are on par with most teens. The author gave just enough background to understand the workings of her vampires. I truly enjoyed Ryan and Constantine. Ryan was adorable and a teenager's dream. Constantine was deliciously dark. Ms. Bell has done an admirable job of telling a story suitable for young adults.

Cynthia Breeding

~ Dawnie, Fallen Angel Reviews

* * * *

The Sense of Honor - Ashley Kath-Bilsky has written a historical romance of the highest caliber. This reviewer fell in love with the hero and was cheering for the heroine all the way through. The plot is exciting, characters are multi-dimensional, and the secondary characters bring life to the story. Sexual tension rages through this story and Ms. Kath-Bilsky gives her readers a breathtaking romance. The love scenes are sensual and very romantic. This reviewer was very pleased with how the author handled all the secrets and both characters reacted very maturely when the secrets finally came to light.

~ Valerie, Love Romances and More

* * * *

Highland Wishes by Leanne Burroughs. The storyline, set in a time when tension was high between England and Scotland, is a fast-paced tale. The reader can feel this author's love for Scotland and its many wonderful heroes. This reviewer was easily captivated by the story and was enthralled by it until the end. The reader will laugh and cry as you read this wonderful story. The reader feels all the pain, torment and disillusionment felt by both main characters, but also the joy and love they felt. Ms. Burroughs has crafted a well-researched story that gives a glimpse into Scotland during a time when there was upheaval and war for independence. This reviewer commends her for a wonderful job done.

~Dawn Roberto, Love Romances

* * * *

I adore this Scottish historical romance! **Blood on the Tartan** has more history than some historical romances—but never dry history! Readers will find themselves completely immersed in the scene, the history and the characters. Chris Holmes creates a multi-dimensional theme of justice in his depiction of all the nuances and forces at work from the laird down to the land tenants. This intricate historical detail emanates from the story itself, heightening the suspense and the reader's understanding of the history in a vivid manner as if it were current and present. The extra historical detail just makes their life stories more memorable and lasting because the emotions were grounded in events. **Blood On The Tartan** is a must read for romance and historical fiction lovers of Scottish heritage.

~Merri, Merrimon Reviews

* * * *

Chasing Byron by Molly Zenk is a page turner of a book not only because of the engaging characters, but also by the lovely prose. Reading this book was a jolly fun time all through the eyes of Miss Woodhouse, yet also one that touches the heart. It was an experience I would definitely repeat. Ms. Zenk must have had a glorious time penning this story.

~Orange Blossom, Long and Short Reviews

* * * *

Moon of the Falling Leaves is an incredible read. The characters are not only believable, but the blending in of how Swift Eagle shows Jessica and her children the acts of survival is remarkably done. Diane Davis White pens a poignant tale that really grabbed this reader. She tells a descriptive story of discipline, trust and love in a time where hatred and prejudice abounded among many. This rich tale offers vivid imagery of the beautiful scenery and

landscape, and brings in the tribal customs of each person, as Jessica and Swift Eagle search their heart.

~Cherokee, Coffee Time Romance

* * * *

Jean Harrington's **The Barefoot Queen** is a superb historical with a lushly painted setting. I adored Grace for her courage and the cleverness with which she sets out to make Owen see her love for him. The bond between Grace and Owen is tenderly portrayed and their love had me rooting for them right up until the last page. Ms. Harrington's **The Barefoot Queen** is a treasure in the historical romance genre you'll want to read for yourself! Five Star Pick of the Week!!!

~ Crave More Romance

* * * *

Almost Taken by Isabel Mere takes the reader on an exciting adventure. The compelling characters of Deran Morissey, the Earl of Atherton, and Ava Fychon, a young woman from Wales, find themselves drawn together as they search for her missing siblings.
Readers will watch in interest as they fall in love and overcome obstacles. This is a sensual romance, and a creative and fast moving storyline that will enthrall readers. Ava, who is highly spirited and stubborn, will win the respect of the readers for her courage and determination. Deran, who is rumored in the beginning to be an ice king, not caring about anyone, will prove how wrong people's perceptions can be. **Almost Taken** is an emotionally moving historical romance that I highly recommend.

~ Anita, The Romance Studio

* * * *

Leanne Burroughs easily will captivate the reader with intricate details, a mystery that ensnares the reader and characters that will touch their hearts.
By the end of the first chapter, this reviewer was enthralled with **Her Highland Rogue** and was rooting for Duncan and Catherine to admit their love. Laughter, tears and love shine through this wonderful novel. This reviewer was amazed at Ms. Burroughs' depth and perception in this storyline. Her wonderful way with words plays itself through each page like a lyrical note and will captivate the reader till the very end.
Read **Her Highland Rogue** and be transported to a time full of mystery and promise of a future. This reviewer is highly recommending this book for those who enjoy an engrossing Scottish tale full of humor, love and laughter.

~Dawn Roberto, Love Romances

* * * *

Bride of Blackbeard by Brynn Chapman is a compelling tale of sorrow, pain, love, and hate. From the moment I started reading about Constanza and her upbringing, I was torn. Each of the people she encounters on her journey has an experience to share, drawing in the reader more. Ms. Chapman sketches a story that tugs at the heartstrings. I believe many will be touched in some way by this extraordinary book that leaves much thought.

~ Cherokee, Coffee Time Romance

* * * *

Isabel Mere's skill with words and the turn of a phrase makes **Almost Guilty** a joy to read. Her characters reach out and pull the reader into the trials, tribulations, simple pleasures, and sensual joy that they enjoy.

Ms. Mere unravels the tangled web of murder, smuggling, kidnapping, hatred and faithless friends, while weaving a web of caring, sensual love that leaves a special joy and hope in the reader's heart.

~ *Camellia, Long and Short Reviews*
* * * *

Beats A Wild Heart - In the ancient, Celtic land of Cornwall, Emma Hayward searched for a myth and found truth. The legend of the black cat of Bodmin Moor is a well known Cornish legend. Jean Adams has merged the essence of myth and romance into a fascinating story which catches the imagination. I enjoyed the way the story unfolded at a smooth and steady pace with Emma and Seth appearing as real people who feel an instant attraction for one another. At first the story appears to be straightforward, but as it evolves mystery, love and intrigue intervene to make a vibrant story with hidden depths. Once you start reading you won't be able to put this book down.

~ *Orchid, Long and Short Reviews*
* * * *

***Down Home Ever Lovin' Mule* Blues** by Jacquie Rogers - How can true love fail when everyone and their mule, cat, and skunk know that Brody and Rita belong together, even if Rita is engaged to another man?
Needless to say, this is a fabulous roll on the floor while laughing out loud story. I am so thrilled to discover this book, and the author who wrote it. Rarely do I locate a story with as much humor, joy, and downright lust spread so thickly on the pages that I am surprised I could turn the pages. A treasure not to be missed.

~*Suziq2, Single Titles.com*
* * * *

Saving Tampa - What if you knew something horrible was going to happen but you could prevent it? Would you tell someone? What if you saw it in a vision and had no proof? Would you risk your credibility to come forward? These are the questions at the heart of ***Saving Tampa***, an on-the-edge-of-your-seat thriller from Jo Webnar, who has written a wonderful suspense that is as timely as it is entertaining.

~ *Mairead Walpole, Reviews by Crystal*
* * * *

When the Vow Breaks by Judith Leigh - This book is about a woman who fights breast cancer. I assumed it would be extremely emotional and hard to read, but it was not. The storyline dealt more with the commitment between a man and a woman, with a true belief of God.
The intrigue was that of finding a rock to lean upon through faith in God. Not only did she learn to lean on her relationship with Him, but she also learned how to forgive her husband. This is a great look at not only a breast cancer survivor, but also a couple whose commitment to each other through their faith grew stronger. It is an easy read and one I highly recommend.

~ *Brenda Talley, The Romance Studio*
* * * *

A Heated Romance by Candace Gold - A fascinating romantic suspense tells the story of Marcie O'Dwyer, a female firefighter who has had to struggle to prove herself. While the first part of the book seems to focus on the romance and Marcie's daily life, the second part transitions into a suspense novel as Marcie witnesses something suspicious at one of the fires. Her life is endangered by what she possibly knows and I found myself anticipating the outcome almost as much as Marcie.

~ *Lilac, Long and Short Reviews*

* * * *

Into the Woods by R.R. Smythe - This Young Adult Fantasy will send chills down your spine. I, as the reader, followed Callum and witnessed everything he and his friends went through as they attempted to decipher the messages. At the same time, I watched Callum's mother, Ellsbeth, as she walked through the Netherwood. Each time Callum deciphered one of the four messages, some villagers awakened. Through the eyes of Ellsbeth, I saw the other sleepers wander, make mistakes, and be released from the Netherwood, leaving Ellsbeth alone. Excellent reading for any age of fantasy fans!

~ *Detra Fitch, Huntress Reviews*

* * * *

Like the Lion, the Witch, and the Wardrobe, ***Dark Well of Decision*** is a grand adventure with a likable girl who is a little like all of us. Zoe's insecurities are realistically drawn and her struggle with both her faith and the new direction her life will take is poignant. The references to the Bible and the teachings presented are appropriately captured. Author Anne Kimberly is an author to watch; her gift for penning a grand childhood adventure is a great one. This one is well worth the time and money spent.

~*Lettetia, Coffee Time Romance*

* * * *

The Crystal Heart by Katherine Deauxville brims with ribald humor and authentic historical detail. Enjoy!

~ *Virginia Henley, NY Times bestselling author*

* * * *

In Sunshine or In Shadow by Cynthia Owens - If you adore the stormy heroes of 'Wuthering Heights' and 'Jane Eyre' (and who doesn't?) you'll be entranced by Owens' passionate story of Ireland after the Great Famine, and David Burke - a man from America with a hidden past and a secret name. Only one woman, the fiery, luscious Siobhan, can unlock the bonds that imprison him. Highly recommended for those who love classic romance and an action-packed story.

~ *Best Selling Author, Maggie Davis,*
AKA Katherine Deauxville

* * * *

Rebel Heart - Jannine Corti Petska used a myriad of emotions to tell this story and the reader quickly becomes entranced in the ways Courtney's stubborn attitude works to her advantage in surviving this disastrous beginning to her new life. This is a wonderful rendition of a different type which is a welcome addition to the historical romance genre. I believe that you will enjoy this story; I know I did!

~ *Brenda Talley, The Romance Studio*

* * * *

Cat O' Nine Tales by Deborah MacGillivray. Enchanting tales from the most wicked, award-winning author today. Spellbinding! A treat for all.

~ *Detra Fitch, Huntress Reviews*

* * * *

Brides of the West by Michèle Ann Young, Kimberly Ivey, and Billie Warren Chai - All three of the stories in this wonderful anthology are based on women who gambled their future in blindly accepting complete strangers for husbands. It was a different era when a woman must have a husband to survive and all three of these phenomenal authors wrote exceptional stories featuring fascinating and gutsy heroines and the men who loved them. For an engrossing read with splendid original stories I highly encourage readers to pick up a copy of this marvelous anthology.
~ Marilyn Rondeau, Reviewers International Organization
* * * *

Faery Special Romances - Brilliantly magical! Jacquie Rogers' special brand of humor and imagination will have you believing in faeries from page one. Absolutely enchanting!
~ Dawn Thompson, Award Winning Author
* * * *

Flames of Gold (*Anthology*) - Within every heart lies a flame of hope, a dream of true love, a glimmering thought that the goodness of life is far, far larger than the challenges and adversities arriving in every life. In ***Flames of Gold*** lie five short stories wrapping credible characters into that mysterious, poignant mixture of pain and pleasure, sorrow and joy, stony apathy and resurrected hope.
Deftly plotted, paced precisely to hold interest and delightfully unfolding, ***Flames of Gold*** deserves to be enjoyed in any season, guaranteeing that real holiday spirit endures within the gifts of faith, hope and love personified in these engaging, spirited stories!
~ Viviane Crystal, Crystal Reviews
* * * *

Romance Upon A Midnight Clear (*Anthology*) - Each of these stories is well-written; when grouped together, they pack a powerful punch. Each author shares exceptional characters and a multitude of emotions ranging from grief to elation. You cannot help being able to relate to these stories that touch your heart and will entertain you at any time of year, not just the holidays. I feel honored to have been able to sample the works of such talented authors.
~Matilda, Coffee Time Romance
* * * *

Christmas is a magical time and twelve talented authors answer the question of what happens when ***Christmas Wishes*** come true in this incredible anthology. Each of these highly skilled authors brings a slightly different perspective to the Christmas theme to create a book that is sure to leave readers satisfied. What a joy to read such splendid stories! This reviewer looks forward to more anthologies by Highland Press as the quality is simply astonishing.
~ Debbie, CK2S Kwips and Kritiques
* * * *

Recipe for Love (*Anthology*) - I don't think the reader will find a better compilation of mouth watering short romantic love stories than in ***Recipe for Love***! This is a highly recommended volume–perfect for beaches, doctor's offices, or anywhere you've a few minutes to read.
~ Marilyn Rondeau, Reviewers International Organization

* * * *

Holiday in the Heart *(Anthology)* - Twelve stories that would put even Scrooge into the Christmas spirit. It does not matter what *type* of romance genre you prefer. This book has a little bit of everything. The stories are set in the U.S.A. and Europe. Some take place in the past, some in the present, and one story takes place in both! I strongly suggest you put on something comfortable, brew up something hot (tea, coffee or cocoa will do), light up a fire, settle down somewhere quiet and begin reading this anthology.

~ Detra Fitch, Huntress Reviews

* * * *

Blue Moon Magic is an enchanting collection of short stories. It offers historicals, contemporaries, time travel, paranormal, and futuristic narratives to tempt your heart.
Legend says that if you wish with all your heart upon the rare blue moon, your wishes were sure to come true. In some of the stories, love happens in the most unusual ways. Angels may help, ancient spells may be broken. Even vampires will find their perfect mate with the power of the blue moon.
Blue Moon Magic is a perfect read for late at night or during your commute to work. The short yet sweet stories are a wonderful way to spend a few minutes. If you do not have the time to finish a full-length novel, and hate stopping in the middle of a loving tale, I highly recommend grabbing this book.

~ Kim Swiderski, Writers Unlimited Reviewer

* * * *

Legend has it that a blue moon is enchanted. What happens when fifteen talented authors utilize this theme to create enthralling stories of love? Readers will find a wide variety of time periods and styles showcased in this superb anthology. ***Blue Moon Enchantment*** is sure to offer a little bit of something for everyone!

~ Debbie, CK²S Kwips and Kritiques

* * * *

Love Under the Mistletoe is a fun anthology that infuses the beauty of the season with fun characters and unforgettable situations. This is one of those books you can read year round and still derive great pleasure from each of the charming stories. A wonderful compilation of holiday stories.

~ Chrissy Dionne, Romance Junkies

* * * *

Love and Silver Bells - I really enjoyed this heart-warming anthology. The characters are heart-wrenchingly human and hurting and simply looking for a little bit of peace on earth. Luckily they all eventually find it, although not without some strife. But we always appreciate the gifts we receive when we have to work a little harder to keep them. I recommend these warm holiday tales be read by the light of a well-lit tree, with a lovely fire in the fireplace and a nice cup of hot cocoa. All will warm you through and through.

~ Angi, Night Owl Romance

* * * *

Love on a Harley is an amazing romantic anthology featuring six amazing stories. Each story was heartwarming, tear jerking, and so perfect. I got tied to each one wanting them to continue on forever. Lost love, rekindling love, and learning to love are all expressed within these pages beautifully. I couldn't ask for a better romance anthology; each author brings that sensual, longing sort of love that every woman dreams of. Great job ladies!

~ *Crystal, Crystal Book Reviews*

* * * *

No Law Against Love (*Anthology*) - If you have ever found yourself rolling your eyes at some of the more stupid laws, then you are going to adore this novel. Twenty-four stories fill this anthology, each dealing with at least one stupid or outdated law. Let me give you an example: In Florida, USA, there is a law that states 'If an elephant is left tied to a parking meter, the parking fee has to be paid just as it would for a vehicle.' Yes, you read that correctly. No matter how many times you go back and reread them, the words will remain the same. The tales take place in the present, in the past, in the USA, in England . . . in other words, there is something for everyone! Best yet, profits from the sales of this novel will go to breast cancer prevention.

A stellar anthology that had me laughing, sighing in pleasure, believing in magic, and left me begging for more! This is one novel that will go directly to my 'Keeper' shelf, to be read over and over again. Very highly recommended!

~ *Detra Fitch, Huntress Reviews*

* * * *

No Law Against Love 2 - I'm sure you've heard about some of those silly laws, right? Well, this anthology shows us that sometimes those silly laws can bring just the right people together.

I highly recommend this anthology. Each story is a gem and each author has certainly given their readers value for money.

~ *Valerie, Love Romances and More*

Be sure to check our website often

http://highlandpress.org

LaVergne, TN USA
02 February 2011
214848LV00001B/39/P